Dear Reader,

While completing my PhD on the history of global Indian migration,
I chanced upon stories from the early twentieth century involving a
small band of South Asian revolutionaries on the West Coast of the
United States. I was immediately drawn to this history; I grew up in
California and had always assumed Indian immigration began in the
1970s with the arrival of engineers and professionals.

As it turns out, in the early twentieth century, men from Bengal
and Punjab—a mix of students and farm laborers—began to arrive
in California. A number of them harbored anticolonial sympathies
that found voice in meeting halls and political groups. They organized themselves into ragtag political parties on the campuses of
Stanford and Berkeley, met and fell in love with American women,
and later, many of them would become major world figures in
India—and beyond.

Set in 1917, *A Bomb Placed Close to the Heart* tells the story of
Indra and Cora, individuals from vastly different worlds who nevertheless meet and fall in love on the Stanford University campus.
As the United States lurches inexorably into World War I, their beliefs in revolution, freedom, and equality become a liability, and the
two must escape California for New York City, where new trans-
formations await them both. Their union, and those of the other
revolutionaries I uncovered in my research, was remarkable: anti-

Asian and anti-miscegenation laws (especially the Expatriation Act of 1907) meant that a woman's citizenship would be revoked if she married a foreigner.

Indra and Cora are based, in part, on the story of M. N. Roy and Evelyn Trent, a great love lost to history. While Roy would go on to found the Mexican Communist Party and become an elder statesman in the Indian nationalist movement, Trent would be mostly forgotten—her life's papers were destroyed when her Auburn, California, duplex caught fire in 1962. Even though time and circumstance would eventually wrench Roy and Trent apart, this book is a testament to the hope and aspiration of their early love, and to the radical world of pre-WWI America. Because the Asian expulsion acts of the 1920s deported many from Roy and Trent's community, this historical moment and these unlikely unions have long been overlooked by both history and literary fiction.

In writing the story of Indra and Cora, I began to explore how two people, still young and unsure of themselves, met and, in that encounter, became entirely new individuals upon the world stage. I write about the kinds of risks they took, the impossibilities of their love—and the ways in which that love changed the very ways they thought about the world.

This book was made because there are so many hidden love stories worth telling. I hope you enjoy it.

Yours,

Nishant Batsha

A BOMB PLACED
CLOSE TO THE HEART

ALSO BY NISHANT BATSHA

Mother Ocean Father Nation

A BOMB PLACED CLOSE TO THE HEART

A NOVEL

NISHANT BATSHA

ecco

An Imprint of HarperCollins Publishers

A BOMB PLACED CLOSE TO THE HEART. Copyright © 2025 by Nishant Batsha. All rights reserved. Printed in the United States of America. No part of this book may be used or reproduced in any manner whatsoever without written permission except in the case of brief quotations embodied in critical articles and reviews. For information, address HarperCollins Publishers, 195 Broadway, New York, NY 10007.

HarperCollins books may be purchased for educational, business, or sales promotional use. For information, please email the Special Markets Department at SPsales@ harpercollins.com.

Ecco® and HarperCollins® are trademarks of HarperCollins Publishers.

FIRST EDITION

Designed by Jennifer Chung
Title page illustration by Vivian Lopez Rowe
Chapter opener art by Jennifer Chung

Library of Congress Cataloging-in-Publication Data has been applied for.

ISBN 978-0-06-330360-7

$PrintCode

Love . . . first really teaches a man to believe in the objective world outside himself, which not only makes man into an object but even the object into a man . . . love lives not only in the brain immured.

—Karl Marx and Friedrich Engels, *The Holy Family*

A BOMB PLACED
CLOSE TO THE HEART

PRELUDE

The train cut through an American darkness lit only by a half-moon, a pale and meager thing hanging over a world beset by halves—a world where she and he were bound, by some hidden power, to walk unsteadily between a vanishing here and an unknown there.

Cora awoke sometime in the night. She and Indra were curtained off from the rest of the train, still separated from each other. She lay in her berth, Indra in his beneath her, his small snores drifting upward in a rough-hewn cadence. The loss-of-momentum jostle of the train as it reached its stops made for a fitful sleep for them both, all the worse from the air condensing into sweat as the night became thick and soupy, ever warmer as the train kept moving them toward their end-of-line destination.

Cora longed to drape her hand upon Indra's side, to feel the warmth of his body even in this sultry heat—sleep always came easily when they shared a bed. But they were kept apart here. And that was that.

Awake now in this great heaving machine, she imagined that the steam it pumped into the night veiled and protected her like a witch's fog and, in doing so, revealed a future without danger, without fear.

(That raised the prospect that if the train stopped, so would its steam, and in its dissolution she would find herself again in a naked and trembling present. That was the fear that wouldn't leave her. Not until they reached where they needed to go.)

She had met Indra by chance at a party she had never actually been invited to and attended anyway—a time of repose that seemed to be now at a great remove. She had entered that small bungalow on Bryant Street, cracked cedar shingles painted canary yellow, tufts of crabgrass and dandelions as big as kittens growing out of the redbrick path to its front door, and within found rooms made humid by too many men talking among themselves, a musky smell combining with a faint backdraft of woodsmoke from the lit fireplace. The house had been filled with a drone lifting from a mass of conversations, filaments of a language she could not comprehend. Walking through that door meant trading the Palo Alto she had known for years, receiving in return some foreign bazaar. She had been one of the two Americans in that room, but, at that time, she didn't feel it, realizing instead that everything heretofore had been a pitiful meandering, as if she were some mewling calf hungry for the sweetgrass, unsure in every step as to where it grew. And there, finally, was the open meadow she had sought.

Indra and his possibilities for a new world had been made manifest by the pull of an uncanny feeling, a tug felt at the base of perception—she had become the object of another's gaze, and she scanned the room for the source.

Back then, he didn't know, couldn't know, that she had been searching. The world had been handed to her like some worthless rock, wet and dripping, mined from the mud. And she had been trying to learn how to work it, how to turn it into something pure—if only for herself.

Sleep continued to slip past her as she sifted through what came before and, finally, what would await her in what could only be an elliptical close to a never-ending story. She could hear Indra shift below her and imagined him singing the Bengali lullaby he had sung to her months ago. Khoka gumalo, he had whispered, para juralo. In that tenderness, she had known she would love him. It was an open question whether she had fallen in love with the man who made himself among other men, or the man who emerged only between her and him. It was perhaps of no matter. She had both now.

She closed her eyes and tried, once again. She had earned this rest, that much was certain. They had all come together. Her repose was the gift they had worked together to give her.

CHAPTER ONE

FROM THE BEGINNING

There had been a letter.

Cora sat on a backless bench outside the campus's newly built Women's Clubhouse. The breeze shivered up her shirtsleeves while the morning sun made weak attempts to hatchet through the bulbous overgrowth of an early-February overcast. She bounced on the balls of her feet to keep away the bite of the chill, cradling the weathered steel of her thermos of coffee with one hand while rolling its cork lid back and forth against her leg with the other. She watched two women crack-bounce-crack-bounce volley on a lawn tennis court across the way until Hazel finally joined her.

"There was a letter?" Hazel asked before she even sat down to join Cora. She was tall and reedy, and with her hair done up in a loose bun, she had the faint look of a single blade of pampas grass.

"There was a letter," Cora said, trying to force herself to sound aloof from the whole situation.

"When did he send it?" Hazed asked, finally sitting down.

"Right after the party, I think. I suppose he sent it in the middle of the night. Do you think Suresh told him where I live? I can't figure out how else he would know."

"And what did it say?" Hazel seemed eager to hear what had conspired, wanting some morsel of friendly gossip.

Cora could remember exactly what it had said, but in the moment it took her to formulate a summary, Hazel cut in. "Look, Cora, you're blushing," she lied, seeking out embarrassment to move along the conversation.

"Oh, shut it, you're imagining things. Here's the one thing I can't figure out—why is he here? He's some sort of revolutionary, right?"

"I asked Suresh about it," Hazel replied. She had been with Suresh for a little under a year. He was a dandyish man who had come to study literature at Stanford from the reaches of Bengal. He was already an accomplished writer, or what passed for it nowadays—several of his poems had been published in respectable but poorly circulated journals and periodicals across the United States. "It turns out that Suresh's brother fought alongside Indra back in India. Indra's a revolutionary through and through. Was a gunslinger against the British." Hazel formed her hands into two finger guns and pointed them at Cora. "Pew, pew."

Cora held up her hands to stop the bullets. "I got that from our conversation. He's a freedom fighter. I don't know how that connects to California at all."

"There's the big question," Hazel said with a nonplussed expression. "Suresh thinks it has something to do with the Germans—"

"Oh dear," Cora interrupted. "This is turning into a play with one too many characters on the stage. A roving mass of Germans enters stage right. What do the Indians want with them?"

"Supposedly, the war in Europe has reduced the number of British army officials in India to the bare minimum. Indra and his ilk think that if they can secure arms and material support from the Germans, they can topple British rule in India."

"Sounds dangerous," Cora said.

"Foolish is more like it. Something like this can't end well. There's too much hope placed in too many far-flung people. Why get tangled up in all this in the first place? It's what I appreciate about Suresh. He keeps his distance from the rabble. He knows it's a doomed fight."

"I didn't know Suresh was a traitor to his own people," Cora said with a sarcastic look.

"I'd call him a realist. Did you see the lot of them at the party? Did you really look at those men? They're scrawny students and half-crazed revolutionaries peddling ideas and newspapers. None of it adds up to anything of meaning. Frankly, they're all likely to get arrested."

Cora took a giant sip of her coffee, but the thermos had kept it too hot, and she scalded her tongue. "Ah, shit," she said, trying to take in a breath of the cold morning air to calm her tongue. "As far as I know, there's no offense against fighting for national liberation from foreign rule, Hazel. Really, it's similar to what you're trying to accomplish with suffrage. Free expression isn't a crime."

"What *we're* trying to accomplish," Hazel corrected. "Sure, speech is free—for Americans. The British can't handle a rebellion from their own servants. They'll use any excuse to arrest them, to shutter their papers and quiet them for good. Suresh told me that.

"Why not return to where you're needed instead? You don't need to play along with their games. We need you here. When you were attending NWP meetings more often, we had hands down the best speakers' series. Plus, suffrage is in the United States, not something across the world."

A group of men hollered as they walked close to the tennis court, already raucous early in the morning, ready for the day, for the world that was made for them.

Cora nodded in a vacant way. Her eyes followed the volleying on the court: the crack of the tennis ball against the racket, the dull thud on the ground, the crack once again. The world itself was fevered, driven mad by its own agonies. The Great War that raged across Europe was cutting a trench of hellfire and mustard gas across civilization. The bubble around the Stanford campus, where people like Hazel and Suresh could quaintly date each other, belied the fact that Congress was declaring men like Suresh and Indra illegal in the United States. And what was more, she had a floundering education to tend to.

She was a graduate student, studying the work of the playwright Rachel Crothers. Her choice of subject had the feeling of some great unseen force playing dice with her life: when she arrived as an undergraduate, the university had lacked any campus housing for its women, and the Greek letter houses filled the gap. During her first year, an alumna who hailed from Nevada and whose father owned some silver mine, who married the son of so-and-so who had founded the such-and-such Bank of California, had sent an open invitation wherein the girls at her sorority were to be given free transportation, a meal, and the chance to attend a show at the Sequoia Club in San Francisco, a social club devoted to the arts and letters of the day. The club had been putting on a series of plays directed and acted by members of the dramatic section, where the men were no more than fops, the women bored mindless, and all of them too wealthy for their own good. Cora had picked a staging at random, or perhaps because one of those erstwhile friendships of early university life, quick to form, quick to dissolve, dictated that was the only date available. Whatever the reason, Cora chose a Rachel Crothers play to attend.

That day she attended a staging of *A Man's World*, where she found herself yearning for the independence and freedom of the protagonist Frank's life, relating earnestly to the shared details of their upbringing (like Cora, Frank had been raised by her father), and connecting so deeply to the play that nothing was the same for Cora after that single staging.

Looking back, it was strange how the meeting of a single person—in this case, she never met Rachel (she thought of the playwright so often that, in her mind, they were on a first-name basis)—could rearrange the entire gravitational assemblage of one's life. Then again, she was quick to fall in love and equally quick to throw herself into the passion this love asked of her.

Before, Cora had been interested in the stage merely as a hobbyist actress. It was something to do, a social activity in which she could take part. But from the newfound center of Crothers's work extended so many orbits. First and foremost came attending other contemporary plays, or at least those she could find in Palo Alto. Though the town lacked a permanent company, the campus meant there were at least some plays on offer.

If Crothers's work touched upon themes central to the suffrage movement, well, Cora too went to campus meetings to understand suffrage, and that was where she met Hazel. And from each stem that extended from the center, nodes would branch in unseen directions: some of the women who attended meetings on women's suffrage were interested in socialism, so she tagged along to yet more meetings. She agreed with much of what she heard, even if the men occasionally got a bit handsy when they were drunk and inspired, and she fell into it.

That life had ended when her time as an undergraduate came to a close. She went to live with her father and stepmother in Sacramento, and attempted to busy herself by writing the occasional theater review for the *Union*, a job she had been gifted because the section editor often dined with her father at the Sutter Club. After a year of sporadic writing, she longed to have again some of the lost verve of her life, so she returned to the campus to complete a master's program in English—again studying the work of Crothers.

She had gotten older, but that world had stayed the same. What had interested her as an undergraduate had lost its luster, if only because it was what she already knew. She had been interested in the stage—not as a true actress or as a playwright, simply as someone who loved watching and thinking about a set of people placed in a space of artificial constraint, each distilled down to their essential humanness. Even at meetings, the content had stayed the same, only the faces were different, save Hazel's. She had wanted the old feeling of possibility back. What she got was akin to a new dress worn by a woman trying in vain to cling to her youth.

"No one's organized anything since the Alice Park visit?" Cora asked, redirecting conversation. "You all miss me that much? In that case I'll think about it."

Hazel bit into a small cheddar sandwich. "Want a bite?" she asked. "I pilfered the cheddar from some socialist who tried to get fresh with me. Dreadful human being, impeccable taste in cheese."

"I'll take half, if you don't mind." Breakfast for Cora was often cold coffee and toast, and today she had skipped the luxury of bread to make it in time to meet Hazel, who was right, the cheese was fantastic, sharp, just a hint of tang, not the wet sawdust she usually bought for herself.

"Well, what did the letter say? The one he sent to you after the party?"

Cora told her how Indra wrote that he had to see her again, he had been thinking of her.

"I'm glad he sent it—maybe it's how he flirts. He meets a woman, cribs what she says, and then makes a move. You never know," Hazel said.

Cora laughed. It was true—she only had inklings of who he was, what he did, why her. There was only a feeling.

"What do you see in him?" Hazel asked.

"What do you mean?" Cora replied defensively. She didn't want to let on what she felt for him.

"Oh, you know what I mean. What do you like about him?"

"He seems like a man who leads men," Cora said decisively. "When he speaks, other men listen."

"Even if he's stealing what you say. So where are you headed off to next?" Hazel asked before Cora could defend him.

"Tuesday lecture, same as always," Cora replied, lying. She wasn't ready yet to confess that after he had sent the letter, she had replied, and the two had agreed to meet for a walk on the campus's Arizona Garden. Even now, she could feel a skip-of-the-heart anticipation when she thought of what was to come, forsaking obligations for want of something new.

"See you Thursday morning?" Hazel asked. Until Hazel met Suresh and began to spend increasing amounts of time with him, she and Cora had been inseparable. They had often stayed up late into the night in back-and-forths that crisscrossed between life and political theory, before falling asleep in the same bed. Sometimes Cora would awaken in the middle of the night and feel part of Hazel pressed up against her—the awkwardness of two adults sharing a single bed—and Cora wondered if the comfort she felt in that darkened closeness was what sisters felt their entire lives.

Cora tried to fill her days with people, a decision to act in stark distinction to what she had lived through as a child when there were few friends she could count upon, which wasn't to say she was raised a loner, simply lonesome—there was a great chasm of difference between the two. Her father had come to the United States as a child from the hollow lands of Northern England and ended up, as an adult, around the mines and in the same line of work in which his father had toiled. Unlike his father, he became an engineer filled with the immigrant fantasy of American riches, often working behind a closed door, attempting to make his money by perfecting the Frue Vanner machine to process ore more efficiently. This dream took him away from her, cloistering him as he attempted to become one thing: wealthy. She thought of herself as lucky, as her childhood was not filled with the beatings she saw meted out to the scampish children of the mines.

Cora agreed that they would see each other soon, and they said their goodbyes. Initially, she walked in the direction of her lecture but soon doubled back to make her way to the garden.

What she had told Hazel was both true and not. In his letter, he had written:

Speaking with you in Suresh's home, everything else fell
away. I have heard much about the importance of qismat,
of fate, of the way in which the designs for our lives
will guide us through every waking day. I have before
dismissed this as nonsense. And yet I write to you now.
What is it about you that leaves me wanting more? It
would be foolish not to ask you.

All that Emerson in high school and college. Good old Ralph
had used the *Gita* to find the universal. She had learned that in a
lecture as an undergraduate. She knew little of India other than
old epics and religious precepts. From what she could remember,
Emerson had done a lovely job, because his gift was the capacity to
strip the foreign of all its alienness, leaving it as something familiar,
something loved. That act was one of such tenderness: to see in the
stranger one's own self, and to invite that doubled reflection into an
intimate space of wonder, the constant configuring of the self and
the stranger that built up all perception.

She read Indra's letter repeatedly, stuck cheek by jowl with others in the reading room, a low hum of whispers batting at her concentration, the research for her lumbering thesis on the presence
of the suffrage movement in contemporary female playwrighting
stretching out in piles of books in front of her. He had taken from
her, and she liked it.

He was handsome, of course, only a few years older than she
and tall too, taller than any other man in that room. When she had
first seen him at the party, standing in the shadow of an archway
near Suresh's kitchen, only half his face was visible: the thick wave
of his coarse hair hastily combed to the side, dark eyes holding proof
of a journey with their sunken bags of exhaustion underneath.

They spoke for hours. One cup of coffee. Another. Then another. She hadn't eaten anything that evening, and she had to stop
herself when the Turk on the red tin container of Hills Bros. cof-

fee upon Suresh's counter seemed to be drinking his own cup with them.

They first spoke about Suresh. He had come down here to Palo Alto from San Francisco after taking a liner from Japan, had been on the run from India, where he fought the British for the liberation of his people.

She told him she was a graduate student on campus, went through the usual, about what she studied and how that had introduced her to the meetings and the protests, but, feeling nervy from all the coffee, she also went off on a tangent about how the individual must live without artificial encumbrance, that suffrage, socialism, free speech, even free love—they were all connected.

And then he had to give an introductory speech to the men who had gathered. There had been a solidity in the conversation they shared, which, when taken away, caved in to a feeling of lack, the awkward feeling of being trapped in her own body, and Cora felt nervous, her fingers fidgety, a feeling like she didn't know what to say, even though there hadn't been a question posed to her.

"Individuals must live without artificial encumbrance," he began.

Her words in his mouth.

He smiled at her, sheepishly, as if asking permission.

She had been standing by the door, where the chilly touch of a light winter's breeze that swept across her legs was a welcome respite from the stuffy heat of the room. It was next to her, the exit she could have made.

She looked at him, and he looked down. It must have been only a second or less that passed, but time had no set cadence, moving between them as an allegro and a largo demanded by some invisible conductor.

All the distances that could form between them were made apparent. He wasn't white, had probably never looked upon a white woman like this, and maybe she even saw a little tremble in his face as he took the ideas from her. In his foreignness, she could feel again the hinterlands where she had been born. Even so, he was the one who spoke, and she stood, off-center and silent.

She gave him an assent as a little coquettish glance.

"The cause of freedom rotates upon the axis of the individual," Indra continued, adding his own spin to her original thought. "We fight for the nation. The nation is a collective of men. The freedom of each of these men is essential to our fight. Freedom from tyranny means not only to banish the British from our homeland but also to give women the right to vote and, yes, to break all the old bonds and make something new."

Amid the roaring applause of those gathered, an intimacy had thus been conjured: he had seen her, was serious about what she had to say, and in this recognition he had taken a part of her. In exchange she was receiving the chance at something. What it was, she wasn't sure. Unplumbed depths could always hide a world entirely unknown.

CHAPTER TWO

He fumbled for the watch in his pocket and found, for the fifth time since he'd arrived in the garden, that the minutes would not vapor themselves away. He had been pacing up and down the same portion of the garden's chalky dirt pathway, avoiding the splotches where it sank into mud, and each time he would pass the same set of four columnar cacti, two on either side of him, all of them a dull green, taller than he by about three or four heads. The garden was empty, which was no surprise because it seemed to be the most hastily put together garden he had ever seen, lacking the beauty and symmetry of the gardens of India. In lieu of the Muslim fantasy of paradise, there was a haphazard arrangement of low stones, large-spined shrubs growing wildly between the cacti, and, at a distance he had yet to reach, a large palm. Still, he conceded to himself that the cacti were rather interesting. He had never wandered into the Thar Desert, hadn't visited the reaches of the Deccan that rarely saw rain, so he had never seen that type of plant before.

Perhaps Indra would have been more amazed at these wonders if not for the fact that he was nervous, and for what—a woman? But not quite a woman. It was a similar feeling to when he was younger and had to take his exams viva voce. He would be judged for this performance. Not by her, but by some part of himself. His life had been in constant motion until this journey, a respite marked by the terrible news of his friend Nitin.

Nitin, I met a woman, he said silently, to no one.

A woman? his friend replied. What good is a woman? Women won't lead our country to freedom.

You should hear her speak. She could move mountains.

His friend laughed. Three steps into the west, and you've already changed.

As a ghost, Nitin was gaining a capacity to lead him into—and compel him from—loneliness. In that vacuum of sorrow, Indra was pacing a garden, seeking out that basic human need that he had once denied himself in service of a greater cause: the tremble-anticipation of joy, of possibility, of someone new.

There wasn't much to do in Palo Alto, in any case. Even with the news about his friend, he wasn't going to give up his mission. He had paid the German consulate in San Francisco a visit on his first day. They kindly told him to be patient, that they were awaiting the capital needed to move their grand design into order.

Indra had come to California to put a plan into action. Not only was he going to traverse the country to catch a U-boat somewhere off the coast of New York and, from there, cross the lines of war into Germany to cement an allyship between the kaiser's government and the revolutionary fighters of Bengal, but he also was to make sure that the German consulate in California kept up its promise to his cadre of nationalist fighters in India: that the country would pay for a cache of arms to be secretly shipped to Calcutta. While Indra could have left for Berlin before the cache was secured, his comrades in India had been burned before, guns never sent out from Java or Shanghai. He had to see proof of these weapons before he could move on.

Indra's plan had been sanctioned by Wilhelm Obermeier, who had said that he wouldn't have to wait long to see the arms cache sent off.

Obermeier was Indra's German handler, spymaster, agent, the one who had dictated his fate from Calcutta through Kobe and now in California. And yet Obermeier was one whom he had never met, was simply the signature at the end of a letter or the initials W.O. at the end of a terse telegram.

Indra felt a tap on his shoulder and turned around. The wild curls of her dark hair were tied up, and the angular lines of her face gave her a severe look when not smiling.

Cora.

Ko-rah. He'd liked the way it sounded when he repeated it back to her at the party, so similar to the Bengali verb meaning to do. When she spoke his own name in return, she said it in the American way, all hard consonants where a softness was required.

"So, do you send letters like that to every girl you meet?" she asked.

"Only the ones whose conversation keeps me up at night," he replied, feeling a little confident, a little haughty.

"How many of those are there?" she replied, not missing a beat. "Ten, fifteen, thirty?"

He fumbled over his reply. "You're the only one I've written such a letter to."

"Oh, that's no good," Cora said. "It's either you're too picky or you're too much of a loner."

He stared at her blankly, his heart dropping a bit into his stomach, the gears and movements of which seemed to be seizing out of beat into a standstill.

Her thin lips broke into a smirk, and she gave him a little push on the shoulder. "The look on your face right now," she said, laughing.

Whatever anxiety he had did not abate quickly, but he laughed all the same. "You know, Cora," he began, "keep that up and I might try to retract that letter."

"Retract?" Cora asked. "This isn't some article published in a journal where you can send angry letters to the editor. How would you go about retracting it?"

"Perhaps I could find it and destroy it, then pretend it never happened. You're making a good case right now to do that. Shall we?" he asked, pointing toward the path, smiling, emboldened by the off-balance precarity from Cora's first volley.

The two began to walk, side by side, just far enough away from each other for the heat of one to dissipate into the air.

"I bet you could find and destroy it," Cora said. "You knew where I live. How'd you find that out, anyway?"

"I asked Suresh. He told me your address. I didn't know it was private information."

"What else did he tell you about me?"

"It never occurred to me to gossip. Now, remind me, you said you were studying a woman playwright, is that correct?"

"Yes, Rachel Crothers. It would be a shame to think of her just as some woman. Yes, she writes about women in *some* of her plays. But she also writes about the changes we're going right now. I think she belongs up there with all the big names, our generation's George Bernard Shaw."

"I don't know much about the American stage. I attended quite a few plays in Calcutta. We have wonderful theater there. It's a city of playwrights and poets. Did you know that in Calcutta, the only women who act in plays are prostitutes? It's not considered something that proper ladies do."

"What are you saying, Indra? That I'm not proper?"

Indra laughed. "I wouldn't have sent you that letter if I thought something as silly as that. No, I think you wonderful," he said, and he could feel the hammer beat of his own pulse as he said it.

"Wonderful," she repeated quietly, with a small smile. "And the same could be said for you."

The conversation paused, as if whatever that which was fleeting between them needed a moment to breathe, to relax, to begin to establish itself a bit more.

"And then what do you plan on doing?"

"Oh, God, you sound just like my father. 'You're a woman of

twenty-four, you must settle down before it's too late,'" she said with a heavy, mocking impression.

Indra shrugged. "It's good to have the attention of your father. When I was younger, it was all I wanted. I have three older siblings and four younger. I'm not sure if I could recall my father saying much of anything when I decided fight for the good of my country. There were other mouths to feed."

"Seven siblings! Dear God. I remember when my half brother was born and I felt like things got a little too crowded."

"Well, I don't want to sound like your father with my questions, I suppose."

"No, no. He's got a point. It's just that—" Cora stopped mid-stride. Indra turned around. "I'm not sure when it happened. I just don't find any of this very interesting anymore. I mean, I still love Crothers's plays, and it was my work on Crothers that introduced me to suffrage, to socialism, to an entire world. I'm not sure if I want to focus on one little thing. I want more than that. I love writing. I'd love to find a way to support myself with my writing work in a bigger way, not just about the theater, maybe taking what I've learned from the NWP."

"I see," Indra said, struggling to keep up with the rapidity of her thoughts.

"It's silly to say this out loud, isn't it?" she asked, turning to face the cacti. "It's embarrassing to hear myself say that I have thoughts and opinions and want the world at large to read them. I think my father was right, that it's time to figure something out. Move to San Francisco and start having a couple babies."

Indra looked at her quizzically. She clearly didn't know the extent of her own talent. "What you said at Suresh's party about the cause of the individual—it was absolutely inspired. That's why I had to share it with others. If you want to make a living through your writing, it's a question of when, not if. And if you're interested in writing something, in a few days' time I'm going up to Berkeley to meet with a few of the fellows working toward Indian liberation there. Some of them were at Suresh's party. Maybe you can come along with me? They publish a magazine in English and Hindustani. The editor will be there too."

She smiled, warm and true, and Indra felt a lightness, if only because he had shared a truth that she, for reasons unknown to him, seemed to be denying. Perhaps what he failed to see was that in his flirtation with this woman, he was looking at a trick mirror. He was attracted to an outline—within the borders of a person, he was coloring in his own imagination.

"That sounds wonderful," she said. "I don't know a single thing about the struggle in India."

"There's what we discussed at the party—you were a quick study. I imagine that the men in Berkeley would be excited to explain more specifics to you. If you have a moment, I'm sure you can find a book at a library. It's called *Poverty and Un-British Rule in India*. It's almost fifteen years old but still reads like it was written yesterday."

"I'll be sure to check it out." She paused. "I do have a question. What does Germany have to do with any of this?"

"Did Suresh tell you this?" he asked.

"No," Cora said with a chuckle. "I heard secondhand, from Hazel."

"I see," Indra said with a chiding air. "Yes, I am trying to meet up with members of the German consulate."

"Why's that? Doesn't seem to be a great time to be involved with the Germans, with all the saber-rattling that's going on."

"It doesn't concern this country," Indra said. "We're just trying to find ways to further our cause. The war in Europe is an opportunity in India. The Germans have agreed to support the fight for national liberation."

"Sounds dangerous. Is it?"

Her voice was smaller than it had been. She seemed fearful, and

Indra wished to do his best to quell that fear, because the last thing he wanted to do was scare her off—to do so would be to lose this (and what was this except for a great bloodrush of feeling).

"Everything is dangerous when you're fighting a great power upon the world stage, but this in particular? Not compared to what I've seen back in India. This is simply a few meetings."

It was true, this was just a few meetings. Again, the thought of Nitin, and of the loss, news delivered the day he was to leave Japan. His dearest friend—his comrade, his fellow nationalist leader—had been shot and killed in an encounter with the colonial police. He had entered the open ocean of this journey with the sorrow of death. A meeting in a consulate was nothing compared to the possibility of dying. And yet, there too were the beginnings of doubt, that this meeting could lead him to the Nitin's fate. Losing a friend side by side in a gunfight often meant pursuing vengeance in his memory, taking care not to squander his martyrdom. To lose a friend from a distance meant seeing all his life's choices as some sort of set piece. Indra wondered, Did it truly have to end this way?

Cora seemed placated by his response, and the two agreed to meet in two days to head up to Berkeley. Before she left, Indra placed his hand briefly upon Cora's lower back. He meant only to lead her forward out of the garden, but she stopped and put her hand on his shoulder. He felt the electric arc surge through his body, and there came the kiss, slow, lingering in the silence of the garden, ended only by the sound that came in the distance, the chimes of the hour from the campus church. She had to attend a meeting with a professor and left him in the garden.

This was madness. Mostly, he saw white women as a right hand of power, an empire built of Lady Macbeths. Calcutta, that city at the crossroads of the world where he had most recently lived, was where almost every race upon the earth could find their place in the city's geography. In Chowringhee, he could walk among the Europeans and Anglo-Indians of his city, each of them passing around him in a hollow way. An international city provided no means for understanding among people, only a way to hear small voices on a street or in the bazaar.

And he knew, if he were to look upon a white woman in any way that could betray a feeling of want beyond perhaps the paid-by-the-hour appointments of Free School Street, the reprisal would be swift, unforgiving—terrible. There was no such admonition against his feeling here. In fact, California seemed to care little about his nation's history, precepts, rules. He hadn't meant to kiss her, yet it happened without his willing it. He had an inkling that things would move fast with her, faster than he wanted or intended. In India, he had been a leader among men, and to be in that position meant to stand alone. Since then, he had crossed an ocean and was now awaiting orders in a foreign land. Amid all this change, some deep part of him was seeking a break from the past, a firm desire to move with another, even if that meant that he would no longer be the sole arbiter of the pace.

The world felt like it had been inverted, a photographic negative imprinted upon his vision.

CHAPTER THREE

At the train station in Palo Alto, Cora got to the platform first and the morning was fine, a warm respite from the cold February rain. She walked a bit farther away from the station's colonnade into the sunshine and toed a small piece of gravel that had been kicked up from the tracks while she rehearsed her notes in her head. After the garden, she had been filled with the energy of possibility—she hadn't gone to meet with a professor and instead had gone to the university library to requisition a copy of the book Indra had mentioned, which she had read quickly, taking notes on how Britain drained the wealth and possibility of India.

The speed of her reading had been dictated by life's twin driving forces: desire and ambition. The book was a way to take her goals—to make her voice and opinions heard—and use that ambition to further please another.

The notes had been rehashed, and she was left to wait. Waiting entailed a number of dysfunctions.

Little hallucinations: any man of his height at a distance was a possibility—that man must, no *that* man is him, no that isn't him, either.

Small paranoias: did he forget? Or perhaps she was the one who forgot. He said today, right? Was the hour correct?

Concomitant agitations: she had canceled on Hazel to come to Berkeley and would have an empty morning if he never showed up.

All erased when she caught sight of the wave of his coarse-textured hair. He hadn't seen her, so she could observe: his hands in his pockets, the seriousness of his face, the way he walked and kept his head slightly down as if in thought, but as he came closer to the platform, he saw her, and even before they embraced, she felt the bewitching calm that it would provide, the way in which touch could ablate swelling anxieties.

In his arms, she reached up to give him a light kiss to say hello.

"Sorry I'm late," he said.

"It's fine," Cora lied. "I didn't even notice it. You seem out of breath."

"I just moved into a new room and got lost getting here. Went left instead of right. Made it here just in time," he said as the arriving train whistled in the distance.

She chided herself inwardly for doubting his arrival. It had never occurred to her that there could be some dull reason for his lateness, but there was so little she knew about him. She had never gone from meeting a man to exchanging letters to kissing him in a week's time, but she already felt at ease with him in a way that seemed to erase the borders between them.

The situation with her family put her in a permanent sense of unease with regard to class and position. Before the days when her father couldn't get his vanning machine to perfect the separation of gold and silver from worthless ores, it had seemed easier. They moved from one mine to another, and there were two axioms to always remember above all others: "Never cross a picket line, and never trust a man who makes his living telling others what to do."

The anxiety began only when everything started to go right, when the money began to do what it did best—alchemize the entire matrix of one's connections and conceptions, including the most basic precepts of the self—and her father quickly became a man who told others what to do. She felt like some sort of discounted Engels, who himself had used the proceeds from his father's textile factory to fund his dalliances in left-wing political theory.

It was this in-betweenness that was perhaps allowing her to feel at ease with someone so foreign. Indra was in transit, crossing a platform between one conveyance and the next, and he, as well the Indians they were going to go call upon, were on their back foot from the very fact that they were disconnected from the country of their birth, agitating for the freedom of a distant land from inside one that wasn't sure if it wanted to keep them around.

Exactly the place she wanted to be.

It was a long journey between Palo Alto and Berkeley. They had to get to San Francisco and then take the autobus up to the Ferry Building, where they could take a Key ferry across the Bay, then the streetcar to Berkeley. If they were lucky, they could get there by midafternoon.

The conversation with Indra moved as easily as the steam and fire of all the forms of transport that took them to their destination. They told each other stories of their youth—she enjoyed recounting to him how she grew up in the hardscrabble mines. He couldn't believe that she had lived for so many young years in such desolate places, and he had such great pity for the loss of her mother. He seemed sadder about it than she ever felt, but she soon learned that his own mother had passed away a year or so ago, and he was speaking of his grief through her loss.

He spoke of his upbringing in India, particularly his brief wanderings as an ascetic. Indra's grandfather had been the village priest, which meant that there was some sort of manhood ceremony when he was ten years old where he had to become a peripatetic mendicant. Temple to temple, he wandered, gurus waiting to tell him the same tenets over and over: renounce the world that passes by as an illusion.

Reading gave way to action, she learned. Indra gave up his religion when he was eighteen and the British announced their plan to partition Bengal in two, to take the power of that region and neatly divide it upon an invisible border. It was an outrage to divide a place upon a simple religious line, one Hindu, one Muslim—he joined the street marches to protest, and in him grew a desire for direct action, a fist that could rise above a simple collection of voices upon the street to grab at and crush the heart of empire.

"These men in Berkeley, they feel the same thing," he told her. "They've made a political party called the Ghadar."

"What does that mean?" Cora asked. She said the word internally: Gha-dar. It sounded all wrong, nothing like how he said it.

"It means the revolution. They're the Party of Revolution. They organized about five years ago. Their members move between here and the Punjab, mainly. They want the same thing I do: total liberation of India from foreign rule."

"Are there many Indians in the Gha-dar in California?"

"There were more a few years ago. Now it seems to be mainly students and writers. They've made inroads with the Sikh Punjabis working the farms in the state."

"I didn't know there were Indians farming in the Central Valley," she asked, curious about a history and people that seemed hidden from her. "Why are they here?"

Indra shrugged. "Why is anyone anywhere? One man has an idea and takes a boat. If he's able to find some sliver of a good life, he writes home. His cousin, his uncle, his nephew, and maybe even his best friend's brother's son's brother arrive soon enough."

Cora chuckled. "Is that why there are men studying at Berkeley as well?"

"For the most part. One man found he could come here and learn without having to bow down to the British at Oxford or Cambridge. The men reading for degrees at Stanford and Berkeley are the same. They don't want to beg their lords and masters for an education."

This seemed, to Cora, entirely different from the countless editorials and articles at the *Union* about the Asian menace creeping across the state, a tide of workers seeking to undercut the wages of good white men.

The two finally arrived in Berkeley near two in the afternoon. As they walked from the edge of the Cal campus to their destination, Cora wondered why she had chosen to attend Stanford over Cal, as the former seemed to be a pastoral destination, cloistered off from greater society. This was a place where city and school moved together, filled with a life that emanated from the Campanile chiming in the distance. As they walked down Telegraph Avenue, she overheard conversations in French, in German, and outside a teahouse, a man slamming down his hand on a table, exclaiming, "Cubism will not survive the war in Europe!" This wonder was not limited to her attention: she saw how Indra too let his eyes wander this way and that with the look of a traveler newly arrived in a strange land, a moving and unfocused stare that confessed there was too much novelty to behold in a single moment.

The meeting that she and Indra were to attend was in a cramped apartment in a brown-shingle foursquare on Dwight, just off of Telegraph, a rather plain building made beautiful by the enormous aloe planted in front, on the left side, setting all the symmetry askew. Its leaves reached nearly eight feet tall, like some ornamental that the gods accidentally dropped from the sky and left there, for it was far more weathered and aged than the building behind it.

Inside was a handful of men who all seemed to glance her way when she entered before returning to their conversations, and that brief feeling of incongruousness made her feel once again like she was at the party at Suresh's. This sparsely furnished bachelor pad must have belonged to one of the men there, and before she could turn to Indra to ask, he had gone up to a man no taller than she, with hair shaved right down to pinpricks atop his head. His round face was made to seem rounder by the small circular glasses he wore. In his shirtsleeves with a red tie, he seemed like some windsock filled with bluster as he waved about a news clipping in his hand.

Indra motioned for her to come over. "This is Cora, she's a

friend of Suresh and Hazel's. She's a magnificent writer at Stanford and is interested in our cause. Cora, this is Govind. He's the editor of the Ghadar newspaper over in San Francisco."

She held out her hand, and he shook it limply.

"Have you seen this nonsense? Published in the *Dayton Journal* last week."

Cora shook her head and thought he was joking, though he seemed filled with too much intensity to be riffing with her.

He slammed down the clipping on the nearby dining table. A low murmur filled the room. "Cora, where is Dayton?" he asked without looking back at her. Indra put his hand on her upper back and smiled as if to say, Courage.

In these spaces, her difference from everyone else blurred the distinction between migrant and native-born. At least she knew the answer to Govind's question. She replied politely that it was a city in Ohio, back east in the country's industrial heartland.

"And do they not have editors in Dayton? Men of understanding and intellect? Or is it a mass of fools publishing nonsense?"

Cora laughed. "You'd be surprised, Govind. There are few men of intellect in the entire United States, let alone Ohio. And even fewer editors capable of turning their muddled thoughts into something beautiful. What's the article?"

"About the war in Europe and questioning India's loyalty to Britain. It explains how much Britain has given to India and how India fails to give back in Britain's moment of need. Give back?" His pencil-thin mustache trembled with his upper lip.

His tirade seemed to be an announcement for the men gathered in the apartment to sit at the trestle dining table, perhaps an elegant piece thirty or fifty years ago, now covered with scratches and scuffs, the yellowed shellac peeling off the dark oak at its corners, and all eight squeezed around its edges. She looked around and remembered what Hazel had said about the men, and for a moment, she thought her friend right. Most of them, save Indra, were flatly unattractive. Not hideously so. No one could ever put a finger upon why exactly they were attracted to anything. It was easy, yes, to describe the bloated or distended faces of the unattractive but damn near impossible to really understand what drew her to anyone in particular.

"It's only one small city in a nation filled with them," Cora said. "Opinions fly around on the wind. What does it matter what some idiot in Dayton has to say about India?"

"Surely she must be joking." A wiry man snorted at Indra from across the table.

Indra interrupted. "This is Singh, here from Patna, a city in eastern India."

"Yes, yes, Indra," he continued, brushing off Indra's introduction with a wave of his hand. He continued to speak only to Indra. "Who is this woman? She should know that every city matters! Ignorance is like a poison that spreads. Typical of a woman to fail to comprehend the nuances of what we're seeking to do."

Cora was taken aback by his rudeness.

"He's right," Govind said. "It's a time of delicate public opinion. Congress just vetoed the president to prevent men like us from entering this country. Our hand is weak. They already see us as laborers stealing their employment. We don't want the American public to think of us as ungrateful wretches undeserving of freedom as well."

Cora took a breath and went through the notes in her head. The conversation fractured into little splinters of low talk among the men.

"Britain drains India's wealth." Cora said above the din. "How can a nation be loyal to a ruler that only takes? Loyalty runs strongest via love."

"So you suggest we counter with a letter to the editor summarizing how Britain drains the wealth of India?" Indra asked with a warm smile.

"No, no," Cora said. She saw how Indra raised his eyebrows in surprise at her quick dismissal. "That book is too old to summarize now."

"Then what do you suggest?" another man asked.

She tried to pull together any notion of what Dayton was like but could imagine only smokestacks and business.

Maybe that was all she needed to know.

"Dayton is a city of factories. Why not speak in the way a capitalist understands? 'The Balance Sheet of British Rule in India.' List everything that Britain has taken—a balance sheet so negative that only a fool could question where India's loyalties lay."

Cora felt Indra stretch out to rest his arm along the top rail of her chair, and when she turned to him, she saw the same look upon his face as when he spoke to the crowd at Suresh's party.

"Brilliant, absolutely brilliant," he whispered to Cora, as if he wanted her to begin writing at that very moment.

"Let's start with the key numbers," Cora said, taking control of the conversation. "Does anyone know how much the British takes in tax revenue?"

"Fifty crores of rupees," said a dreadfully thin man whose sunken-in eyes gave him the look of a walking skeleton.

"That's Anand. He studies political economy at Berkeley," Indra whispered.

"I don't know what that means. What's that in dollars?"

Anand scribbled on a piece of paper in front of him before looking up. "I believe it's roughly a hundred and sixty million dollars."

"Great, a hundred and sixty million. And what's the average income?"

"Average income per capita," Anand corrected. "Five paisa. Two and a half cents."

She motioned for something to write with. Anand ripped off a page for her while Govind slid a pen down the table. The nib was worn and the black ink streaky, but it was enough to note down the figures. "And how much do they spend on things that benefit the people—say, education?"

"I don't know the exact figure offhand," Anand replied even as he completed further calculations. "For the sake of argument, let's say something on the order of twenty-five million dollars."

"And how much on the army?"

"It must be near at least a hundred million dollars."

"Okay, so we have some expenditures. What do they give back? There must have been some recent crisis they haven't attended to. They don't sound like very benevolent leaders."

"Twenty million people have died from famine. Eight million have died from disease. An Indian's life is worth less," Indra said.

"That's terrible. Twenty million! We can take these numbers and turn them into something a reader can understand. They want to talk about the war? Let's talk about loyalty. They have used India's money, and they have used the men of India as soldiers to conquer Afghanistan, Egypt, and Africa," Cora said, taking from what she had read in the library. "And I bet they're sending soldiers to the war in Europe, right?"

"Of course," Indra said. "Always more soldiers sent to die abroad."

"Men of India die for the war in Europe and receive nothing in return. How's that for loyalty?"

"I think we have our response, gentlemen." Indra said. He straightened up and patted the back of her hand. Govind nodded from the head of the table. Singh said nothing, glowering.

There was a shared Remington in another room. Cora had no professional experience as a typist, but she knew none of these men had ever typed their own work, so by default she would be the one to bring the ideas to a printed page. The break was nevertheless welcome. She was all steamed up on argument and intelligence.

Her life, outside of this moment, had the feeling of a motor car stuck at a crossroads, and when she looked at the map she had used to get to that point, she instead found something useless, jottings of locations superimposed upon old notes. This feeling today, this was hunger, a glimmer of another world she had only heard of once or discussed, one filled with suffragists and anarchists, the Alice Pauls and the Emma Goldmans, women who took men as lovers or ignored them altogether. What they shared was a Cause, an encompassing force that cleared away the muddle and filled life with vitality.

Because she was an outsider, she probably would have to work twice as hard to go half as far as any man could, and by the same token, any mistake that she made pulled her down three times as far as the same mistake by a man. She hadn't before thought herself capable of recalling, with almost mirrorlike quality, the reading she had done. She had been driven to want to understand, to recall, to translate the foreign into something recognizable. And from that want, the skill had appeared.

To debate among these men, she had to be focused, attuned to the matter at hand. She couldn't let herself slip, because if she did, all the roles would be reversed, and she would be revealed as the foreigner among them.

The first echoes of doubt came from her past, from the mines. Near Trinidad in Colorado, there had always been the Chinese, living away from all the others in their China camp. Cora couldn't remember ever actually speaking to any of them, though there was perhaps the obvious language barrier. She had once wandered into their camp. A white girl of about six was given a wide berth in spaces like those, and she felt the eyes of all the men upon her, as though they were horrified that if something happened to her, the terror unleashed upon each and every one of them would be nothing short of absolute.

She had wandered right into the open doorway of one of the log-cabin hutments, and the single room, filled with cots, the ceiling blackened from smoke, smelled distinctly of fish and vinegar. Before she wandered back out, she noticed someone sleeping on the other side of the room, the drone of his light snores floating into the air, keeping time with each raddled breath. She stepped into the room, and a floorboard creaked out her arrival. He awoke but never got up—he lay there and stared at this stranger with wide eyes, fearful of what awful portent she had brought to him. Cora had stood there, frozen, until his gaze was enough to shoo her away.

Cora was being drawn into a new room, but it was difficult to shake the feeling she had felt in the mining camp, that she was that unwelcome white girl, an imposter.

Cora could hear wisps of conversation and laughter from the other room. Half the time she couldn't understand them, and the other half she found that they often preferred English. "Listen, Indra," she heard Govind say, "if you try to keep away from meat here, you'll quickly starve. There's no dal or chana or anything resembling a decent vegetable. Eat, heartily. If you ever go back to India, no one needs to know how you kept yourself alive."

He too was being made to change.

As she typed up what they had drafted together at the table, she felt the sublime nothingness of the task at hand—the complete absorption of what had to be done. Some unknown amount of time passed, the only proof of it being that the direction of the shadows had slowly shifted across the room. It was done: "The Balance Sheet of British Rule in India."

Indra had walked up behind her. "Incredible," he said. "Simply incredible. You said before that you wanted to earn your living as a writer—how that has not happened yet is beyond me. I've never seen someone so quickly synthesize an idea into a manuscript."

He seemed so pleased, as if she had somehow done the most intimate of favors for him, and in a way, she had—what she had made was proof of a fundamental understanding building between them.

If she could suspend the movement of the world, she would press herself upon him and dissolve into him. This Feeling translated into want, and this was base, not too far from how a cat could abandon everything, even its own kittens, when it felt that it had to go find its satisfaction.

"Kiss me," she said to him.

"Here? Among them?"

There was no one in the room, no one near the doorway, no one to see them.

She kissed him, holding him tight against herself. It was quick, almost too quick. A good kiss was like dancing, to know when to lead, to know when to follow, but most of all to have that unspoken rhythm shared between the two, a syncopation that dissolved the boundary between self and other, erasing all endings for want of a forever beginning.

There was a charged feeling between them now. She wanted nothing more than to be alone with him.

"Come," Indra said. "Let's show this to Govind first. It's a long journey back to Palo Alto."

The two of them walked back into the other room together.

She handed Govind the typewritten article. "This is far too important to waste upon the fools of Dayton," he said.

"I disagree," Cora stammered. "I think it's in a clear language that they can understand. I think it would be essential for the cause to have the men and women of Dayton understand what the freedom of a nation actually means."

"This is too valuable. We're going to translate it into Urdu and Punjabi. We'll publish it and send it to our people. And we'll print the English version too. Before we can reach the men and women of Dayton, we need to be sure that our own people know everything of this balance sheet."

From this came a fantasy of readership: sunbaked and weathered hands, tired from a day tending the peaches of the Central Valley, would read a translation of what she wrote. The students at Berkeley and Stanford would soon get their own copies. And there would be copies that would go on to New York, to Europe, and perhaps even to India itself (if the British didn't intercept it en route)—there was a whole mass of individuals across the known world who could read that piece of paper. Even if only a fraction of that number remembered what they read, held fast to the list of facts presented so cleanly and neatly, then perhaps a slice of that fraction could be called to action, called to fight for the cause of justice, to take up arms for freedom. This was little like writing a review for a man's weekend entertainment.

She was dizzied by the sense of possibility. There was a capaciousness inside of her that she was only beginning to fathom. Once started, she did not want to stop. There was something here that could fill her in a way little had before. She had to write again.

CHAPTER FOUR

It was well into the night by the time they made their way back to Palo Alto. The conversation between Indra and Cora was beset by the intimacy of sleep. At first she was leaned up against him, and he could feel the anticipation, equal parts trepidation and excitement, all tingly nerves down to his fingers. They kept their hands mostly to themselves, his resting upon her legs, hers in his lap. By the time they got on the train from San Francisco, he could see that the day had drained her, and when she began to fall asleep, he contorted himself a bit lower so that her head could rest upon his shoulder.

Under his breath, remnants of a lullaby that his mother had sung to him as a child: "Khoka ghumalo," he sang quietly. "Para juralo / borgi elo deshe / bulbulite dhan kheyeche / khajna dibe kishe?"

"It's beautiful," she whispered, already half asleep. "What does it mean?"

"Aren't all lullabies about how the world is terrible? Children are sleeping, and in the silence, soldiers come in from another land while the birds eat the grain harvest, and the mother wonders, how will we ever pay what we owe?"

By the time he had completed the dry explanation, Cora was already asleep.

Looking at her, helpless, quiet, and vulnerable, he felt a desire grow again within him. He could see down the neck of her yellow tunic to the white of the camisole underneath, and he slowed his breath.

Like in the Arizona Garden, he was surprised by how much he wanted her, now even more so because she seemed so capable with the cause that illuminated his life. In India this had never been a possibility. A wife meant a woman who would defer to him always, someone who would stay quiet as he spoke, or wouldn't be in the room at all. But someone who would be his equal? Who could match or even best his intellect? There she was. Sleeping on his shoulder. He closed his eyes to calm himself. He had the pity common to the waking for the asleep—he didn't want to move in any way that could rouse her. He had to remain as still as he could, and as he did, he sifted through what Govind had told him about the German plan.

"A man can spend a lifetime waiting for these fools, Indra," Govind had warned after Indra told him about the guns. "They played us low down over and over. I doubt the weapons are coming. If you want to go to Berlin, I think you should go now. Talk to them directly, see if they can help us. If you want to stay, there won't be any guns waiting for you. She might wait with you. Help you pass the time." Govind grinned like a schoolboy just discovering that underneath their clothing, all the women in the world were naked.

"She's here because I thought her brilliant—and she is, you heard her. Do you really think they're going to burn us again?" Indra had asked.

"I've been with the Ghadar long enough to see good men go on foolish journeys across the world only to find themselves arrested or abandoned on the other end—just two years ago the British executed the Ghadarites who returned to Punjab, and did the Germans come to save us then? We're nothing to them. Their way of thinking is simple. The enemy of my enemy and all that. Nothing they do with us adds up to anything more than a vague gesture of support."

"It's February now. I'll give it a month to hear from Obermeier and the consulate whether these guns will ever be sent off," Indra had replied, a little offhandedly.

"A woman is a good a reason as any to stay." Govind laughed.

Indra was irritated with his casualness. This had nothing to do with a woman—it had everything to do with the freedom of the nation. He changed the subject by pulling out of his jacket pocket a small newspaper clipping folded over two or three times. He handed it to Govind. "I told no one I had arrived, and yet this was in the *Chronicle* in San Francisco just a few weeks ago."

MYSTERIOUS ALIEN REACHES AMERICA— BRAHMIN REVOLUTIONARY OR GERMAN SPY?

"They must have someone here," Indra said. "They've been watching me since I left Calcutta. I didn't think they would cross the Pacific."

"Brother," Govind said with a casual air, "of course they're watching us."

Indra was taken aback by his response.

"We're always being watched," Govind continued. "This is a place of refuge. This isn't India. The British have no power here. This is a place of freedom."

"Wait, who's watching us here?"

"The usual—CID," Govind said. CID had been the bane of Indra's life in India, a law enforcement group made to track so-called criminal elements all over the country, and recently, he supposed, across the world. "It's a small office in San Francisco. One man for the entire region from Vancouver down to Los Angeles."

"Who is it?" Indra asked.

"Lewis Hopkins."

"Never heard of him. What does he look like?"

"What do all British men look like? Short, expensive suit, too much pomade in his hair."

Indra laughed at the description. "Should I be afraid of him?"

"No, brother, I'd be more afraid of your Germans never showing up."

On the train, Indra wondered what he would do after he secured the guns from the Germans.

He had met Nitin Chatterjee at the Bengal Technical Institute
ten years ago, before Indra dropped out. The two went together to
the hills to train on how to shoot. From that day on, he had always
been there for Indra. It had been Nitin who had most recently bailed
him out when he was arrested after their group had looted fifty
pistols and forty thousand rounds of ammunition from a British armory. Obermeier had heard about the brazen attempt—it was what
got Indra out of India.

From death, Nitin whispered in Indra's ear that Govind was
wrong, that the guns would be there, that Indra shouldn't abandon
the plan he had died for. Indra had lost friends by time or circumstance. Their voices, their names, their faces, all of it faded slowly
and inexorably from memory. The death of a friend was a curse.
Indra knew he was going to hold on to some part of him, forever.

Govind had also told him about a silent protest they were going
to conduct in San Francisco. The priest at Vivekananda's mission
wasn't sufficiently approving of the Ghadar, or something along
those lines. What good a silent protest could do was beyond Indra.
Power only listened to power. He would go with them—he had the
time to pass—but maybe he'd bring Cora with him.

As soon as he thought her name, she began to shift in her seat,
as if able to read his thoughts. She yawned, stretched. Adorable.

"Almost back," Indra said.

"It's too late to go to my house," Cora said.

"Too late?"

"I'd have to wake up the house mother to get in. It's okay, I told
them I'd be staying in Berkeley with a friend tonight. No one's going
to miss me."

The intensity of desire returned, now mixed with a touch of

trepidation as to what might transpire between them. "We'd have to sneak you past my landlady," he said, thinking aloud. "I don't think she can hear anything over her snoring."

"That's fine by me," she said.

"You know, it's a little presumptuous of you to have thought that I would let you stay with me," Indra said with a mocking air.

"Better to presume than to be chastised by a house mother and gossiped about by other residents."

Indra was staying on Ramona Street, just a ten-minute walk from the train station. He had scoured the classifieds in the *Daily Palo Alto Times* and been lucky to find a pauper's room to rent just down the street from Suresh's. His room was on the first floor, and the landlady's was thankfully on the second, on the other side of the house.

"You weren't kidding about the snoring," Cora said as they entered. They tiptoed to his room. Inside, the streetlight came into the room as a golden embrace through the thinness of the curtains. The house had been built eight or nine years prior, but the window had been poorly fit in its frame, allowing coughs and whispers from passing strangers to shake themselves through the corners. In one corner of the room was a porcelain sink where the cold-water tap could close only to a constant drip.

She sat down on his narrow bed and he next to her. He began to kiss her.

"What is it?" she asked as he pulled away.

"One thing, I'll be right back."

"Where are you going?"

"I'm going to clean up," he stammered.

He left his room quickly and drew the bath, didn't even wait for the water to warm up, simply hopped in and began to wash. It was an act born of nervousness—desire could be paired with unspoken lack, that his body, when stripped of its carapace, would be seen in all its bare fragility. He got out of the tub almost as soon as he got in, like some wayward animal who had slipped through the ice into the lake below. He returned to the clothes he had worn before, beads of cold water dripping from his wet hair down to his collar.

"What was that?" Cora asked, clearly confused as to what he had just done.

Govind had made a comment about the mission in San Francisco, how mainly white women attended the services. "They seek knowledge," he had said. "They seek something esoteric. A smattering of the East to enliven their dead little lives."

In the same way, he thought of something vaguely spiritual, assuming that was what she wanted to hear.

"It's like prayer. When we pray to the Goddess, we wash ourselves before we do so. None of the dirt of the day should greet Her when She receives us. In the same way, I come to you."

He began to kiss her: the base of her neck, down her spine, down to the small of her back. Entwined, a heat was shared between them as pleasure built unto itself over and over. When he was above her, he saw the dark skin of his hands caress the whiteness of her breasts until the breath came out of her lips in small gasps for more.

He was something out of the East shrouded in a touch of mystery. In love, there were still parts to play.

CHAPTER FIVE

There came the quiet thereafter in the darkness, his room aglow from the streetlamps outside.

In her heart of hearts, Cora wished to experience her body as a man would, to accept it as a thing made of light and air and humors always leaking. Among many other reasons, she loved Hazel because it was with her that she could be the man she wanted, if only privately. And some of it was deathly serious, but mostly it was puerile: learning to sing through a belch, passing wind in an airless room and laughing at the result. These little titters of the body were important: those as far back as Boccaccio had known that people were beings in the world and not minds locked away in a jar, that lust and the scatological and ambition and joy all lived next to one another.

It was a downfall too, this belief, for one of its logical ends was that she should experience a climax in the same way a man could. She once had loved someone—Henry, the last man she had dated back when she was an undergraduate, the grandson of a business magnate who had been partner with someone more important, someone glossed by history as the Cattle King of California. The business partnership of an ancestor bequeathed to all future generations the freedom and the glory of fantastic wealth, if only because the power of compound interest had long ago supplanted titles of nobility in the new world. Henry seemed to wish to squander that wealth, preferring socialist and anarchist meetings, learning the ins and outs of a cause. They had met at one of those meetings.

It was with him that she became a woman who no longer said no, becoming known among all as one who said yes, so every meeting after that decision was handsy. No one ever said it to her directly, but she had become an easy rider, because men are terrible gossips, and they were always talking about who would sleep with whom, who was the one who took free love a little too seriously and as such was an easy lay. In this, the Indians were a welcome break from the socialists. No one knew her past.

On the surface, she supposed she supported free love, supposed she agreed with Emma Goldman that a free heart had no place in the prison of marriage. The problem was this: to a man, free love only meant free whores, and who was to change that point of view? And even if that were possible, it was women like her own mother who would always suffer the punishment of love and childbirth, for on the day Cora was born, there had arisen the stench of a death from the mess of her meconium and afterbirth.

In this, folks like Sanger were right: first the need for free contraception, then maybe free love could be considered. Where to find that free contraception was another question, so instead Cora trusted in the veracity of the advertisements she had seen in the paper, purchasing a bottle of Lysol over at Eagle Drug on University Avenue, dutifully mixing it with cold water into her douche after she made love.

She ran her fingers through Indra's hair, the base of each strand still feeling a light touch of damp. His body had been different than what she had ever seen before—his fleecy chest, skin neither tan nor darkened, instead shaded. All these differences excited her, like praying to the Goddess. Religion had been mostly inconsequential to her life thus far—the camp preachers from her youth were always half drunk on Sunday morning anyway, just like the parishioners who had stumbled into the pews, lips still wet from the bottle, each hoping for some sort of salvation that wasn't an underground explosion or a mine collapse. Mankind could use some of Christ's teachings, but the rank hypocrisy of every believer kept her away. And yet when Indra spoke of a god, it felt new, foreign, exciting.

She kissed his neck, feeling a day's stubble under her lips.

"I think I'll be here at least another month," Indra said to her. "There's no rush to Berlin. My meeting with the consulate will probably be delayed. I'll message my contact tomorrow. I'll know for certain then."

The announcement of a time line disappointed her, for what had begun with an attraction was revealing the joy of matching patterns of thought. She didn't want to let it all go.

She tried to wear a mask of upbeat interest even if her heart hung low. "Are the Germans supporting you too? Financially, I mean." She curled up lazily next to him like a resting cat, or perhaps an errant question mark, and ran a hand upon his chest. He was absently tracing patterns on her upper back, wrapping the ends of her hair around a finger. There was a feeling of safety in all this.

"To tell you the truth," he said, "I have only about a week's worth of money left. Finding this room cost more than I had thought."

"I'd be happy to help out, if you need it," she said. Her father sent her an allowance every month that could easily cover both of them.

"It's no matter," Indra said curtly. "I saw a satisfactory job in the classifieds." There was an edge of hurt in his voice. It was the sound of pride, of a man who didn't know how to ask a woman for money.

"Really?" she replied, almost a little suspiciously. "Doing what?"

"Washing dishes for a fraternity."

Cora let out a laugh. "Washing dishes! Have you ever done that before?"

"When I was living underground in Calcutta, I learned quite a few things. Not the least of which was taking care of myself."

She wasn't convinced by his answer but didn't press it further.

"Govind told me about a protest they're planning. Would you like to attend?" he asked, seeming eager to change the subject. She yawned. It was late. She didn't push it.

Indra relayed the story he had learned from Govind of the swami and how they would come up and meet the same folks they had seen in Berkeley, that they would stand together in a silent show of force, a protest built up by the presence of bodies standing shoulder to shoulder in the rear of the hall, eyes like gunsights set straight at the swami.

"Reminds me of the Silent Sentinels," she said, feeling the weight of sleep pull on her attention, knowing she would have to wake up around dawn to sneak out of his room. "They're in Washington right now, you know. They're protesting for women's suffrage, each of them posted outside the White House, staring Wilson right in the eye and not saying a word."

"Have you ever protested, Cora?" he asked.

Warm memories lifted in that space between sleeping and wakefulness. "Mostly around the National Woman's Party. I've been involved for a few years on the Stanford campus. We'd stage marches for the suffragist cause along University Avenue or the County Road. Occasionally, the mayor would bring in the police and send us all to the lockup for the night."

"You should be right at home in Govind's protest, then."

She was going to say something in reply, but sleep was coming upon her fast. In the days to come, there was probably some deadline to attend to, an essay for one of her courses, a handful of meetings with professors. It would all have to be pushed aside for now. The potential for academic failure didn't keep her up, for that world felt haggard and pale in comparison to the thrill of experiencing something completely new.

CHAPTER SIX

He and Cora were to take the Peninsula from the Palo Alto station up to San Francisco, and in the station, Indra thought of how he had always loved the train. Near his village, there had been a track that ran on a levee surrounded by rice paddy. The nearest station wasn't for miles, and so the train, when it came around, ran through at full speed, steam billowing out of its engine, steel moving upon steel to propel its people ever forward to cities upon the horizon.

It came through twice a week, eleven in the morning, rarely early, only on occasion late. And if not distracted by school, he would run to the paddy, risking his bare feet to be suckled by a leech or bitten by some other insect lying in the shallow waters. All to glimpse it for the few seconds it moved through.

The sound always came first, and even though it moved so quickly when right in front of him, from a distance it would saunter into vision, beginning first as a plume, more of an abstraction than a mode of transportation. It was a great heaving beast, snarling and sighing out a garbled message to him from afar, but a boy could never stop the movement of something so large. For the rest of the day, it was like he remained in its steam, and he was left to imagine what it was meant to tell him: whether his destiny was to ride it to his destination, or instead he was to speak with those riding inside it, each of them going somewhere important, somewhere far, somewhere that wasn't the smallness of the space occupied by his feet. Either way, he would tell himself that the train could bring him some new life away from being a middle child in a backwater village.

He tried to convince his siblings to come with him, and perhaps they would, once or twice, before boredom fed their evasion—it was always the same, after all: the same train, going one way or the other. Even so, it was breathtaking for Indra, every time. In the end, the only one who would follow him was Sunil, a boy from his village so dim-witted that people lovingly called him the idiot, and less lovingly spoke insults right to him, which he always took with a smile.

All the others were content to let the train pass, save him and the idiot. It seemed to him curious, now, that this was the way of things.

Before he got to the station, Indra had sent off a missive to Obermeier, had decided to ask him point-blank when he would be meeting with the Germans about shipping arms to India or if he should just proceed to Berlin without meeting. It should have been time to make haste. The proposed deadline for the arms meeting was a few weeks away, but the kaiser had recently declared unrestricted submarine warfare in the Atlantic. And then the headline in the paper: *GERMANS SINK U.S. SHIP*. The Germans had sunk some merchant ship off the coast of Italy. The ship had been submarined and destroyed. No fatalities, thankfully. Indra had never thought of the Germans as stupid, but he couldn't see the endpoint here—everyone was incensed. Just the other day, he had overhead a conversation between two drunks about "the Huns" and how they "oughta punch 'em right in the nose."

For now, a train was an invitation to relax, stationary behind glass, watching cattails sway in the empty sweep of marshland, a landscape dotted by small shacks growing into disparate huddled meetings of homes as they reached the next station, then reverting back into lonely dwellings spread out upon the hills to the west. As they came close to the city, the mass of buildings outside began to match the growing number of those entering the train.

"I used to come up so often for the Panama-Pacific Expo when I was an undergraduate," Cora said with a nostalgic air. "Rodin at the French Pavilion! Walking around the Palace of Fine Arts, it was such a place of love. And the food! French croissants next to Chinese almond cookies next to Mexican tamales. It's the closest I've ever been to traveling abroad."

"Sounds like you had a lovely time," Indra absently replied, wondering in passing with whom she had attended the fair. "Did you go with Hazel?"

"A few of the times," Cora said in a way that Indra could infer that she went with another man. He didn't know how to ask about that part of her past, and so he didn't. She continued, "It wasn't without its oddities. Ford set up a Model T assembly line at the fair. The mass of humanity, just gawking at men at work. Bizarre. And then there was Lincoln Beachey."

"A friend of yours?"

"God, no. You've never heard of him? The world's most famous barnstormer. Son of the city too. Bet half the country's seen him do his tricks on his airplane. He does this great act over the Bay, with loops, flying upside down, the crowd going nuts. They said two hundred and fifty thousand people were watching him fly. And then he does his signature move, the dip of death, and loses control, and hits the water at a hundred and ninety miles per hour."

Indra was taken aback. He didn't expect the long drone of a simple memory to end in such a dramatic fashion. "And was he okay?"

"It's a strange thing to watch a man die, Indra." She put her head on his shoulder. "Have you spent much time in the city?"

"Not really. The longest, I suppose, was the night I arrived."

That first day in San Francisco three weeks ago was nothing more than a passing dream. When he had left the liner, his false identity was easily accepted at the port, and he headed straight for the German consulate in the city, asking for directions, taking two streetcars that traversed the hills of the city. He was dressed in a well-worn gray cotton suit. In his single valise were two black suits of fine Chinese silk in contrast to his usual well-worn gray one, picked up in Shanghai while waiting for a cargo boat to take him to Japan. It had been a tip given to him by Nitin back in India: the tailors of China were second to none. It was Nitin who knew more of the world. It was he who had been most comfortable in it.

Along the way to the consulate, he caught glimpses of the daily lives of his fellow passengers: complaints about work, a tired housewife saying that "the price of milk gone up a penny again," a thin man with a threadbare jacket trying and failing to catch the streetcar, left behind huffing and puffing against a telegraph pole. In this listening and seeing, Indra saw the same everyday life of Calcutta, Shanghai, and Kobe, all transposed. Life in a city could be conducted only through so many permutations, leaving Indra to note how the mundane could find its own recurrence.

The German consulate, built among palatial homes and set behind tall iron gates, was stately red brick, an imposing architecture of orthogonal lines and symmetry—it made Indra think of the neighborhoods of European haughtiness back in India, and thus gave him a vague sense of distaste. After a wait of nearly an hour, he was able to exchange a few words—without sitting—with the balding and severe Bricken, some consular official in a morning suit who had previously been mentioned by Obermeier. His colleague, the consul general Bapp, was quite busy with official business.

"I'm glad you were able to make it, Mr. Mukherjee, or should I call you Mr. Thomas?" Bapp said, laughing. For his journey, Indra wore mahogany beads with a pendant cross around his neck, becoming the missionary Pierre Thomas—a fake persona.

"Indra is fine," he replied, sounding polite and wooden, as if he were talking to a British police officer back in India. "I know you must be busy, and I don't want to keep you. What news do you have of our shared plans? Of the ship to leave port here?"

"No news, I'm afraid. We should have some new developments in two or three weeks' time. You should hear from Mr. Obermeier then. Perhaps then we'll know better as to when the ship can leave port. From what I can understand, though, big things will be awaiting you soon. Big things. Until then, stay here for a while. You'll find there's much to do and see in and around San Francisco. I'm sure Mr. Obermeier has given you enough funds to cover your stay."

Being told of a delay so offhandedly made him feel small and unimportant. He searched for something to feel as if he mattered to these people. "There isn't much. Is there anything the consulate could provide to help allay my costs?"

"At the moment I don't have anything set aside for you, but once you're settled in, telephone us, and we'll see what we can do."

He tried to shake the feeling, but knew he could only feel better if he were among familiar faces. Suresh's brother had idolized him back in India. Maybe Suresh would feel the same. Indra telephoned the English department at Stanford, knowing that Suresh was studying there, and made his way down to Palo Alto the next morning.

FROM THE GRAND DEPOT AT THIRD AND TOWNSEND, WHERE THE BUILDING'S BRILLIANT terra-cotta tiles reminded Indra of Bengal's Gongoni canyon, he and Cora took a series of streetcars, passing first through the city's Chinatown. For a few blocks, the hard sounds of consonants went undeciphered and, as an increasing number of people pressed against each other in the carriage, he had the brief impression of being back in Shanghai or Kobe.

Later, as they passed Pacific Street, Cora let out a laugh. "You ever heard of the Barbary Coast?" she asked.

"I've never been to Africa," Indra said, confused as to what she was talking about.

"No, no, the Barbary Coast here. All the way down Pacific

Street to the wharves. It was a nightlife district. Someone once told me that before the earthquake, every street was brothels next to dives. Completely leveled after the quake. Nothing left. When they rebuilt it, they filled it with nightclubs. You ever dance the Texas Tommy?"

"I'm not much of a dancer. I didn't know you were one either."

"Really, never danced the Texas Tommy?" She smiled, gregarious, full of life. "There was a year or two when everyone from San Francisco to Oakland and down to San Jose was dancing the Texas Tommy. The band gets that swing going, and you find your partner, and you're on the move." She hummed along to some song in her head, snapping her fingers to the beat.

"Sounds like you had a wonderful time," Indra said. Dancing had never been a pleasure of his.

"Here's what we're going to do, Indra, we're going dancing. I'm going to teach you the Texas Tommy. I promise you, I will." She laughed in a warm and generous way, and Indra smiled along with her. He had never taken her for a dancer, and he knew little about the daily life she had lived up to their point of meeting. She was a great unknown, two dimensions slowly revealing a third, a depth of a history. There was an Indra who hated to dance, but he found himself wanting to join with her, wondering when and where the day would come where they could move together to the beat set by a raucous band.

They finally caught a car up a steep hill he recognized from his first day, going into a neighborhood of grand mansions housing the moneyed proprietors of the region, and there too were consulates of foreign governments, and he knew that among them was the German consulate, that maybe Obermeier had received his telegram and was at that very moment was penning a reply, and soon the guns would arrive, and it would finally be time to leave for Berlin.

Before they went on to the Vedanta Society, Cora and Indra were to meet up with the Berkeley cadre at a cafeteria for a quick lunch, the perfect place to split the meager dollar or two between them—money saved on tipping a waiter could be used for another cup of Hills Bros. coffee, after all. A few of the group were already seated inside. Indra and Cora grabbed a single tray and slid it upon the rails, picking up a chicken pot pie and two cups of coffee.

Conversation with these fellows was lively and quick, each of the men fiercely intelligent. They had been talking among themselves about how North America was losing its patience with those from the Asian continent. Canada had turned away the ship *Komagatu Maru*, filled with Punjabis, at the port of Vancouver only a few years prior.

"That chutiya Wilson wants us out. Look what he's doing, trying to include India as part of Asia," said Bishen, a short and wiry man who was at the Berkeley meeting, but had spoken little. "Says we're not Aryan."

"It doesn't affect us, nah?" Dihrendra countered. He was dressed smartly in a suit and a fiery red turban. He hadn't been at the Berkeley meeting and Indra gathered that he worked at the newspaper with Govind. "The law says if you're a student or a teacher or an author or an artist or a man of science, you can still come in."

"It's the labor unions!" a paunchy Naranjan yelled. He studied political economy with Anand at Berkeley and didn't realize that his bushy mustache was filled with crumbs from a piece of toast. "Don't you know your history? Ten years ago, in the Washington State in the north, near Canada, a lumber mill hires some Sikhs, and the whites, they beat six of them with lathis. Then all hundred of the Punjabis leave town. They don't want us working their jobs. Whites only!"

"He has a point," Anand replied, grabbing one of the dinner rolls on the table. "They don't want us working in their factories, their mills, their fields."

"Anand, I hope you're eating more than a roll," Cora interrupted. "You were only eating a slice of bread the last time I saw you. It's an easy way to get scurvy, like some *Robinson Crusoe* pirate. Here, take a bite of this pie." She cut a piece of her portion of chicken pot pie, plopped it on Anand's plate, and soon was dividing up the lot for the rest of the men.

"When I first came to Berkeley," Naranjan continued between mouthfuls of Cora's pie, "they wouldn't let me stay in the first hotel I went to. They said, 'Whites only, go there, that hotel is for blacks.' You are either white or not white. That's what comes first. Being a workingman second."

"It's like caste," Cora said. "The white man sees you as the lowest caste in America. Treats you with contempt."

"That's preposterous!" Singh countered. "What do you think you can say about caste in India? From your chair here in America, you think you can pass judgment?"

Indra could see that Cora was hurt and trying to hide it. If she was to sit with these men as her brothers, she had to endure the kind of insults so common to family. It was hard to ignore the look on her face as she tried not to betray her emotions. Her face was drawn into neutrality, every muscle relaxed into something close to a scowl at rest. He knew, under the surface, she was livid, and could see the faintest red appearing in her pale cheeks.

From what Indra could gather, Singh was some Bihari hothead, always eager to find someone to put down. He had tried and failed to read for a degree in law at Oxford and returned to India, where he was caught up in a revolutionary fervor, coming to San Francisco to continue with the Ghadar movement.

"That's enough, Singh," Indra said. "You let your anger get the best of you. She has a point. I've only been here a short while, but even I can see that Americans talk and talk and talk about the color line. The color line and the caste line are close enough to be the same."

"Indeed! It sounds like you've read Kesariji's recent book on America." Anand said. "He says that in America, punishments against the black man are made by the mob, not by the law. He is placed on the funeral pyre and burned alive, or he is hanged from a tree. Now, tell me, how is this different from our small villages, where the Shudra is beaten for his shadow falling upon the Brahmin?"

"It is completely different," muttered Singh. He had been castigated into silence, nursing his wound in the corner.

Indra saw again how Cora could guide conversation with these men. He had to stop himself from glancing at her with a smitten schoolboy face, lest these men lose their image of him as one who had taken up arms to fight.

"Did any of you ever come across Mangu Ram?" Naranjan asked. "From Hoshiarpur district in Punjab. Father was a leather worker. Said himself that when he came to California and joined with the Ghadar, it was like he had entered a completely new society. We were all equal in our fight."

"Are there many like him in your organization?" Cora asked.

"He was the only one, I think," Naranjan replied. "It never occurred to me to ask. Live and let live here."

"It makes sense. In America, you're grouped on one side of the color line. It wouldn't make sense to continue with divisions from the old world. Not when there are bigger things to fight," Cora concluded.

Indra had thought, perhaps incorrectly, that she still had much learn. She was proving herself to be the student who came to class somehow already knowing what to say, perfect marks achieved effortlessly.

"What happened to Mangu Ram? Is he still part of the party?" Cora asked.

"He left California two years ago on a mission to Manila. They gave him the fake name Nizamuddin—"

"They must love religious names," Indra said, interrupting. "They turned him into a Chisti and me into a missionary."

"He was supposed to receive a shipment of guns to take home," Naranjan continued. "The ship never showed up. Arrested by the British, rescued by the Germans in the middle of the night."

Govind was going to meet them at the Vedanta Society, but if he had been here, Indra would have given him a knowing look, that this story of Mangu Ram was a rejoinder to his warning that the Germans didn't care for them. Maybe Govind would have rolled his eyes in response, as if to say the man wouldn't need to be rescued if the guns had actually been delivered.

When they left the cafeteria and made their way up one final hill, Indra turned to look upon the brilliance of the San Francisco Bay in the distance. Its waters seemed serene in the clarity of the day, marred only by small blue-black clouds of exhaust, engines moving upon the Bay, steamers taking workers from the eastern reaches of the area into the city. Above these boats were cliques of gulls that hung and dove, looking for scraps to steal from the lunches of the dockworkers up and down the piers.

It was a beauty he had never seen.

"It really is something else, isn't it?" Cora said. "Every time I see a view like that, I think I don't ever want to leave a place like this."

There was something about what she said that struck him with a touch of anxiety. For the first time, he felt an inkling that he would be waiting for his German contact for some long and protracted period of time, that in this waiting he would soon gain Naranjan's belly from one too many chicken pot pies.

He looked to see that no one from the group turned around as they kept on standing. When Indra had led men like those walking in front of him and Cora, he had sacrificed his happiness for a greater good. There was something from his time here that he already wanted to keep close, both here and during what came next. He slipped his hand into hers. "Wait till you see the sunrise on the Bay of Bengal. That'll give this a run for its money."

He saw how she smiled at the thought. He did too.

CHAPTER SEVEN

It was hard to miss the Vedanta Society building. The first two floors looked like any other building in the neighborhood, rolling bay windows and gingerbread trim, but it was the third floor that seemed to have lost its mind in some fantastical journey through the Eastern realms of the known world.

Rimmed by a columned terrace and archways of a vaguely Oriental style, the building was topped by a series of domes: at one corner the turret of an ancient castle, at the other the teardrops of a Russian Orthodox church, at another the sloped roof of a Swedish hut, and still another looking like the hat of some Mongolian hunter once set out upon the steppes, now lost and forlorn on some other continent. Perhaps the architect had asked the society the simple yes-or-no question if they wanted to dome their building, and the only response was *more*.

Inside was a small hall with perhaps seven or eight rows of wooden pews, no different from any other church. But the pulpit had been replaced by a small elevated stage. On the stage was a statue of a man seated cross-legged, placed under some sort of intricately carved awning, itself covered with fine red and orange cloth.

"Cora, a pleasure to see you here," Govind said, reaching out to shake her hand. He had been the only one who met the group here at the society.

"What a building," Cora replied. "It certainly stands apart from the rest of the neighborhood."

"We had high hopes for this place. We thought it would be a grand meeting place for others interested in our cause. But, as Indra must have told you, things have gone awry."

"He told me a little. Are we sitting near the front?"

"No, no. A wall near the back. Leave the first pews for his acolytes and devotees. The ten of us are enough to send a message."

Those disciples began to file in, mainly women, most of them seeming to be on the precipice between womanhood and dotage, needing something that could take them away from a life without purpose. Children raised, husbands comfortable, grandchildren a few years away, and hours upon hours of empty time all in front of them for the taking.

They had the same searching, yearning look as those some of the true believers she had seen in John Scullion's home, of those looking for the divine truth from the theosophists, men and women searching for something to take them beyond the life they knew into a divine revelation, a group waiting patiently for a spirit to enter them, to draw them to speak in a tongue whose language was twisted by an Eastern syllabary.

The swami came in. He saw them standing at the rear and his wide nose flared. He shook his head but said nothing. Cora looked over to Indra and Govind, who kept their stone-faced scowls but nevertheless seemed to have relaxed after the swami's modest tell made it clear that he didn't want them attending his service.

When Indra had mentioned the swami, she had imagined some pasty and wiry man—anyone against the cause of freedom had to suffer from some lack that could only manifest as a starved body. But she was surprised to see that he was quite tall, and quite healthy too, his doughy stomach framed by a sash the color of a winter tangerine tied at his waist.

She was still hungry. She hadn't wanted to give away part of her meal, but these men didn't seem to know how to take care of themselves. She could put up with a lot of things, but the inability to

take basic care of oneself was not one of them. She had been forced
to learn it at a young age—it wasn't as if she knew innately how to
launder clothes, or clean a room, or cook a meal. Put in an effort!
Learn, for God's sake! She could grab each of these damned men
and shake him like a new mother could shake a baby to death: the
exasperating love that could turn on a dime.

The service itself was entirely in Sanskrit, though pamphlets
were in the backs of the pews, and Cora wondered if she could
thumb through one of them, but it would perhaps ruin the protest
if one of the ten suddenly broke character to sift through temple
literature. Without any guide, her mind wandered in and out of the
present moment.

Mr. President, you say that the want of liberty is the fundamental need of the human spirit.

Mr. President, what will you do to advance the cause of freedom?

Mr. President, how long must women wait for liberty?

On the other side of the country, the Silent Sentinels were holding their placards in front of the White House, protesting for each
and every American woman to have her God-given right for freedom and the vote.

Mr. Swami, why will you remain silent on the march for freedom?

Perhaps this was a moment in history when the selfsame ideas
of freedom were appearing like some divine epidemic, outbreaks in
disparate countries across the world. And she was gifted the opportunity to feel its effects in varying places—an entire world brought
to her.

Translation was always an act of love.

The swami kept intoning in Sanskrit. Sometimes what he said
would interest her, the cadence and the sound, a language more
like the beat of a drum. She thought about what she had said to
Indra, about teaching him the Texas Tommy. She meant it. After

days spent cloistered with ideas—fickle words upon a page—few things could be better than feeling the presence of her body with another. There were times when the seriousness of all things had to be broken, to let the band take control of the moment, all noise and raucous laughter that whinnied in her ears long after the moment passed. There could be a luster and a joy in finding that breathless release from the day.

In the same way, she was a little jealous of artists. Unlike those cloistered in libraries, they were able to live between body and result, a life that opened up through the hands. At one of Scullion's parties, she once met a Swiss woman who had graduated from Stanford and then gone up to San Francisco to study at the Art Association. This artist was about to head off to South America for some reason or another, Cora couldn't remember, but what she did recall was the awe that this woman could live across continents in search of the next canvas, that time in the studio was counterbalanced by a train, an exhibition, a journey ever outward from a point of origin.

Her thoughts were broken by the sounds of pews creaking, feet shuffling, the brief stretch of all things once still as the parishioners stood up. The swami lit a few candles on a steel platter—the service was on its way to ending. She glanced to her left, and Govind seemed to be so pleased, a self-satisfied look of victory on his face. But the look on Indra's matched what Cora felt: victory over what, exactly?

The service ended. The women at the front stood up. Almost all of them had gray-at-the-roots hair and were dressed in severe autumnal colors, in dresses with high collars and long sleeves. Their desperation for something beyond the life they lived seemed so clear to Cora—she saw in them a version of herself that could exist if given the chance to take root. Among them was a man she hadn't noticed before, short and trim in a tweed suit, as if he were going hunting after the service. He turned briefly to glance at all of them in the back row, and as he did, Cora had the feeling that he was scanning their faces a bit too closely. He soon turned to face the swami again, and as he did, he put his bowler back on carefully, so as not to upset the gracious amount of pomade used to comb his thin blond hair.

The ten protestors walked outside, none of them willing to stay to receive the blessings from the fire that concluded the ceremony. They milled outside the door like little chattering pigeons pleased that they had managed to scrounge a whole salami from the trash.

"I believe we sent our message," Govind said.

"What message?" Indra asked. "We said nothing, we did nothing."

"Didn't you see the look on his face?" Naranjan asked excitedly. "He saw us, he knew what we were doing there. He'll think twice next time he tries to cross us."

"I thought he wasn't sufficiently supportive of the cause of independence?" Cora asked. "How has he crossed you, exactly?"

"The head priest there is nothing but a charlatan and a thief," Govind said, growing excited. "That slick priest is the rudest man I've ever encountered, hiding behind his so-called tenets of faith so that he may treat us—"

"Slow down," Indra said. "What can one priest do to offend someone like yourself?"

"It's different here, you know. They're not just priests. They're powerful. Whites, like those women in the front row, come to men like him. They're all women of some means."

"Wouldn't you want him to spread the word?" Cora asked. "Thread the line between spiritual and national liberation?"

Govind grimaced. "He's sabotaging it. We had plans to buy and renovate a small house in Berkeley to create a home for the Indian students on and around that university. We had even found a donor to provide us the funds for the home. A Mrs. Kinnie."

"Was she here tonight?" Indra interrupted.

"No, unfortunately not," Govind answered. "She's the type

who never stops being a mother. She's old. Ancient. And still she seeks out more and more young men to foster. She has a fondness for Indians."

"I had no idea about this. She was the snake and he the cunning charmer. Convinced her we were nothing but rabble-rousers. She pulled her support for the Berkeley house after speaking with him."

"And that's all you did?" Cora asked. "Stare at him?"

"No, of course not," Singh said, sneering. "We've also published several articles about him in the Ghadar."

That was something, Cora thought. At least they were coming out publicly against the man, not simply staging impotent protests. But when Cora looked toward Indra, she saw grave annoyance on his face. The others clearly did too.

"Oh, look alive, Indra. You'll be in Berlin soon," Govind said. "You'll be fighting again like you used to. We're not in India here. We can't behave as we would wish. We can speak as we want, but we're guests in this country, and if we try to bomb this building or shoot someone, we'd all be deported in an instant, if not hanged here. Deportation is a quick trip to the firing line back in India. We can write, we can organize, but the grand moves are reserved for elsewhere."

"You're right, grand moves elsewhere," Indra said. Cora could see his thoughts were elsewhere too, eyes searching some unknown horizon. "I have to get going," he said in a softer but decisive voice. "Thank you for bringing me along and showing me this. Cora, would you like to come with me or stay with these fellows?"

Cora agreed to leave with him but didn't ask where. He gave the group a perfunctory goodbye and fell quiet as they walked uphill. They didn't take the streetcar this time, and she huffed and puffed a bit as they walked. Indra seemed to be lost in his own train of thought. She wanted to ask him what was bothering him, but everything between them was too new, and she didn't yet have the language to pierce through his shell. She knew if she didn't, that silence would grow, maybe even eat away at the little they had together, so she finally asked him.

"That was so boring," Indra said, exasperated.

"Govind had a point: there's only so much to do. Open violence doesn't do anyone any favors here."

The final climb until they reached the top of the hill—the sidewalk was so steep here, the city had carved steps into the concrete to assist in the ascent.

"When I crossed the Pacific, I brought my gun. It was an old Enfield looted from an armory after the army began to replace their pistols with Colts. I never went to an operation without it."

Cora was shocked at Indra's admission. She was no stranger to a gun—they were common enough back in the mines, although those were often rifles used for hunting. A gun in a city seemed illicit, an invitation to disaster. "Do you have it with you now?"

"No, I don't. It feels so strange to be without it. It's like I have to relearn what it means to fight a greater power—what it means to disobey without the force of arms. I'm not sure if I like it. Home was a place of action. I understand that this isn't my country, and we can't just go around shooting guns. If standing around and being quiet in the back of a room is what counts as successful, I don't want to be part of it."

They reached the top of the hill, and the path flattened. The conversations she could catch among those in the neighborhood gave proof to the wealth that was here: tidbits about maids, drivers, cars, and she thought she even heard something of the Bohemian Grove. The sun continued to shine in the heavens, and the breeze, upon which floated the laughter, conversation, and midday hustle of others, felt like a balm against the strain of reaching that point. As she caught her breath, she managed to ask him a question: "Does that mean you're leaving, then?"

He didn't answer. She wasn't sure if he had heard her.

She had fallen for Indra. And she had fallen for him not only because she was attracted to him as someone wholly other than herself, but also because she was falling for the idea, still faint but becoming more real, of becoming some new version of herself that existed only with him. She had been to San Francisco countless times, and never once had she realized that there was a temple built for Hindu worship right up the street. What other rooms, what other wonders, were there waiting for her?

She knew Indra liked a challenge. She stopped walking. He didn't realize it for a few strides, had to double back once he did.

Men loved talking about the beauty of violence. She had seen it at a few socialist meetings: bum anarchists would show up and go on and on about how one little bomb could change the world. It was maddeningly stupid. They read their Johann Most and their Luigi Galleani, and suddenly, they fell in love with the possibility of being more than little men feeling lost in a great big world by marrying nitroglycerin to fire through the fuse.

Every bombing was the same. The smolder would finally dissipate into the air, and once the smoke cleared, the police would always find the hand that had thrown the bomb, and the murdered politician would eventually be found again in his successor, and life would continue on as old, except now the police raids would grow more frequent, the batons would hit the skulls a little bit harder, a satisfying crack upon each head, just like what had happened in San Francisco the previous summer.

"Do you know of Thomas Mooney and Warren Billings?" she asked. When Indra said no, she went on, "The Preparedness Day parade last summer. Someone set off a bomb at Steuart and Market, killed nine people. San Francisco's a union town, but it's run by a bunch of backward-looking reactionaries. None of them voted for suffrage back in 1912. Anyway, San Francisco is Sunny Jim's city, and Sunny Jim is a capitalist through and through. They arrested Mooney and Billings on a lark. They were fighting for labor, fighting for the little man. Ended up being scapegoats. Thankfully, even Wilson saw it for what it was. Got rid of the death penalty for Mooney. They're still up in San Quentin. Rotting away.

"Even if you had a gun or a bomb, it doesn't matter who's guilty or innocent. Once someone lobs the bomb, they start the search for a scapegoat. I don't want to see you hanged up at San Quentin or any other prison. It's not worth it."

"It's always a possibility," Indra said, hands in his pockets. He looked up at the sky, squinting against the sun. Without looking down, he began again. "My friend Nitin Chatterjee, he had taught me everything I knew, and I learned recently of his death back in India."

"I'm sorry to hear that." She reached to touch his arm, and he let himself be touched. She slid her hand into his and they stood for a moment, holding hands.

"He was shot by the colonial police. A scapegoat. A victim. I don't want to meet his same fate, but I don't want his death to be in vain. I'm still learning what to do, Cora. I'm still not sure."

They started walking again and turned left onto yet another hill. She knew Indra had to find some third way, some path that would take him between either giving up the cause or giving up his life.

"Where are we going?" Cora asked.

"The German consulate."

"To do what, exactly?"

"I sent my contact a message. Since we're here, I want to call upon them to see what's going to happen and when."

"Indra, it's Sunday," she said quietly, so as not to upset him with her corrective. "Surely the building will be closed today."

Indra looked sheepish, admitting he hadn't considered it, and indeed, when they got to the building, they found it inaccessible behind a locked wrought-iron gate. He looked so embarrassed, unsure of himself. She rubbed his back as they walked away.

"It's okay," she said, choosing to ignore what had just transpired. She wanted to help. She wouldn't let on that she was witness to a man utterly confused about what lay before him. "Let's go home."

CHAPTER EIGHT

KGPE UAINR ZALAL PPIAI. WIQ UYMQBE YECMCB YGAFW HGBT. XRCM
MSCGP HYRID U WMSGKQNIFXC.

That's what the letter had said. Unsigned, of course. No return address. Postmarked from Chicago, Illinois. It was an Obermeier message, as if Obermeier himself were some sort of small and petty god, blessed with omniscience yet forced to communicate with mankind through the smallest of acts, a Shiva whose only power now was to manifest as a stalagmite lingam in some lost cave.

And like all mysterious and small acts sent from the gods, this one had to be pored over to be deciphered. A hint had been entrusted to Indra prior to the journey: "and we shall say forever, Bande Mataram."

They had preferred simple ciphers to communicate back in India, and this seemed no different. Indra took a sheet of paper and drew a table.

	1	2	3	4	5
1	B	A	N	D	E
2	M	T	R	C	F
3	G	H	I/J	K	L
4	O	P	Q	S	U
5	V	W	X	Y	Z

He rewrote the message as one long block of letters:

KGPEUAINRZALALPPIAIWIQUYMQBEYECMCBYG

AFWHGBTXRCMMSCGPHYRIDUWMSGKQNIFXC

And then, he broke it into pieces of five:

KGPEU	GAFWH
AINRZ	GBTXR
ALALP	CMMSC
PIAIW	GPHYR
IQUYM	IDUWM
QBEYE	SGKQN
CMCBY	IFXC

Using the table, he turned the letters into numbers:

34 31 42 15 45	31 12 25 52 32
12 33 13 23 55	31 11 22 53 23
12 35 12 35 42	24 21 21 44 24
42 33 12 33 52	31 42 32 54 23
33 43 45 54 21	33 14 45 52 21
43 11 15 54 15	44 31 34 43 13
24 21 24 11 54	33 25 53 24

Which he then transposed into several tables:

3	4	3	1	4
2	1	5	4	5
1	2	3	3	1
3	2	3	5	5
1	2	3	5	1
2	3	5	4	2
4	2	3	3	1
2	3	3	5	2
3	3	4	3	4
5	5	4	2	1
4	3	1	1	1
5	5	4	1	5
2	4	2	1	2
4	1	1	5	4
3	1	1	2	2
5	5	2	3	2
3	1	1	1	2
2	5	3	2	3
2	4	2	1	2
1	4	4	2	4
3	1	4	2	3
2	5	4	2	3
3	3	1	4	4
5	5	2	2	1
4	4	3	1	3
4	4	3	1	3
3	3	2	5	
5	3	2	4	

Which he then turned into new pairs,
matching the numbers up vertically:

32 41 35 14 45	35 15 12 23 22
13 22 33 35 15	32 15 13 12 23
12 23 35 54 12	21 44 24 12 24
42 23 33 35 12	32 15 44 22 33
35 35 44 32 41	35 35 12 42 41
45 35 14 11 15	44 44 33 11 33
24 41 21 15 24	35 33 22 54

He could then take these numbers and reference his
original cipher key once again:

HOLDU	LEART
NTILE	HENAR
ARLYA	MSCAC
PRILA	HESTI
LLSHO	LLAPO
ULDBE	SSIBI
COMEC	LITY

Giving him the final message of:

HOLD UNTIL EARLY APRIL. ALL SHOULD BECOME CLEAR THEN.
ARMS CACHE STILL A POSSIBILITY.

Indra was aghast. The amount of work he had just laid out, a half hour of patiently matching letters to numbers back to letters in the confines of his room, only to be told to wait further—something that he had already been doing.

An old habit: he burned the telegram and its decryption in the sink and went to open his window to clear the room of the smell of fresh ash. Outside, he watched a few spindly men, probably students, walking at a slow, methodical pace not unlike a drove of donkeys seeking home, talking loudly about that evening's smoker at the economics department, that there would be a fair amount of free food at the party. None of them smiled, and yet Indra imagined them happy, futures wide open, still an immense plain of human possibility.

Not even in Japan, where he was unmoored in a culture and language not his own, had he felt as between and betwixt as he did now. If Indra hadn't been safely abroad, he would have been dead, like Nitin, or at least arrested again, left to rot in some cell. The conclusion: to be alive was a gift. He had been given a chance to escape, and he was going to make the best of it. He was going to trust the process laid out in front of him.

One delay, another, now a wait for a little over a month. How to pass the time? He surely didn't want to go back to the Ghadar. It had been something great only a few years ago. But after the Lahore Conspiracy, it seemed much smaller. The moves they made were tantamount to chess pieces not being played, instead rotating in circles in a single square of the game. It depressed him to see men of great talent and potential reduced to being happy with what they got.

He went to lie on his bed. To pass a month with a beautiful woman. Not a bad thing.

A passion was, at first, two individuals finding their own pleasure in the other. What had passed between them was ceding to something more: an invitation into frailty and mutual aid. He had been told by his German handlers to wait patiently, and so it would be, because to wait was to invite more of her into his life. Whatever had brought them together, they were becoming intertwined now, bound by the weight of an uncertain future.

In any case, he was on the edge of running out of money. He had just come from Suresh's home to seek help in that regard. When Suresh had first arrived in Palo Alto, he'd gone door-to-door looking for work, asking anyone who answered if he could clean their house, finally finding one who said yes. Suresh told Indra that he had learned more about America in the hour it took to find his first job than he had in the years since. Some, he said, would simply say no and close the door—a simple arrangement. Others would see this dark-skinned man and launch into a tirade so fierce, he would scuttle away before they had a chance to close the door.

Indra had expected Suresh to give him advice on where and how to find a job, not on the status of Indians in America.

"Remember this," Suresh had told Indra over a cup of coffee. "Color is as important to an American as varna and jati. The Brahmin who is polluted by the mere shadow of a Sudra is the same as the white who sees a man of color leave his place. We're in a protective cocoon here on this campus, for the most part. It gives Hazel and me a measure of freedom. The world outside of this college will see you as nothing more than a nuisance."

Indra had been confused as to what Suresh was trying to say. "I've heard of this," he said. "There's a division between black and white, but our ancestors were Aryan. Surely we're more white than black?"

"You'll find that they see you as both when it suits them. They'll trust a Chinaman as they trust a faithful dhobi—they'll have him launder clothes, perhaps even in their own home. If that same man leaves behind his father's career, gains an education, and comes back to marry the white man's daughter, why, he's equal to a black man now."

It was odd advice, considering both Hazel and Cora, but Suresh seemed tied to America now. He had nothing but ire for the nationalists these days, seeing them as wanting to be a different boot to place upon the necks of the same tired and poor people. Indra scoffed at the characterization: it made quite a difference to be ruled by one's own people versus a foreign power. Perhaps it was because Suresh was beginning to feel like America was a home for him that he felt compelled to live within its own prejudices, navigate it as an immigrant would, one yearning to be accepted and loved by his new home.

Indra, on the other hand, was a sojourner. What did his landlady say? He looked handsome, like a Sicilian. Same skin color, and as tall as the best of them. If anyone asked, he was from Sicily. Or maybe he would just say nothing at all. From now on, he was from nowhere, a flickered apparition living among people for a short while.

There was a feeling he had on the boat coming to California. There had been that woman at dinner who had called him cosmopolitan. He wanted to learn from her, wanted to see what she could teach him at this moment. Maybe becoming cosmopolitan also meant finding the world in the smallest of places. Cora knew people in this small and unassuming town. He would go to her and ask to meet some of them, hear what they had to say. The world beyond could wait, if only for a moment.

Nitin laughed. Waiting with a woman, are you? A waste of time. You don't need to ask permission from the toffs at the consulate. The guns aren't coming. Go East, go to Germany on your own.

Were you ever lonely, Nitin? Indra asked, changing the subject. Did you ever find yourself needing something else?

Don't be a coward. We have to lead men from strength. And if you're asking if I ever needed the company of a woman, why? I could pay one by the hour.

Indra thought this to be such a cold life, even though it had been his only months ago. You're gone, Nitin. And now, I'm not like you anymore, Nitin. I need something else.

You're growing soft.

Indra felt a pang of embarrassment at the admonition. He wasn't growing soft. He was growing older.

A search for stability could be reckless in its own way, a million more reasonable paths cast aside for want of a vision of a life that could be. And it was within that could-be where the danger lay: could-be was a mirage, a flimsy belief in the capacity for expectations to somehow transmute from fantasy into reality. Maybe the truth was that life could grant only half-hearted resolutions to the perplexities arisen from chance encounters.

Or maybe it could offer something more.

CHAPTER NINE

A stable life needed to be built upon a foundation of money. There was a job posting to work in a kitchen at a fraternity house near campus. There, Indra met a bald and stocky Japanese man who scowled at him when Indra introduced himself. He was probably no older than Indra, though his hands, lined with small scars, told his story of years spent working in kitchens. His white chef's coat was stained with the blood of the afternoon's meat, giving him the look of a butcher rather than a chef.

"You can wash dishes?" the cook asked.

Indra was nervous—even while in Kobe, he could never figure out how to charm or chat with Japanese men. "Of course," he said. He had never washed dishes in his life. It couldn't be that difficult.

Soon the lunch rush began, and the dishes piled up—bowls, plates, spoons, forks, most with food still on them.

What was Cora doing at that moment? Indra wondered. He wanted to help, wanted to show her that here, in the safety of this campus, the world could quiet down.

"Pay attention!" the cook yelled. "Can't you see? You're not scraping the food before you put it in the basin." He pulled out a plate from the sink, grease and leftovers dripping off its edge. "You're doing it all wrong, and too slow. These dishes need to be cleaned faster, better!"

When his boss wasn't looking, Indra ate a piece of bread or a vegetable that was untouched on a plate sent to him to clean. Good food was increasingly becoming a luxury, and he relished his opportunity to eat for free, but every bite taken was a moment away from the job, so he tried, double-time, to scrape the wet remnants of remaining food off the plates into the trash. It was no use. New arrivals kept piling up. At the end of lunch, when the cook came to check on the cleanliness of each dish, he had only one reply to this disaster of a first day.

"You're fired," he said.

"Fired?" Indra asked, somewhat unsurprised.

"You're dismissed from the job," the cook barked, handing him a single dollar before trying to shoo him out of the kitchen. "It's clear you've never done this before. I won't be needing you for dinner."

"What did I do wrong?" Indra asked.

"First you scrape, then you wash in hot water with soap, then you rinse, then you dry. You've dried nothing! All these wet dishes, who's going to dry them?"

"A good point." Indra laughed with a forced charm as he reminded himself that there were always more fraternities. There were more places to practice this newfound lesson in dishwashing. "One that I won't soon forget, my friend. Before I go, I have a small question for you. I've been in California for two months now, and I haven't had a single grain of rice. Bread, yes, potatoes, too many, but rice? I miss it."

"I fire you, and you're asking me about rice?"

"I was going to ask you, whether or not you fired me. It seems like this is my last chance. As a fellow rice-eater from the East, I figured you would know."

The chef eyed him up and down before seeming to relax, as if Indra's move from employee back to civilian lent a hitherto unknown comfort to their interaction. "I like Takahashi's, up in San Mateo. Small general store, mainly serves us Japanese. If you just want any rice, there's a small general store for the Chinese south of here, in Mayfield. I think his prices are too high. Another bigger store down in San Jose. Never been."

All it took was a smile and a casual air, and the cook's hard exterior gave way quickly. Faux-charm had its place. "My friend, being in your employ may not have worked out, but my stomach and my spirit thank you. There's nothing more I want than a bowl of rice."

He smiled as he left, and couldn't wait to rush to Cora to tell her the story. He wouldn't disappoint her with a story of failure. It was better to make her laugh with the image of him fired for being unable to properly wash a dish, then patiently asking where to find a bowl of rice. With her, he would resolve to take himself less seriously. To become someone of the world, relishing all of its strange ways. For now, he went to the next fraternity to try to find work: a job was a thing easily lost and gained.

INDRA SOON HEEDED THE COOK'S ADVICE AND TOOK THE TRAIN A FEW STOPS UP TO SAN Mateo, wandering from the station down the crowded shops of B Street to find the market the cook had recommended, until finally, there it was, a simple grocer squeezed between a Chinese laundry and a blacksmith's shop. Inside, the place had a briny smell of the sea, emanating from the shrimp sold as bait, alongside lines, lures, and poles for those willing to work to catch their evening meal. He made a mental note to himself to try to save up for some gear—now that he ate meat, he could save a dollar by trying to catch his own dinner every night.

He was going to treat Cora to a homemade meal of rice. In his newfound hemmed-in life, this kind of meager offering was one of the few things he could gift her: a table and a warm bowl and a few friends.

Behind the counter were shelves filled with cans of fermented goods and bottles of black and clear sauces. Lining the scuffed wooden floor were heavy canvas bags filled with white rice, and in the shop were two men in oilskin jackets and rubber boots, speaking to the proprietor in Japanese. For a moment, Indra felt that he had been pacing Kobe's wide and crowded avenues, seeking out some market stall to find a meal that could placate his tired body.

He had been in that city only a week, a brief respite on the way to California. It was the first time he had traveled into the distance, and he'd been doing so as Pierre Thomas, a French-Indian novitiate from Pondicherry heading to Paris—via a stopover in the United States—to further his studies in theology. He was a new man with a new identity, a fresh passport in his pocket, complete with an American visa, all supplied by the Germans.

As a ten-year-old, he had attended a Scottish Presbyterian school in Calcutta and struggled to remember the precepts drilled into his head: the trinity, the crucifixion, God the Son, God the Father, God the Ghost. The number three must have been important, so Indra completed his costume with three purchases in a back-alley Christian bookstore in Kobe: a thumbtack-size golden cross to pin to his coat's lapel, a wooden crucifix to hang from his neck, and a copy of the Bible bound in fine black Moroccan leather to carry wherever he went.

When he finally left Japan, he was surprised to see his ticket was first-class. He had smuggled himself from India to China and onward to Japan among the barrels and boxes of cargo. He could have barricaded himself in his cabin when going to America, but hiding away would draw attention to him through the small-town gossip that could form on a ship, so he lived with ease out in the open. Or perhaps it was because any time alone would lead his thoughts on that circuitous route back to the past, back to Nitin, and it was true. Silence invited the embarrassment of death—the same questions: Why did I live, why did he die? Fighting among men was a constant competition of who was braver, stronger, most capable of handling the pain—who was the man among boys. And to die was to be crowned the manliest of them all.

"Can I help you?" the shop's proprietor asked Indra in English, taking a break from his Japanese conversation with the other customer.

Oh, keep speaking in that language, Indra wished to say, content to pause and remember, if only for a moment. He made some excuse that he was browsing the fishing gear. The two men seemed to look through him with a suspicion that could only mean they knew a man who fished when they saw one, and Indra was not among them, not one who could lean against a pier's railing for hours on end, waiting for tension in the line, betting time against hunger that there existed some vestige of life in the opaque waters that lay beyond.

Dinner had been such a pleasure on that liner, a small, flitting flame of a city filled with impromptu associations, saloons, divisions of class, berths lined up like apartments on a neat street, each filled with Japanese officials headed to Honolulu or San Francisco, the remainder being American missionaries (and how dreadful a town of proselytizers could be). On the second night of his journey, Indra found himself sitting next to a young American woman in the cavernous dining room humming with the white-noise murmur of conversations and the sharp clink of silverware against worn ceramic plates, the place lit brightly with electric lamps.

"And where are you from?" The woman seated next to him asked this question as if she already knew the answer. She ran her finger around her wineglass's rim, causing it to respond with a low tune. Her name was Jane and she was headed to Washington from India. She told him how she had finished a stint as a clerk in an American consulate. Indra had never expected to dine with a blonde and fair-skinned woman—there simply had never been any opportunity in India.

"Pondicherry," Indra replied with the coolness of a practiced lie. The domineering Anglo-Indian teachers of his high school days had trained him on how to eat in the European fashion, but it had been years since he had done so with ease, so he had to focus on using the cutlery, a long-dormant second language in which he stumbled to find fluency again.

"Ah, lovely," she said, turning herself in her chair to face Indra. "I was posted in Madras for three years. Tell me, do you speak Tamil? I've picked up a few words myself, and I'd love to practice. It'd be a shame to lose the language so quickly."

Indra swallowed hard. "No, I don't," he said with a weak smile and returned to cutting the boiled potato on his plate, taking care to avoid the sausage placed next to it.

"You're from Pondicherry and you don't speak Tamil? How can that be?"

Indra felt caught in his own lie—with a member of the American government, at that. He put down his knife and fork and cleared his throat. On the exterior, he remained cool, even looking at her with faint disdain, as if she had been the one to get everything wrong. "Ah, you're quite mistaken. I'm Bengali. I was born in Chandernagore, making me a subject of the French. I relocated to Pondicherry only a few years ago to further my studies."

"Of course," she said, putting down her wineglass. "I've seen you reading your Bible on the deck. Rumor on the ship has it that you'll be joining a monastic order—is it true?" She leaned forward to place her hand on Indra's forearm.

Indra felt a gut punch of excitement from her touch, a surprise so sudden and so sweet that he hoped she did it again. "They've spoken of me, have they?" he asked with faux surprise.

"It's hard not to notice such a studious and well-kept young man on board a ship as small as this one," she said, parting her wine-colored lips to smile. "Tell me, though, where are you headed?"

She kept on asking him questions. He could have slowed the conversation by turning a few of them back to her, but there was something about that touch, about being forced to weave a tale on such short notice, something intoxicating about being the center of attention, when he didn't know if anything he said formed an edifice that could withstand the pressure of lie upon lie. "Paris," he said. "I hope to further my theological studies there."

"And join a monastic order?" she asked in a pleading tone, as if trying to glean valuable information.

"That I don't know. I leave my future up to God."

"You must get this all the time—you are quite the cosmopolitan," she said, leaning back in her chair and looking up to the saloon's ceiling. "Born in one place, living in another, traveling the world. And you seem at such ease with it too."

Indra thanked her with a smile, wide, real, and genuine. No one had ever called him that before.

"If only I weren't headed back to Washington," she said. "I'd come right with you. Traveling to Paris with a Christian gentleman from India. I can't think of a better adventure."

"Fate, as it were, brought us together here for a short time," Indra said. "Perhaps that's all we can hope for."

"And I'm glad to share this journey with you," she said warmly.

Dinner was over, and Indra said good night. He went alone to the main deck for some air. A godly Pierre Thomas couldn't lust after a woman, couldn't risk his cover, given to him so carefully by Obermeier.

Looking over the railing into the darkened expanse that stretched all around, he buzzed with the potential of what the woman had called him: cosmopolitan. Above, the sky was filled with the pinprick brilliance of thousands of stars, not a single breath of air between him and the heavens. And then the resound of a stranger playing some piano, its notes dancing upon the empty expanse of the blackened sea.

The two men at the counter finally left the shop, and Indra could idle no longer among the lures. He walked over to the counter and rummaged through the pockets of his trousers. "How much rice can ten cents get me?"

"It's sixteen cents a pound, my friend, one pound minimum."

Indra again jangled the coins in his pocket, made fewer after the trip on the train. "Would you take fifteen cents for a pound? I haven't got a penny on me."

The man looked Indra up and down with annoyance. "Let's just make it even. I weigh out a pound, take a few spoonfuls off the top, and we'll call it fifteen cents."

"Anything for a bit of rice," Indra said. He couldn't help himself. "I haven't had a spoonful since Kobe."

"Ah, so you've been to Japan!" the proprietor responded, suddenly animated in his conversation with his customer.

"Only passed through, on my way from India."

"I haven't seen Japan since I moved to California in 1898, nineteen years now. Tell me, how was it?"

Indra didn't know how to answer such a broad and vague question. "Beautiful. Bustling. Grand buildings built in the Western style, and yet the streets filled with the pride of the only unconquered peoples in all of Asia."

"Here, I'll give you an extra cup," the man said, pouring a bit extra into the small canvas bag that would hold Indra's rice. "My name's Tokutaro, nice to meet you."

Indra beamed and gave the man his hand. "Indranath."

"From India?" Tokutaro asked, eyeing him up and down. "Don't look much like a workingman. Why are you here?"

"Don't be quick to judge. I just came from washing dishes, my friend. Anyway, I'm just passing through," Indra said. "Here for only a small while."

"Washing dishes and just passing through, huh? That's what I told myself. Worked across the bay in the salt ponds, supervising the men during the harvest. So many Japanese and not a single store to serve them. Opened up my own shop back in 1911. You look like you could have an eye for business. Maybe you'll do the same for

Indians."

Indra laughed. "I don't think I'll be here long enough." Suddenly, the store felt a bit too small, its unmoving air suffused with rotting ocean spray was enough now to make him feel a bit nauseated. "Thank you for the rice, Tokutaro," he added.

"Come back soon, Indranath." He waved. "And if you open up that store, don't do it too close to mine."

Outside, Indra took in a deep breath of the fresh air, but there came a confusion of what he was actually doing in California. He should have been fighting for his people—which ostensibly he still was. Indra had once sworn it was nobler to die for country than to live under the boot of foreign rule. To die for what? The world was starved now of Nitin's light, of the width of his beautiful smile, of his endless capacity to help. The world was more than shoot-outs in Calcutta. Part of him always knew this.

To be called out so succinctly by the woman on the ship: cosmopolitan.

In India, his life had a singular direction: the fight for freedom and independence. That cause had rarely taken him far from home, and now the world was opening up. As he wandered through it, he wanted to see more of it, take what it had to offer. And not alone either—he hadn't realized the depths of his own loneliness, but given the chance to love another, he didn't want to lose it.

Nitin, he called out into memory. There are other ways to be a man. It's not all dandies or boxers. Trust me.

There was no response.

His world, right now, was haggling for his daily rice at the counter of a shop. But more would come, soon. He just had to be patient, wait for early April, and together, he and Cora would see what would happen next.

CHAPTER TEN

I have a surprise for you," Indra had told her.

The surprise, it turned out, was that Indra was going to cook everyone a meal at Suresh's house, and so Cora sat next to Hazel in Suresh's kitchen as Indra conducted a grand experiment in cooking rice.

"I haven't seen you in well over a month," Hazel said with a knowing air. "How's your thesis coming along?"

"It's coming along great," Cora lied. She hadn't given up on her thesis yet, but it was true that she was putting in far less effort. Perfunctory trips to the library. Her eyes would scan the words over and over in the books in front of her, and nothing would stick. Each word scribbled onto the page was agonizing, and it was through pure strength of will that she finished what she had. Her mind had been incapable of settling upon the thoughts in front of her, instead flirting with the air, the clouds, the sound of rain tapping against the library's windows.

"I've been working on it quite a bit since I last saw you," Cora said.

"I'm sure you have," Hazel said with a little smirk.

"What's that supposed to mean?" Cora asked, perhaps a little meanly. She knew the question. She had seen it in countless others: the doldrums of love. Women falling into the same pattern of being courted, the inevitable nuptial vows, and finally disappearing through a dissolving of the self into his interests, his needs, the rear-

ing of his children. That initial spark always came from a fundamental boredom, a realization that there was nothing to do in this
world except find a man and become his.

"Are you sure none of you know how to make a pot of rice?"
Indra asked from the stove. "There was a cook in my childhood
home, Bhika, and he always made it look so easy. He would wash
the grains and put them on the chulha, and lo, a bowl of rice."

"I've only had rice a few times," Cora said. "A high school
classmate had family in the Carolinas. She would always insist that
we eat a bowl of Hoppin' John around New Year's."

"Americans name their foods the most bizarre things," Indra
said. "Is there a Dancing Jane?"

The women smiled at the joke. Suresh broke out into a chortle.
"Walking Tom?"

"Sitting Harry," Indra replied. The two kept on chuckling,
making different permutations of their joke, attempting to busy
themselves with stirring the rice, opening its lid, changing the heat
from the burner.

"It's just that I haven't seen you much at all in the past month.
You've canceled every time for our morning chats."

Cora didn't appreciate her friend's tone. "I remember the same
when you met Suresh. I didn't see you for a whole month!"

Hazel again smiled in a lording way, as if to say, I see what you
did there, I see you made the comparison to Suresh, and I see too
that you've removed all the obligations from your life to make room
for a man. And so, backed into this admission, Cora decided to be
honest and said in a low voice: "We seem to get along so well. It's
been lovely."

"Well, I am glad to hear that," Hazel replied.

Love, especially in its earliest moments, was supported by a
moral framework of friendship and sisterhood, and Cora would be
lost if Hazel said anything but a note of support.

Beyond the simplicity of the conversation, there was yet more feeling. The last month had changed everything. Cora knew it would be silly, girlish, to confess that part of her was always focused upon him, was waiting for the time when they would be together again. That's what passion entailed: the skip-of-the-heart dance of anticipation that every telephone call, every letter, every knock on the door, could be the other (and the concomitant anguish when it wasn't).

"Don't lose yourself too much," Hazel chided gently. "What you're doing with Crothers is new and interesting. It's worth your time and energy to finish your thesis."

Cora agreed, if only because Hazel herself was finishing a master's degree in history, and Cora felt like, out of respect, she shouldn't outwardly belittle the somnambular routine of attending lecture, completing the readings, writing an essay in response, awaiting her marks from the professor, and repeating it all again.

That rhythm and cadence achieved no real ends.

It wasn't like they would be able to keep studying forever. A woman's formal education was to examine maybe fifteen branches of knowledge, only to graze upon their surfaces, never to go deep. What was valued instead was that skill needed by all women: to be able to converse freely, if passively, with men. And by proceeding from a university education further still into a master's degree, both of them had done something unladylike, which of course in this day and age was grudgingly accepted by the men around them, who were often happy enough to have the company of a woman in their masculine halls (enough so that Cora always had to keep her guard up to discern those whose attention was limited to texts at hand and those who suffered from the misplaced loneliness of men among men), but the expectation was there: that she would soon leave them for her proper place.

"You know, I had the strangest feeling the other day," Cora heard Indra said to Suresh. "It felt like someone had searched my room. Same feeling I had back in Calcutta."

Suresh laughed. "Sounds to me that you have a landlady who likes to snoop," he said.

Indra laughed in reply before he turned around. "Come here, Cora. Try this rice. I think it's done."

Cora pushed her chair back and went to the stove. It was a bit too chewy, too wet. He had probably put in too much water, but Cora could see how much effort Indra had placed in the pot and didn't want to dissuade him. "It's great," she said. "I think you've done it."

Indra smiled and took a bite of his own creation. "It's a bit chewy, not quite what I'm used to eating. As long as you like it, I'm happy."

Cora smiled to assuage any of his doubts. It was interesting, the possibilities a little lie could provide. A lie could build confidence, push another toward reflection, open things up where the truth could be only a drag upon them both. Lies had their place. They always did in love.

FROM THEIR BOWLS OF WATERY, CHEWY, UNDERSEASONED RICE, THEY LEFT SURESH'S house and walked to Indra's room, where they could have a brief moment to themselves before his landlady came back from a game of contract bridge.

His bed sank in the middle, acting as a miniature force of gravity bringing them together. They had seen each other naked, and he had kissed every small crevice of her body, finding joy in the details that she rarely saw (the mole on the small of her back delighted him every time—she could feel his fingers drifting down to it, kisses that started near the base of her neck would end upon that feature). They had felt the arc of passion pass between them and witnessed the awkwardness of the body. (This awkwardness was always limited to her body: she had to surreptitiously wash their encounter out of her. His actions were always limited: Pass me that towel, she would say, and she would clean up proof of their union left upon her stomach.)

"Before dinner, you mentioned something about someone being in your room?"

"Oh, Suresh was probably right. Just my landlady snooping around. It used to happen all the time in India. Though it was usually the police doing it."

"Really?"

"It's what they did—I learned how to hide things quite well."

"That's no good of your landlady," she said, glancing at the closed door of his room. "You're sure it was her, right?"

"Who else would it be?"

He had a point—she didn't know why she was so worried about it. She changed the subject. "Do you want to go back up to Berkeley? Go back to San Francisco? I know you said it bored you. There must be something," Cora said, trailing off as she ran out of ideas.

It was as if he didn't hear what she had said. He continued to stare at the ceiling, but his face took on a dreamy, unfocused look, as if he were on the verge of falling asleep. "You said you knew something of India from before we met. What was it?"

She launched into a summary of the texts she had read over the years, most recently, of course, Tagore's *Gitanjali*, everyone was reading that now. Beyond that, her knowledge had come about through the transcendentalists. Again, the role of chance: old Mr. Williams, with his beard so long and gray she wondered if he had been part of Emerson's coterie. He insisted upon reading both the transcendentalists and their interlocutors, and from there came the chance to read the *Gita*, the *Ramayana*, the *Mahabharata*. And had she not read those, she never would have had the positive association of India. To her, those pieces of epic literature captured the human spirit far better than anything her own culture had to offer. She laughed at anyone who tried to argue that the dreadful and dry *Beowulf* was any competition.

And then there was the sublime cosmic order of all things.

"Karma," she said. And even though there was some true feeling within her, what came out was a recounting of facts and figures, as from a schoolgirl in a classroom. There was nothing that made her feel more confident than having the right answer at the right moment, letting one thought slip gracefully into the next with the ease of a pickpocket. "It's a tremendous, beautiful philosophy," she said. "Inescapable justice. No one else can alter it, touch it, change anything about it. Not the divine, not man—no one. It gets at the heart of everything. We have to do what's right because it's so."

He seemed pleased by her answer. He nodded, eyes closed.

"I first learned from my father," Indra said. "He taught me Sanskrit. He was the one who switched my knuckles if I couldn't read a verse correctly. He was also the one who first showed me a light unlike any other. You must know that India today is different. I wish our problems were only philosophical."

He turned to her now, his face knitted into seriousness. "I told you about this earlier, my contacts have confirmed that our meeting here will finally happen sometime in the beginning of April. And then I'll finally be able to go. When that time comes, will you come with me? To Berlin? I somehow feel more intelligent just standing next to you. Imagine what we could accomplish together."

He was always going to leave. When they met, he'd told her he was here for a short while only. From the start, they had been doomed to meet and move on. In his question now, an invitation to keep on.

There had been a Cora whom he had met, but as she grew closer to him, she was ceasing to be Cora and maybe become (cora), some small thing that held him close and fed him and made sure he could grow. A woman was a chrysalis to a man. She could be a Cora only at a distance, and (cora) with him.

"Of course," she said to him, drawing closer. She kissed him softly.

Even though they existed in a zone of relative safety, she had seen the headlines, seen how the Germans were sinking more American merchant ships. There was an outside that could threaten to kill them. "The war, Indra. How do you plan on getting through the front?"

"The war is on the front. We're going to sneak behind it to make our way to the capital, to meet with a few other officials. We'll discuss our plan to make a decisive move against the British. I hope that the German government will provide our men the means to fight off the British."

Though she was scared, the truth was that some fundamental fear was slipping away from her. She had spent her entire life wandering: in the mines, confused in the prim and proper world of her private schooling, and finally, her work on the playwright, the subjects it had introduced her to—socialism, pacifism, the suffragist cause. To move about with Indra felt like a fundamental desire, a curiosity so great that it gnawed at her constantly, like an apogee of hunger experienced after a life of fasting. He was offering a journey to a Cora far in the distance, a blurry figure upon the horizon whom she had to meet in order to become who she was.

She still wanted to seem tough. She pushed back gently. "To tell you the truth, this all sounds so risky. Are you sure it's going to work?"

"Nitin taught me that sometimes we have to place our faith in power that moves beyond us. I have to hope that these Germans are men of their word. And I have to act upon that."

"I'm sorry I won't be able to meet Nitin. He sounds like he taught you a lot."

"I'm sorry too. And to be honest, his death has thrown into question a lot of what I believed to be true. Before he died, I would have told you the best possible thing that could happen to India is for it to be filled with the guns needed to fight off its captor.

"I don't want to die, Cora. I don't want those I love to die. But I don't want to end up as effete and pointless as those men in the

Ghadar. Nitin once told me something, and now I feel it: the weight of freedom is too much for one person to bear. Maybe it'll all make more sense when we leave."

We leave. Her heart was being branded, no longer was it her own. That "we," said so quietly, was an exclamation, an eruptive force capable of rearranging her known world into a new asymmetry—an affirmation built solely of him and her—and in this union there were no equals. Who held the future, she could not be certain.

She looked at him and saw for the first time what he actually was: a man, a fragile thing, now a light burning brightly but ultimately something that could easily be stamped out. Ashes upon the breath of an angry god.

"I want to introduce you to two people I know: John Scullion and David Dawson," Cora said.

"Dawson? Stanford's president? How do you know him?"

"It's a long story. He came to a play I acted in when I was an undergraduate, and he became a mentor to me."

Dr. Dawson had held weekly salons when she was an undergraduate. Her invitation had come after he'd attended a staging of Shakespeare's *Macbeth*, in which she'd auditioned for the role of Lady Macbeth and been given the minor (though dreadfully important, she reminded herself) role of Lady Macduff.

"And the other?"

"A theosophist. Poet. Playwright. General man about town. Met him completely by chance. He hosts the loveliest parties. Both of them think they're more my father than my father."

(She was not stupid. She recognized that at a certain point, some men finally realized they would never again attract a young woman, and some of them, especially those in and around the American university, would transubstantiate this loss into an erstwhile fatherhood—they would not only mentor and educate but also protect the object of their desire, ensure that she was forever on the right path.)

"I really think you should talk to them," she continued. "Both do a lot against the imperial cause. Dawson with the Philippines. Scullion with Ireland. They might have something to say to help you figure all of this out."

Indra kissed her gently before sleep overtook him. His confession felt like a gift, and a gift was a little world unto itself, a proof of love transubstantiated into an object—that which touched him was to touch her, and the thing was no longer the thing, instead becoming a memory. To be given his secrets, his vulnerabilities, was to be given all that lurked underneath, the alchemy all the more potent because she needed no object. The mere thought of him was a hasp upon her heart, for she knew what he kept hidden. She had part of him now, and this burden was a delight to bear.

Henry, who had given up the cause and was now a successful lawyer for a bank in San Francisco, married to someone who looked exactly like Cora, had asked her once in the dark: "Weren't you bored living among the miners?"

That question was when she knew that he wasn't the one she could love forever. It was proof that he hadn't been paying attention to what she had said.

The miners? Never. On Sunday, the only day they ever could rest, she could tell that they adored her, even from the distance of a walk with her father. They saw her as the daughters they had left behind to come to the camp, where they lived a life inside the earth, burrowing like cursed moles, hoping against hope that they could return to the surface unscathed.

Was she ever bored? These city men. They acted as if a mining town couldn't be as bustling as any other city. There was a school, there were people. There was a lively smallness to both Trinidad and Butte, and when she reached the edge of town, there was always the great nothingness of the arid west, a place where she could hold her breath in the dark and hear no sound of humanity in reply, and on moonless nights search frantically for the vision of her own hand in front of her face. Nothing in those landscapes was as lonely as when he asked that question, proving he listened to few of her life's stories, leaving her wondering if there could be any connection between a man and a woman beyond the fleeting physicality of one body pressed up against another.

Her world had been beset by loneliness since her first few breaths. If anything, she knew that Indra always listened closely, even if what she said was later turned into his own words. This was an exercise in trust, a way of cracking open the carapace of life itself to find soft flesh and warm comradery. Whether this vulnerability would invite hurt, she couldn't yet say. She closed her eyes. She hoped for the best.

CHAPTER ELEVEN

Gaspar de Portola. He was the first civilized man to lead an expedition into this area. He made that rough ascent along the ridge and gazed down past the scrub to the San Francisco Bay. If you look down from that same ridge today, you'll see the fruits of modern industry: steamers along the water, trains running up and down the peninsula. Back then it was only scrub and patches of thicket along the creeks. Yes, there were the savages, living in their communes, trading baubles for glass beads with the expedition. It was Portola who gave name to the city here. He found a tall redwood and thought it appropriate. Simpler times. El Palo Alto."

Indra nodded vacantly. When Cora had described Dawson, Indra had expected someone who, first and foremost, looked like someone important, and in this, the university president did not disappoint. He had the gravity, the severe look of a man who knew that people hung on his every word, and, under his coat, a paunch that seemed to link his physicality to his authority.

And yet he was still tied to the university, and he droned on like a professor in a lecture.

Indra had taken lately to walking the Stanford campus, pacing the paths lined with thin palm trees, the lovely whitewashed Spanish mission–style buildings with red terra-cotta tiles on the roofs— structures that were old only in their referent but otherwise quite new in their grandeur, students going from class to class, and he an observer to it all, without much to do save ruminate, only a few to speak with, time slowed down to a surreal pace where he wasn't sure what time it was absent sunrise or sunset or a shift at some job, and he could never quite be certain of the day of the week.

Given this time and space, a luxury he hadn't been afforded since those months spent wandering after his upanayana (and in that roam, how he discovered the needs of Mother India), he would begin to hear again the past, much like the nishi of Bengali folklore who trapped and disappeared lone travelers by singing to them in the voice of a loved one. Time had passed, and yet Nitin didn't cease his song. All it took was a passing laugh, the color of a flower, the sound of a bell, and there again was the ghost.

Indra read that the firefight between Nitin's cadre and the government forces lasted seventy-five minutes. Twenty-five government goons were killed. In the end, they ran out of ammunition. A gun is only as good as the bullets it's fed, Nitin had told him. Always keep your ammunition close. No ammo, no cover. A fatal shot.

Seventy-five minutes, Indra, you should have heard it, Nitin said to him. The roar of gunshots for over an hour. Oh, how we fought! Do you remember how I showed you how to hit your target? You were a boy then. No aim, no idea how to steady your hand. You became such a sure shot. If you were there, you could have saved me. You would have killed that officer.

No, no, no, Indra argued. I would have died alongside you.

Shaheed, Nitin said, smiling. The way we all should die.

The dead can't lead the living, Indra sneered.

Every day there was more of a stutter in Indra's step. It was common enough to say that they would fight till their death, but when death finally came, those left behind had to sift through the wreckage.

He would find his own way to avenge Nitin's death. He had to win some measure of justice for his friend, that was sure. He had recently gone through his suitcase to hold his own Enfield and found that there was a weight to it he hadn't felt before, and he almost immediately hid it away again. There would be few answers in its chamber.

A proper monument to someone whose zeal and joy were the best mankind could offer wasn't something to be built with gunpowder and steel. There had to be something new.

When memories of Nitin didn't fill the day, there was the reconstitution of memories just past. Her laugh, her touch, her body, even if she had been gone only a few hours, he wanted it again. As her presence delimited his world, it was like he was a child once more, separated from his mother, yearning for her to appear so as to soothe his mind made anxious by her departure. He had made love to women before, but he had never felt for another an infatuation found in daily travails, the passing of a boring day filled with invocations to her, a desire built first from a glance and now into a want felt at every empty moment. To love like this meant that every time he was alone, he was not only beset by the spectral presence of the departed, but too the ghost of a love still living. Time apart turned every task at hand into one completed in a doubled way, part of him with her, repeating conversations over and over in his mind, eagerly anticipating the next meeting, never saying a word about any of it.

He needed her, and this truth betrayed everything he stood for: show no weakness, for it could be used against you. That's what Nitin, and all the men they led, believed to be true.

Nitin, you're wrong, Indra said. There's pleasure to be found in weakness, the strange euphoria when breaking open a bruise.

That felt like so long ago. In this small city he was entangled with another upon a bed, bodies softly curled against each other, creating a cradle.

A cradle was as much a feeling as a place.

She was home now. Even Tagore knew the home as the sacrosanct space for any true Indian, its order and cleanliness managed by Wife and Mother. In the West, Wife and Mother were something different, and this chasm felt so wide he didn't know what to do except ignore it, walk along its edge, and pretend that it wasn't there. A white woman knew nothing of making an Indian home, and why should she? Cora was learning about the struggle for Swaraj, not the ways in which a roti could be rolled out.

The home she offered was the only home he had, not only here but anywhere. His mother, his poor mother, dead when he was released from prison a year ago. All that time spent being a man had led to a year behind bars, and after the initial beatings, that time had eased into a time of reading and learning for him, completely cut off from the outside world. And then to have been set free by want of evidence, and to have learned that his siblings had seen his mother to the pyre. No one said as much, but he suspected it was his fault, the shame of having a son in prison was perhaps too much for her, even if the reason he was sent there was built upon the surest foundation of honor and dignity.

Perhaps that was why he so quickly leaped at the opportunity to leave India.

When he was with Cora, he was laid bare, Indra Mukherjee was something that no longer existed, merely the softness of skin yielding to desire by kisses quick and light, all yet before the dive deep, effacing all sensation save one, to reach, to reach, to find destination in feeling until they were together, he dark, she as white as pearls, and yet even that did not matter, for they had each other, soft pleasure giving way to quiet in a dark room lit only by the streetlamps shining through threadbare curtains, halos of orange light framing soft, whispered conversations.

"To see the savage beauty of this land in that clear California light," Dawson droned on. "Have you noticed the light here? Nothing like it back east—not a cloud in a sky so piercing blue. That clear light, you can't find it anywhere else, everything here is so vivid. It brings a true clarity to your thoughts."

The man spoke with the plodding cadence of an orator, measuring every word by the milligram to make sure even the dimmest among the imagined crowd could understand that what he said was of the utmost importance. Give a man enough lecterns and publications, and he would cease to understand the distinction between public and private personas—even ordinary conversation would fill itself with the pious platitudes of a sermon.

Indra was, of course, a little jealous. He wanted those lecterns and publications for himself. At the moment he couldn't say whether or not he had noticed if the light had been clear. It wasn't quite on his mind.

"What about those you call savages?" Indra finally asked, interrupting Dawson's monologue. "They had seen the beautiful light. They had probably seen that vista countless times. This is the same problem of the British in India. Just because a man of Europe sees something for the first time doesn't mean he's discovered anything at all."

"And here I was, thinking I was talking to myself," Dawson replied. "Surely you must know the difference between a man of intellect and a man who can do no better than to scrounge around in the bushes for his next meal. You're a man of civilization, the kind of man who belongs on a campus like this, who can take himself to the brink of knowledge and return to his race to better it."

Cora had mentioned that Dawson was at the forefront of the eugenics movement. It had come out of his research on evolution and fish. Only the strongest beget the strongest. Pure Darwinism. Dawson believed in the maintenance of clean, educated stock, so that each race could be bettered only by the best. When Cora had described it, Indra had found himself agreeing with the precept: a free and independent nation could be led only by pure men, both in heart and ideas. Racial mixing was the product of a colonized mind, a man who found in his own people something unworthy of his love or, even worse, was guilty of what Vivekananda had exhorted: placing all things European above his native country.

Before Indra could open his mouth, there was the electric

shock—with one step into the West, he was becoming that man. When he and Cora made love, one fact remained: the darkness of his skin was made even more apparent against the paleness of hers.

The neatness of Vivekananda's argument seemed to fall apart in the reality of his own life. There was something about Cora that brought him to her, but that something had no name, no description, save desire, and it seemed now to Indra that desire was chance, something he had no control over, something that seemed to have crawled out of the cracks and folds of daily life to present itself not as some infinitesimal annoyance, no, it was the fundamental premise from which all things now emerged.

"Cora tells me you've been deeply involved in the anti-imperialist movement," Indra said, trying to change the subject. Dawson took a deep breath, ran the fingers of one hand over the large white mustache that drooped over his mouth. I know about you and Cora, Indra imagined him thinking, and I think it's disgusting. But we're not here to talk about that.

"Deeply involved. I opposed American annexation of the Philippines at the turn of the century. We have no business trying to rule over those who have no concept of democracy. Imperialism is a scourge upon this earth. We are best when we do not meddle in the affairs of other races."

"I agree! Britain has no business being in India, and now, by draining India of her once boundless riches, she takes any possibility of uplift from the Aryan race of my country."

"Indeed, indeed." Dawson nodded, and when he did, the thinning white hair atop his head had this way of following, as if it were some supportive echo of Indra's statement. "I've always enjoyed speaking with you young men. It's why I talk to Suresh, and a few of the others who pass through Palo Alto, about the need to fight imperialism. You should know I use the word 'fight' metaphorically here. From what I understand, you are no pacifist."

"Pacifism!" Indra spat. "That word has no place in India. Britain will not bow down to peace. She will never take seriously those who do not fight. What we need are arms, ammunition, means of making war. Only when we place the sword upon the neck of a Britain kneeling before us will she recognize our right to self-determination."

"Of course, of course. A grand way of thinking. One must make war to achieve the ends you seek. Let me ask you something. When you fight, Britain fights back, correct? When you shoot one bullet, her police and armies shoot ten back at you, right?"

"I've been in a firefight, if that's what you're asking."

Dawson let out a guttural laugh. "Not at all! I don't question your martial capabilities, young man. A man as tall and healthy as yourself could hold his own, I'm quite sure. What I talk about here is risk. You surround yourself with the best your race has to offer, and you arm yourself to the teeth. You plan a raid, you go in guns blazing, and the police shoot back, and their aim isn't horrendous. They strike you, or they strike one of your friends. And in an instant, you've taken out, for all generations to come, the best stock your race had. That man, if he had no children, leaves no inheritance for your nation."

Dawson's words were a gut punch, describing perfectly what had happened to Nitin. Nitin was surely the best of the best, and the fact that his presence was deprived for all who were to come was the truest tragedy that had befallen the revolutionary movement since Indra had become part of it.

"From the look on your face," Dawson said, speaking slowly and with care, "it seems like you know exactly what I am referring to."

"We've lost men we never should have lost," Indra replied with a cough, masking the emotions that threatened to choke forth. "And you're right, I'll grant you that."

"I believe in the truth of eugenics. It's my lodestar. And from that, I believe in the cause of peace. War, whether it's between you and the British or the damned war in Europe, only serves to kill off the men we need to make ours a better place."

"How then do you propose we make our way to freedom? We've found that Britain listens to our guns. I see almost no proof of her listening to our voice."

"That, my young friend, is not a question that I must answer. I'm here to seek out men like yourself, to ask you the questions that no one has asked before. It's up to you to find the solution, the way never before found. It's what I meant to tell you with the story of Portola. He charted the path for himself and along the way gave name to all the nameless places that had yet to be mapped. That's the task set before you."

The two exchanged a few more pleasantries before their conversation ended. Indra walked out into the day, making his way to a different fraternity to serve lunch, and as he did, he looked around as if for the first time, noticing now that the light was as clear as he had ever seen it, the way every new leaf of spring seemed to be illuminated from within. This clarity did nothing to settle his muddled thoughts: everything that was once built of solid stone, that seemed to him to be a basic precept, was filling with cracks, threatening to collapse into complete and utter ruin.

CHAPTER TWELVE

They were getting ready to leave Indra's room to go to John Scullion's party. Cora was standing in front of the mirror, attempting to put her curls up in a French twist.

Scullion had invited them to a Saturday-evening gathering at his house, nicknamed Temple Square,. Cora wasn't exactly sure of the guest list, but she gathered there would be the usual: poets, students, professors, artists, students, a smattering of hapless bohemians stuck in their dreams, and perhaps a few writers—she had first been invited to one of his parties after publishing a theater review in *The Stanford Daily*. An evening at the Temple was often spent in casual debate and discussion on poetry, art, and Irish independence, all colored by a dash of the occult and plenty of good wine. Tonight was going to be Indra's first visit.

Scullion's house was in the same part of town as Suresh's home, at the intersection of Emerson and Coleridge. Even though he had named his place grandly, it was a simple brown-shingle home, four gable-roofed dormers proof of its four residents. John and his wife, Mabel, were originally from Dublin, had kept both the rhythm of their Irish accent as well as a fierce love of their homeland. Their boys, Russell and Sigurd, had been born in Syracuse, New York, where the family had first settled after crossing the Atlantic.

Originally Irish Theosophists, they founded the Temple of the People in upstate New York before moving west. Some of the Temple group settled in the aptly named Halcyon, down near San Luis

Obispo, where they had formed a tranquil intentional community.

Every time Cora came to the Temple, Scullion, with his white beard, wild hair, and tanned skin looked every part a Walt Whitman crossed with a John Muir and topped off with a bit of Irish mystic, would try, in an offhand way, to convince her to join further into whatever was going on. In one of their early meetings, he handed Cora a copy of the Celtic play he had cowritten with Mabel. "Promise me you'll read it through," he told her. "In the next staging or reading or whatever we can afford to put together on our shoestring budget, I want you in it, whatever capacity you think is appropriate. Don't answer just yet. Never say no, never say die, my dear, I want you in it."

He hadn't staged the play yet—there was always something grabbing at his attention—but he never did forget about it either, and every time they had a moment away from the chatter and the noise of the conversation at large in the Temple, he would tell her, "Front and center, my dear, right upon the stage, once we get the money, I want you there."

And Cora would smile. "Never say no, never say die, my dear," she would reply.

If any one of the guests in his home suffered or struggled, or had a love for those who did, Scullion would treat that person with reverie and care. Perhaps it all came from his theosophical core, his belief in the ever expanding light that could birth a new consciousness. Cora had read his poetry, published in various small literary magazines, where he went on in wonder about how a universe that was filled with a vast darkness could still birth something as blindingly beautiful as the sun. Even in the most dreadful of situations, there could be that seed of light from which something greater could emerge. That belief, that universal love, suffused with good humor and a warm smile, brought her back again and again and again to the Temple.

Scullion believed wholeheartedly that there was something new forming in the West, a new kind of civilization appearing around the Pacific, something that could not be matched by the bonds of horrific history forged around the Atlantic. This new civilization would invite the Oriental races and their knowledge and—he had this terrific way of putting it—there would rise a new sun of a different kind, and we will greet this light as the Indians worshipped the Sun.

"What's the matter, Indra?" Cora asked as she finished up her curls.

"Nothing, nothing at all. Why do you ask?" Indra replied, getting up to give her a light kiss.

A man of many talents but perhaps never to be a card shark. When she was a child, she would observe the men among the mines who trusted what scraps of money they had (or worse, the scrip that kept them fed) to a shuffle of fifty-two cards, and when she would see them play, each had a gargoyle look from which he would never waver. Indra, with his tells and his wandering eyes and the sighs under his breath, no, his savings would be wiped out in an instant—a good thing he never gambled.

If anything, she wanted his burdens to be her own. That was the naïveté of young love—it was the lie all lovers told themselves, that they alone could fix everything that afflicted the other, that she was the balm and the splint, the cure and the inoculation. She put a few pins in her mouth and rubbed his back for a few moments following their kiss. A man who had fought an empire, traveled across the world, nervous to meet a few artists and poets. It was laughable, really, though she did not utter a word.

Indra hesitated to leave, feeling an animal hunting upon unknown ground, each step balanced upon that thread-thin line between self-assured and cautious. He was seated upon his bed, watching Cora from her reflection in his mirror. Part of him wanted to resist finding a footing in Palo Alto and stay with her that evening. They had such few uninterrupted stretches of time together, and wasting it on a party felt like a betrayal to their bodies. As she finished putting her hair up, he saw the nape of her neck as an invitation. He kissed her again. They could find something better to do.

She pulled away and made to leave. Too late.

Indra hadn't had much to do with the theosophists, though it was hard to travel among the nationalists and not read something by Annie Besant, who had come to India only when Indra himself was a boy, ostensibly to discover some transcendent theosophical truth and instead finding something better: a place among those fighting for an independent India.

It was a curious thing, how these women from abroad could come and find a home among the Indians and, in Besant's case, go even further by taking up the mantle of leadership. It had been Besant who founded the Home Rule League, who had purchased the *Madras Standard* to turn it into an organ for self-government. She too had seen the war as an opportunity. If England asked for help from India to fight its war in Europe, the payment would have to be in self-rule. She had the gall to make real demands of the country of her birth, boldly siding with those who had been treated as a conquered people. Their plight was her cause.

It was what he had come to admire most about Cora. She had plenty to lose. For a white American, siding with the Indian cause meant that she was turning against her race. Indra felt a sense of pride at this too. She had made that decision for him, because of him.

Cora had called Scullion's home Temple Square, but when they arrived, Indra saw how the house was no different from Suresh's: a small bungalow fronted by a splendid orange tree filled with round citrus past their prime. The grass around the tree was littered with the fruit, a few of them split open by animals, a few others rotting, covered with blue-green fuzz, as they dissolved back into the soil.

The two walked along a small path to the side of the house and into the backyard, where the attention of the small party was

drawn toward the far corner, to a magnolia tree covered in an efflorescence of open, plump blossoms of pink-white flowers, some
at their glorious peak, others already beginning to wilt, corners of
brown appearing on the petals, falling to the ground where Scullion
was speaking. He was reciting some sort of prayer, some incantation
to the divine light that emanated from within all, that blessed all
equally with its holy wisdom. It was a bit silly, this religion. These
white folk had been born into Christ's world and grown bored of
it, looking to the East for some sense of wisdom and mystery. Still,
Indra would rather they look to India for divine inspiration instead
of knee-jerk hatred and petty insults. If he allowed himself to be a
bit more giving, he could even see the impressiveness in religion as
horticulture, grafting India's ancient teachings onto Blavatsky's rav-
ings to create a whole new faith from which to worship.

Someone's young child, a boy of not more than four or five, ran
by them, all shaggy brown hair and big wide eyes, still a little plump
in his cheeks, not long from being put in his first pair of trousers. He
bumped into Indra's leg, then continued on as if nothing had happened. Indra found the boy's energy cute and reached down to pat
his head before the child ran farther away, and after he did, Cora
looked at him and the child with a quiet grimace that caught Indra
completely by surprise.

"Do you know the boy?" Indra asked.

"No," Cora muttered before the expression was completely
erased by some purposeful energy that he could not see or understand. "I want to tell you something," she said in a low whisper.
"This is something I thought about before I even met you, Indra. I
should have told you it earlier. Let me now tell it to you straight. I
never wish to have children. I don't want my mother's life."

"I see," Indra said, caught off guard by the unexpected comment. Clearly, she was feeling confessional, vulnerable. He wished
she hadn't said something in public. He had to say something. "I'm
so sorry. You should know that I agree with you. What happened to

your mother was awful, and I'm sorry. The decision to have children is weighty, one must come into it with clear eyes. I cannot imagine supporting a child now." He was prattling on, unsure now of what he was actually saying.

"Did you ever work with any theosophists in India?" Cora asked quickly, seeming to want to change the subject. "I've read so much about Annie Besant. Did you ever meet her?"

Indra was relieved to leave the discomfort of the confessional behind, especially considering they were surrounded by so many. He was surprised to hear the comparison to Annie Besant, since he had just been thinking of her. It was one of those connections forged in a relationship that made the other feel as if they were of one mind. Coincidence had no place among lovers, all was evidence of the hand of fate, of the fact that they were meant to be together.

"No, our paths haven't crossed, but Cora, I've always thought of you as similar to Mrs. Besant, making our fight your own." He smiled and watched as a contentedness spread over her face, relaxing her into the party. The divine light had been invoked, and the gathering was fracturing into small cells of conversation, each layering upon the other, until all Indra could hear was a wave of human sound, punctuated occasionally by the high-pitched wane of a laugh.

The compliment was a clarion bell over the general hum of conviviality that suffused the cool early evening. A lover's gift: placing her in a matrix of relations—she was like Annie Besant, Annie Besant was instrumental to the cause of freedom, and the cause of freedom was central to Indra's life. Whether or not she connected each point so intricately in the moment was beside the point. One's own self-confidence could be built through such affections, identifications, and symbols of relations that connected one life to another.

Indra's wonderful trick was that he made her feel important without having to do a single thing. She had wandered into a life on the Stanford campus: her courses, her friends, her meetings, the preview of a world at large given by monumental figures like Dawson and Scullion. She was a passenger on some dreamlike train, and her arrival could only occur when she willed it into existence. Until then, she was to remain in transit.

And then came Indra, and though he never said as much, she felt as if he saw something in her, as if she were somehow famous and connected to every person he needed to meet. It was an intoxicating thing to be made to feel marvelous, to feel as if she lived a life bigger than she had known. That itself was a destination.

"Come with me," she told him. She led him from the fringes of the party and into a small parcel of a conversation. "Hullo, Henry, hullo, William," she said. "This is Indra. He's come here from India."

"India!" one of them exclaimed, either Henry or William, he wasn't sure. "My God, that's a long way. India! Truly the birthplace of all the ideas worth living by. What brings you to Palo Alto?"

Indra looked at Cora, briefly, a small glance of sure-footedness between them.

"Working for the freedom of my nation has taken me far and wide. I'm here to"—he paused for a moment, a chance to think of some way to phrase what he was looking for—"Drum up support among those interested in national liberation."

"How absolutely marvelous," one of them said. "You're in the right place. John Scullion said something about Irish freedom the other day. You know, I'm thinking of setting the idea of his thought-forms in a composition."

"Really, how do you think you–"

Right when the conversation began to pick up, right at the moment when Indra's introduction ended, when the conversation ceased to center upon him and returned to those who were originally talking, she took him away.

"Dear, there's something over here I'd like you to see."

"It was nice to meet you, Indra," one of them said as he and

Cora shuffled away.

"I was interested in what they had to say about ideas and music," Indra said in a whisper.

"We're not here to talk with just one or two people. I want you to meet everyone. You're here to meet people. Think of it like a coming out for you into a new society. Meet as many people as you can. If any one of them interests you, you can always return to them—here or in time."

Indra, of course, was a quick study. After the musicians and an introduction to a sculptor, Indra seemed to develop his own cadence. She could hear the way he described himself: "Indra Mukherjee, pleased to meet you, I'm from India."

Their eyes would widen a bit. Being from India in a room of theosophists made him close to a celebrity, and he would lean into his background. He spoke of his guru, of reading the *Gita* and memorizing the ancient mantras in Sanskrit, of leaving home at age ten to wander his village in search of truth. And if Cora was honest with herself, it *was* fascinating and otherworldly to hear of a spiritual journey beginning at ten—the perfect age to begin wandering, that point when she herself had taken the precepts from her father and begun to look for them in the world, test them for their value, and these tests would become the foundation for her own understanding of each and every gear upon which the world turned.

Of course, he never mentioned the abhorrent specter of caste that had led him to take such a journey, that he was a Brahmin who sat on top of the racial pyramid (and even though every face in that room was white, each would be aghast at the notion of an inborn superiority). Indra played the game well.

By the time he reached the last introduction, his story had ossified into something standard, a calling card among a set quite different from that of the revolutionaries he had hung around with in India. A party was always a chance to wander, not only between people but between different versions of oneself. This could be an opportunity for him: to make his name among the cultured and the interesting.

Spend enough time in rooms filled with Scullions and Dawsons and their acolytes, and anyone could pick up how strivers spoke to each other. She soon grew weary of the constant conversation, however, and let him mingle on his own while she went out into the backyard for some air. Only as he watched her head outside (the pleasure of watching a lover unseen, the chance to see her as a stranger would, the neutral look of focus upon her face, leading to questions like: Did she always frown like that or was it just now?, and putting away the desire to shout her name, to grab her attention for his own) was he able to take a minute for himself.

"You are quite the cosmopolitan," the woman on the liner had told him. To make that leap from a man of a nation to a man of the world, it was as if Cora knew he wanted it, and she wanted it for him, the transformation he desired, and though she probably had been content being an American in her small corner of the world, he knew that she would work as faithfully as he toward the fruition of a desire he had never told anyone. She was right again. He was glad they had come to the party.

He went into the next conversation with a newfound lightness in his step. How lucky he had been to find in America a woman who intrinsically understood the value of seva—selfless service to the man she loved.

Everyone had a glass of wine in their hand, lips and teeth stained red from each sip taken as they talked. Indra had dutifully abstained from alcohol and meat for his entire life. He had eaten a lifetime's worth of meat over the past few weeks. And here, inside this party, the final sanction seemed to have little meaning except to take him further away from the people around him. If they all had a glass, why not he, he who would stand among them, who would take from them lessons back to the struggle from which he was forged.

Temperance! he could hear some of his compatriots yell. *Only a clear mind can fight for freedom!*

It was a bit of horseshit. If he was to fight among the men of India, he would need to gather brothers from Madras to the Himalayas, and in order to appeal to this mass, he would have to stand by them in their habits and interests, and everyone knew that these habits included a tipple (or two or three) of country liquor distilled to take the edge off a long day.

There were bottles in the kitchen, and he poured himself a glass. He looked over his shoulder, as if someone from back home were watching, as if someone would report the transgression straight to his dead father, who would come back to admonish him for the sin of enjoying himself at a party.

He took a sip.

It was bitter. Not like a karela dal. He had always assumed wine would be sweet, with its deep color so reminiscent of juice squeezed from overripe fruit, but here was a drink drained of all its sugar. It wasn't bad, though each sip left his mouth feeling strangely dry.

"I get the best bottles from near Halcyon," someone said with a hint of an Irish accent. With a mess of curly hair tinged with white, a small beard, and deeply tanned skin, he was a handsome man, one of the few tall enough to look Indra straight in the eye with his piercing blue eyes. "It's where we're building the true temple of the people. That's along the coast, near San Luis Obispo, well south of here. It's beautiful, rugged land, where the rolling hills meet the sea. I always tell Cora she's welcome there any time she wishes to go. John Scullion," he said, holding out his hand with a smile.

"Indranath Mukherjee," Indra replied. "I've heard much about you."

Scullion beamed. "All lies, I'm sure, unless they were compliments, in which case they didn't go far enough."

Indra laughed. "Cora tells me you fight for the cause of Irish Home Rule?"

"If there's one truth in life, it's that every last Britisher can go straight to hell, though of course, as a theosophist, I don't necessarily believe in hell, and the Catholic faith can go to hell, for all I care." He laughed again, taking a drink from his glass.

Indra stared for a moment at Scullion's half-empty glass and wanted to take the conversation further, if only to untangle the knot that had formed deep inside of him. "Tell me, how do you fight for Home Rule from here, from California?" Indra asked. "I believe in being at the center of the fight. Something like the Easter Rebellion. What they did was remarkable."

"That's true, and those martyrs extinguished the light of their life and have joined into the universal body of God, and may their memory be forever chanted throughout the cosmos," Scullion said, and Indra was unable to tell whether the man was drunk or constantly spoke in such overwrought and strained terms. "Let me tell you this. When the British took our country, they banned our language, they banned our poetry, they banned our music. What better rebellion than to celebrate what they've taken from us?"

"Surely the bullet of a gun has more importance than a poem?" Indra asked, taking another drink from his glass, now half empty. He had last eaten a meal that morning, half a stale bun he had taken from his workplace kitchen. He knew now what was meant when it was said that alcohol could loosen the tongue.

"That is not the question!" Scullion exclaimed, growing excited with the conversation, and it seemed as if his nose, ruddy from rosacea, grew even redder as he spoke. "I know you're just poking the beast here. Every poem and bit of song keeps alive what has been taken from us, what they've attempted to squash and kill. Without it, we're just like them, hollow devils, roaming the earth, finding new land from which they can suck the marrow dry—blight, blight, blight."

"Of course," Indra agreed. "Do you know of Vivekananda? What you just said reminds me of his teachings."

"That's quite the compliment, young man, and you'd be hard

pressed to find a man here who didn't know at least some of the teachings of that wise saint. You know, when he came to tour the United States, he spent three months near San Francisco. You're not the first Indian to come to California, and by god, you won't be the last."

"I was recently at his mission in San Francisco. Do you think Indians will continue to come to California, given the recent restrictions?"

"Laws will change," Scullion replied placidly. "They always do."

"Do you think that's true?"

"There's something special about this part of the world. We're building a new kind of society. We look to the East and bring the best of its thought here. Halcyon couldn't exist anywhere else. I know you're not long for California, I know there are other horizons yet for you to explore. Take from here what makes it special. Don't be entombed in the ways of the old world. Mix from here, from there. Make something new." He looked out the kitchen window. "Ah! It's Stephen. Beautiful composer. Wonderful man. Excuse me, I need to go have a word with him."

The sun had long set, and the kitchen was flooded with the pale yellow light from two electric lightbulbs. Electric light was such an extravagance in India, and here, it seemed like every house was adorned with it.

Indra was a bit stunned by the conversation—new ideas feeling like an out-of-body experience, a disembodiment where he looked down and wondered whose hands and feet and mind had replaced his own. He kept going through the party, feeling piped from that conversation with Scullion. Or maybe it was the wine feathering all his edges.

Cora stood in the shadow of the house, long since ready to go but content to let Indra continue his conversations throughout the party.

"He's a charming man," Scullion said, emerging from a conversation at the other end of the yard. Cora agreed, a quiet nod and a smile.

"Let me tell you something, Cora. Mabel and I are equal partners. In everything. The collection of plays? Half and half. The damned publisher wanted me first on the title page. Don't let the size of the name confuse you. We both worked on that as equals. And we *are* equals. The light of the universe doesn't choose to shine upon one person over another. When the light appears to us, it shines before us all. Do you understand what I'm trying to say?"

Cora gave another smile. "Of course," she said.

"Of course you don't." He laughed. "You hide from the light, Cora. The light shines upon you, and you shrink away from it. You spend too much time in the shadows. What I'm trying to say is that you won't be as much as he is until you recognize your own greatness."

That was all there was to say. She stayed and mingled for a bit with Scullion, but the conversation was over—he had made his point and said his piece.

When Cora went back inside, there was Indra, holding a small glass of wine.

He had never drunk alcohol before. Complete teetotaler, for all she knew. Violated some Hindu precept to drink. Here he was, with a glass of Scullion's red wine. Indra let out a laugh, louder than she had ever heard. His lips were tinged with dark purple like an old bruise, and she wondered if this was what mothers felt when they let their boys went out into the world and they came back with habits gathered from the darkest corners she could have once sworn her boy would never explore. He was an easygoing drunk, all smiles and kindness. That was at least a relief.

In every conversation that night, there hadn't been a scant bit of eye contact between those Indra had spoken with and her. The only reminder she was there at all was that Indra had kept his hand upon her, a light touch on her back, as if to say, This is mine, and because she's mine, I get to choose when she talks or when she gets to be part of our conversation.

She tried to shrug off the feeling. He would never say that.

(Maybe he was thinking it.)

Hidden away, close to the center of any desire, was always the lack she felt about herself, the fear that she was of no great consequence.

No, that was nonsense. He was learning, he was in his own world in each and every conversation, learning how to hold himself in the middle of a room.

And she was his guide. He could only be himself among others because she had shown him the way. Had she not, perhaps he would have been the man she had seen at Suresh's, the man half in shadow, able to give a speech yet unaware how to float from person to person to become something that remained in the minds of others at the close of the party, conversations all forgotten save the story of the man from India.

She was a woman. And a woman in the one thousand nine hundred and seventeenth year of the lord was made to hide in ambition's shade. As a child, she'd wanted more, but the door had been closed. With Indra, the door was open, and yet all feeling was similar when she crossed its threshold.

All the great thinkers were wrong—there was no such thing as a grand eternal occurrence. Everything repeated itself upon every mortal day.

CHAPTER THIRTEEN

As he sat at dinner with Suresh a week later, Indra's thoughts were colored by the article he had read in the *Chronicle: GERMANY PLANNED ALLIANCE WITH JAPAN AND MEXICO TO WAGE WAR ON UNITED STATES.*

"I thought Hazel and Cora would be joining us tonight," Suresh said. "It looks like our women are content to go to that suffragist's talk. Hazel was so pleased to see Cora return to the NWP fold."

Suresh and Indra were seated at a table in a nondescript greasy spoon on California Avenue down in Mayfield, nursing a cup of coffee and a bowl of stewed beans. The restaurant bustled with students and workers at the close of a day's shift, and though the town was as dry as Palo Alto, everything in the area was blessed by the pleasant smell of boiling wart from the steam beer brewed at the nearby Mayfield Brewery. Indra was glad he didn't have to debate whether he could order a small beer with dinner. Though he was coming to enjoy an occasional tipple, he still feared vice in the face of a fellow Indian, for gossip could spread fast, and he didn't want his name dragged through the mud.

He had telephoned the consulate again, a little fearful about a potential shipment of arms covered with German fingerprints. They had been casual about it, nonchalant. "We remain hopeful for early April," Bricken said. "Things are in motion that we cannot stop at this point. We don't believe this news will amount to anything. The United States is committed to remaining neutral."

Read the amazing letter, the article announced, *that has fallen into the hands of the United States Secret Service. The letter details the German plan to snarl the United States in a war with Germany and Japan.*

There was a pit growing in Indra and, in that, a foreboding feeling. "If I could cook, or even better, if we were home, I would have gone to my favorite corner to buy us some kachori." He laughed.

"Brother, can you find anything simple, even some bhaat or masur dal at the grocers here?" Suresh asked earnestly.

Indra at first had thought Suresh soft. His brother had been a comrade in arms, but Suresh had seemed to shy away from the gun, preferring the world of letters instead. Not a natural-born fighter at all, slow to take a first step, always looking around the room before opening his mouth, seeking the most ideal outcome without ruffling too many feathers. Maybe now, in this isolation and exile, Indra would be made to soften into another version of Suresh.

RAILROAD APPEALS TO TRAINMEN'S PATRIOTISM, another headline read. The rail brotherhoods were threatening strike, and the war was being used to sidestep the possibility. If this war could stop the great upheavals of capital, it could stop everything, even the forward motion of his journey. Indra remembered what Tokutaro had said at Takahashi's. Indians needed a place to shop. It was work that could keep him alive, but what was living if one didn't feel enlivened? He resisted the pull: it wouldn't be his business to take up. Instead he replied to Suresh that he had no idea where to look for dry goods from their homeland. He wasn't cooking much anymore either, no longer employed by any fraternity at all, having lost his last job after being asked to fill in for a sick cook, and the entire group of men throwing away the under-seasoned lunch in disgust (he only later took up Cora's lessons on how to properly cook a roast).

He now kept house for a professor of Persian art he had met at Scullion's party, and though the professor was always eager to speak on the history of India, Indra felt that his wife was less than enthused with Indra's ability to clean (how was he supposed to know that sweeping the home's dust into the street was considered illegal and impolite in America?) and that another firing would come soon enough. One job and then another, finding small routines to pass the time, to keep madness and boredom at bay, to hope against hope that something would come down the pipeline from his benefactors.

"Someone told me of something out in Stockton," Suresh replied, taking a sip of his coffee. Indra had finished his in a quick drink, but Suresh always nursed his cups until they were long cold. "Punjabi store. Dal is dal. Can't be that different. It's near the gurudwara they've built there. A day's journey, there and back."

"It'd be worth it, I miss the taste of home," Indra replied. Home was farther and farther away. Without the Germans, there would be no oceanic voyages, there would be no possibility of a ticket anywhere. The longing for a familiar meal was the island peak of a mountain of hopes hidden under the surface. There was nothing wrong with his life with Cora in Palo Alto, but he longed to be with her out in the world itself, and without that greater shared experience, he couldn't say whether she would love a man reduced to normal size. That's what they had been doing for the past two weeks: he working his short-lived odd jobs, she returning to her studies, trying to make up for some lost time, and in between, calling upon friends, going to parties, spending the night with each other. In short, daily life. A routine like that couldn't be kept up forever. There had to be something else.

"Remind me, how many years have you been in California?" Indra asked.

"It'll be six years soon. When I came here, I thought I would study for a year or two up in Berkeley and then return home. Time slipped away."

"Do you think you'll stay much longer?" Indra asked with a measure of fear, wondering if his stay too would stretch on into years.

"I can't imagine going back."

He knew that Suresh had established a life beyond his degree, that he and Hazel traveled up and down the California coast, attending parties filled with writers and journalists. Surely that wasn't enough to anchor him in one place. Indra asked if Hazel was enough to keep him grounded in Palo Alto.

"Palo Alto? I'm not sure if I'll stay here longer than my degree allows. It's a small town. There's so much more of his country to see, even of this state. You only spent a day or two in San Francisco. There's also Los Angeles—beautiful city filled with artists and actors and writers of all kinds.

"Hazel is a good woman from a good family. We have a life here I would have struggled to make anywhere else. We went down to Los Angeles a few weeks ago, and she introduced me to a writer, who then introduced me to his literary agent, and now I'm corresponding with an editor at a publishing house in New York. They're interested in my writing, Indra—I think it has something to do with Tagore. They want more voices from India. It's an opportunity that only appeared to me here. Love and work, Indra, the two make a gravity that keeps one anchored.

"And what about yourself? You've been here since the end of January. It's now mid-March. Are you staying or leaving?"

That question. It was like when he asked Cora in the Arizona Garden what she was going to do after her studies. "My contacts say that early April is still on, that they hope to deliver me something then. What can I do except wait to see what they have?"

Suresh's eyes widened. "You've seen the news. The telegram! War is imminent. It's a matter of weeks now."

Suresh was right, in a way. The telegram from Zimmermann was all anyone could talk about now. The Germans, in their infinite wisdom, had been trying to convince Mexico to invade the United States. The code had been broken by British intelligence and the message passed on to the United States, where it had only recently become public news, and now every voting man and politician was seeing blood. This little note of aggression and intrigue seemed to drive opinion more than any sinking ship, and the opinion was that the Americans should go to war. The Germans had tried and failed to play one nation against the other: a longing for freedom in one corner in the world was an advantage to be played. Here the Mexicans, there the Indians, they the chess player leaning back in his chair, Indra a piece among many to be played.

A feeling not unlike what he felt when he heard his mother had died while he languished in prison. A feeling that he had taken entirely the wrong path, and the punishment was not only the diversion, the time lost to finding his way back, but also to suffer the loss of what he had loved.

"Be careful, Indra, you see what's happening," Suresh continued in a low voice, his eyes shifting around the room as he spoke. "They're shaking their swords now. There's more talk of entering the war every day, and when the Americans finally enter the fight with the Germans, what will you do?"

"What can I do, Suresh? I'm here because of them, and I'll leave here because of them. For better or worse," he said.

"We'll have to think of a way, if the worst comes, to keep you safe."

"Have you seen the news from Russia?" Indra asked, changing the subject. March had been an unceasing parade of headlines showcasing how the world was ready to burst in an explosion of war and the changes it could bring. The revolution in Russia was complete—what had started merely a month prior had come to its conclusion.

"The czar is gone, looks like the revolutionaries have won," Suresh said, returning to full volume. The mere mention of Germany in a public place seemed to set him on edge, bringing out the Suresh who had no appetite for drawing attention to himself.

"You side with the czar?" Indra asked.

"I'm not sure I trust the communists, not yet. We'll see."

Indra wanted to add more but lacked a firm understanding of the nuance—he was a nationalist, knew that a country deserved to be ruled by its own people. Of the true difference between a socialist and a communist, of how a government by the people could operate, he had only glimmers of an understanding.

"How are things with Cora?" Suresh asked, as if he could read through Indra's pause, knowing that there was nothing more to say about politics and the world at large.

"Wonderful," Indra replied, and it was the truth: between the parties, the introductions, her work with the Indians, he had no reason to complain, he thanked his lucky stars every day that they had met.

"I can see that look of bliss on your face. That's a happiness a man feels in only two situations: after a good meal and knowing he'll go home to a good woman. Hazel says she's lucky to have what little time they have together tonight. Cora's thrown herself into your world, Indra, and you've become part of hers. A rare thing. Now, what are you going to do for her?"

"What do you mean?" Indra stammered.

"Marriage! It's not done through the families here. It's the man's job to ask."

Indra nearly choked on his water. After gaining some composure, he still had nothing to say. Marriage was an end to a story. Cora had mentioned she didn't want children. Maybe that meant she didn't want to be married either. "I could ask you the same. What are your plans for Hazel?"

Suresh let out a coy smile. He could see right through Indra's paltry attempt to redirect. "You'll see soon, maybe in the coming summer."

"Really? You're going to marry?"

"That's all I'll tell you—for now. Think about it, Indra. A woman like Cora doesn't come twice in a lifetime."

STDYUSP KSRII EZLS SDWN RNP FMRYNLN. GDCZ TGM HZRRT.

After dinner, there was a note from Obermeier waiting for Indra in his room. Of course there was. Obermeier had to have an opinion after the Zimmermann telegram.

It was like his petty German god heard Indra had been doubting his existence and sent a burning bush as a reminder. No postmark, no stamp, just an envelope and a piece of flimsy carbon paper. Indra had no idea how Obermeier's note had been delivered to his room, whether his landlady had slipped it under his door or someone had come inside when he had been out.

For the first time, he could muster only bitter resentment for this god-tyrant. Maybe Obermeier was some strange fiction made to keep man in check, and its purpose was to keep Indra locked in some predefined place until they really needed him, but that moment would never come. Maybe Obermeier was a single person, or maybe he was a collection of individuals amalgamated into a single name. Indra had placed so much faith in the mechanisms of power turning to his advantage, and only here, alone in a foreign land, could he feel the paucity of that belief.

There was no denying it from the note: his prospects were dimmer, were nothing more than irrational hope, and he instinctually went to his suitcase to look in the pocket of his good suit, and there it still was: his gun, unused for months. He hadn't even taken the time to clean it, and there was a chance that the thing wouldn't work when he needed it most—but he didn't know if that moment would ever come. He was slowly moving away from that old life, and proof of that was found with his penknife. The once-light wood of its handle had been darkened by the sweat of his palms, the initials *I.M.* inscribed between the scuffed metal of the rivets. The knife now had a permanent place in his pocket, the perfect tool to peel a potato, to scrape caked-on dirt from a floor.

From his room, he went on campus to meet Cora, finishing up

her time with Hazel and others in the NWP. As he walked her back to her residence, they talked about how this news of the telegram was shaking everything they had once known.

"You've done yourself a favor staying here as long as you have," Cora told him in front of her house with a look of relief. Then she looked around and lowered her voice, and he knew exactly what she was going to talk about next. "I don't see how it's possible for you to go to Berlin now. This telegram, it seems serious. 'He kept us out of war!' It's all meaningless. Everyone's looking for blood now."

"It should be fine," Indra said, taking a breath. "They assured me of my safety. They planned for this. In case of emergency, they would cut off all contact. They would burn the evidence."

Any guilt from lying was assuaged by the look of relief on her face.

"I'm so worried for you. What comes next?" She leaned into his embrace.

He kissed her on the forehead. "Something with you, I imagine." He smiled. The truth was enough to placate her. He watched as she entered her house, and he knew that Suresh was right. The future collapsed, the future opened up.

Deciphered, the note from Obermeier had read:

SUCCESS STILL LIES UPON THE HORIZON. KEEP THE FAITH.

It was laughable, really, to believe them at this point. They would insist upon something happening even if their own legs were being blown off by the drumfire of mortar on the front. Keep the faith—yes, he would keep it, he would keep what was beginning to mean more and more for him every day. Suresh was right. A woman like Cora didn't come twice in a lifetime. Indra would be a fool to do anything to lose her, to experience the kind of regret that could seep through his bones for a lifetime to come.

She was all he had now.

CHAPTER FOURTEEN

There was the quiet thereafter from making love, the heat still radiating off two bodies at rest, furtive whispers of pleasure since passed, the clean smell of soap around his neck, the muskiness of his body, her hand tracing absentminded designs on his chest. The easy rest following pleasure could always open her mind to wander, flit from one thought to another, but he, who usually kept his eyes closed (that small, satisfied smile), now had them wide open, and she watched as his eyes followed some unknown trail of thought along the fine cracked lines of plaster on the ceiling. Inside desire made manifest, there was no thought, only some intersection between sound—the utterances made beyond language—and feeling. And when it was over, and they again lay side by side in a moment of fragility, that was when they could speak, loosened, unburdened by whatever held their tongues in the waking day.

"When we get to Berlin, I want us to have a flat together, none of this going here going there, sneaking around."

"Of course we will," Cora said. "It'll be a place just for us. And maybe we can make it a place to gather, like Scullion's. Artists, thinkers, people of all kinds."

"And I can impress them with my roast, right? Now that I'm an expert."

"I don't think we would inflict your roast upon anyone." Cora laughed. Indra fell into himself a bit, grew silent beyond the gentle ribbing the joke provided.

"What's the matter?" Cora asked. He was lying on his back, she curled up next to him. She felt his fingers trembling as his hand rested upon her side.

He didn't answer, and she didn't push it. He turned his head to look at her and asked in a whisper, "Do you love me?"

"Of course," she said, knowing that the question was not the end of his thought, merely the opening for something else. She waited quietly for its arrival.

"When we leave this country together, nothing should come between us. Will you marry me?"

The "yes" that escaped from her was hardly a breath, and he turned his body to face hers, and the kiss was yearning. His question hadn't come as a complete surprise. On their way back from the previous night's talk, Hazel had mentioned as much. "Do you still think of him as a leader?" she had asked.

"Why do you ask?" Cora had replied.

"That morning before you went off to meet him in the garden. You said you saw him as a leader of men."

"You knew I went to see him?"

"Oh, come now, Cora. I'm not dense."

Cora laughed at her friend—secrets had a way of being shared between them. "I think there's a whole world outside of California. I think he can take me there."

"Oh, most definitely." Hazel said, rising some impatience in Cora.

"Don't be coy, Hazel. Speak clearly."

"Suresh tells me that something might be in the future between you two," she said, smiling. "He also has a mistrust of men with their head in the clouds. Believing in some grand cause makes men full of themselves. Overconfident."

Cora interrupted, ignoring the little remark about their future. "You don't see how hard he works, even when it doesn't come easy. He's been trying to find steady work. He keeps at it. That grit combined with what he's already done—I see a future for me. Not here. Something grand. It seems silly, doesn't it?"

"Dreams always are, to a point. Suresh also says that underneath all the bluster, he's a good man. I agree with him."

He's a good man. He'll be a good husband too. Next to Cora, Indra's fingers finally ceased their trembling, and they moved again, now across her body, drawing lines down her chest, down, farther, farther still, and they returned to motion, finding themselves lost in pleasure once more.

BY VIRTUE OF BEING AN INDIAN, HE DID NOT ENCUMBER HER WITH THE OLD WESTERN traditions of a courtship and a proposal, and for this, she was glad. He would not follow up what was said in bed with getting down on one knee, lacked the money to purchase an engagement ring.

She couldn't wait till they were done with this period of paucity and want. Every job of his would end in an unceremonious firing a week or two after its start. He never came back angry—it was never anyone's fault but his own that he was shown the door "You can't blame them for not wishing to employ a dishwasher who leaves food on the plates," he said, laughing. And she joined him. He never harbored any bitterness toward his former employer. His laugh, that generous, true laugh, deep and resonant, was more evidence of his fundamental goodness than anything else. What a wonderful and silly life they were living. In a few days' time, he would try again, the process repeating until the professor of art paid him a pittance to clean house.

There came a light touch of unease from the thought of being married. A woman was the property of her father, whereupon she passed a certain age, she was bartered into the contract of marriage and there graduated into becoming the property of her husband. The suffragists had been fighting against the tide of history, each trying to undo the dominion of one sex over the other, to amend the laws, to give way to something new. What began in Seneca Falls could continue into a constitutional convention. Cora resolved quickly to have her own wedding reflect this struggle in some way, swapping the theories and praxis of ownership for one of equality, a declaration of a partnership, of an equal say in the life of the other.

She had been thrown into a fever dream of planning. Western religion would play no part in her life and wedding, though she recognized that India was a land of spiritual tradition, and even if he mentioned little of his faith, he must have held close to at least some precepts of being a Hindu. He had told her that there were no separate ideas of religion and secularism in India, that daily life and the divine were enmeshed so tightly that to break the weave was to rend the entire fabric.

She was not him, and she could not bring herself to believe in a god, for how could there be a god who let loose the wicked suffering upon the world? No, there was only man among man, one tearing at the flesh of the other with his teeth, another begging for some scrap of human dignity, while the fat and the proud slept through it all.

Still, to make Indra abandon his faith entirely felt like a betrayal.

The day after his proposal, Cora hustled over to Temple Square and found Scullion in his backyard, playing what to her looked like a piccolo, but what he explained was actually a fife. When he played, he closed his eyes, and his fingers danced upon the instrument, and what emerged was music for dance, an air that matched the day's clear bright sunshine and the buds of bright green that had begun to appear on the maples.

He congratulated her warmly when she told him about her betrothal and asked if he might be willing to host the ceremony. She sketched out what she envisioned: a simple meeting of equals that would avoid the traditional ways in which a bride admitted to a subservient role to a groom. Rings and vows, that was it. She hadn't asked Indra if he approved.

Scullion said he would be delighted. "Perfect harmony between

East and West, and perfect simplicity too. It's a balance, my dear. The invitation to Halcyon is always open. You must go with Indra. It would be absolutely lovely for the both of you. A honeymoon! And don't forget, just because you're married doesn't mean I don't want you front and center, my dear, right upon the stage. Once we get the money."

Cora smiled, warm and generous. "Never say no, never say die, my dear," she said.

"Would that answer apply to my invitation to Halcyon as well?" Scullion asked.

For the first time, the invitation seemed like such a delight to Cora, and she longed to say yes, to go on a honeymoon with her husband-to-be. Her voice was stopped before it even reached her throat. She didn't know if Indra could leave, if he was still waiting for his German contact, even as the country rattled toward war. She felt, for the first time, the way in which marriage could constrict one's own dreams, and she said to Scullion, "I'll have to discuss it with Indra."

"Of course. You'll have to discuss it with your husband." And he gave a wink.

IN THE END, THEY KEPT A FEW OF THE TRADITIONS. INDRA BOUGHT THE RINGS, AND WHILE she had said that anything would do, even silver bands, he insisted that the bride had to wear the traditional gold, so he went out to find two dull twelve-karat bands at a pawnshop, cheap enough to buy with money from his most recent job, with enough left over to have them resized and polished into something new by a jeweler near the train station.

Hazel kept Cora from seeing Indra on the morning of the wedding, though all she wanted was to see his face—something to calm her nerves. "You can see him when he becomes your husband," Hazel teased. "Don't ruin the surprise."

Maybe it was the feeling of possibility that could come forth only in the verdant sunshine of spring, but love was winding its course through the lot of them. There were rumors that Suresh was going to finally propose to Hazel, though there was no date set for their wedding. Suresh, however, had been poisoned by the West. He was planning some grand proposal for his wife-to-be.

Cora eschewed the bridal white with its strong whiff of celebration of a virginal woman. She wore a simple dress of peach, something she and Hazel had picked up from a secondhand shop on University. She had called her father to tell him the news, to invite him and her half brother and her stepmother to the ceremony. The conversation was cold and distant. He said he would think about it. A few days later, a reply came in the mail. They would not attend. Still, he had included a generous gift for them to begin their life together. The leaden feeling swam heavy in her gut. She pushed it down as best she could. At least he'd written. They were thankful for the money.

She cried with Hazel before the ceremony. A wedding was one of the few moments to bring others together to celebrate life. No one was going to throw a party for her publications, her meetings, her endless days, but they would pause and commemorate this. And yet a cause for celebration was a moment afforded to ponder absence. None of the friends she had made over the years in Los Angeles and Palo Alto would be there, though many had written with such warmth and kindness, expressing gratitude for the invitation and congratulations for the day, and that was it. She had never asked Hazel how she managed with Suresh, though it had to be true: Cora was white, Indra was not. Mixing up this division had gulched her off into some third space, neither above nor below ground, instead in that loamy and wet place where the mist just touched the surface.

And she thought of her mother, how could she not? She was older than her mother had been when she died, now by months. All the scrapes and bruises of childhood left unkissed, passing into womanhood among men who lacked a curiosity about half the world, both knowing nothing about what it meant to be a woman and without a willingness or care to learn. Thankfully, she had come of age in Los Angeles, and it was through friends that she learned what was coming, the tittering about the menarche on the horizon, the gossip of who'd had it and who had not, realizing that she would be going about her business when one day she would begin to feel a little strange and then she'd be marked by blood. It was the ruddy-faced and heavyset housemother at her school who had given her a no-nonsense primer on the mechanics, a routine lesson made clear and concise by the number of girls who required her knowledge. The housemother had gifted Cora the cloth that looked and felt like a baby's diaper, said to pin it to a string that she tied to her inseam, told her how to boil it clean, to prepare herself for the peculiar smell upon the stove. Above all, she reminded Cora that this was normal.

Every year presented another milestone, another day to remember the absence, to remember that it was her own birth that had taken her mother away from her, that life could be callous and cruel from its very beginnings. She had no token with which to honor her mother's memory, no memento to wear on this day. There had been the few pictures, the locket she had found among her father's possessions when she snooped around the house, but those were all his. She knew little of her mother's wedding day. A snippet shared here and there: they got married in Connecticut, or perhaps it was New Hampshire—somewhere in New England—and then they took the great trip west.

And so, all she could do was cry—words unspoken—with Hazel at this lonely world, and sew into the reaches of her heart a wish for all this to be different, for there to be other worlds in the offing that lacked the baseness of life as she had hitherto known it.

And when the tears were finally dried and the puffiness of her eyes lessened behind a swipe of witch hazel, she went out into a day where the high-spring sun shone with a beautiful clarity, and the magnolia in the backyard of Temple Square was past blossom, filled now with buds starting to crack open into small, curled leaves of green. And it was under that tree that she and Indra stood before only the smallest smattering of their friends: Hazel and Suresh. Curiously absent were some of the other folks from Berkeley and San Francisco—they had all said they would come but failed to show up.

Loitering near Scullion's house, looking out of place with his officious air, was Dr. Dawson, and Cora's heart leaped with joy, as if it were her own father sitting in the audience.

WHEN CORA HAD FIRST SENT DR. DAWSON A LETTER THAT DOUBLED AS AN INVITATION, his reply was a note to meet her in his faculty office. She arrived there, and he asked if it was not best to walk outside, the fresh air a balm against the lassitude of the indoors. It had been pouring rain. The two sat on a bench in one of the columned archways, looking out at the dreadful weather. When he spoke, he looked forward and did not turn once to look at her.

"Indra is a good man," he said gravely. "He knows that the church of imperial government is filled with false prophets and cunning priests. He knows that the only good government is government by the people. That maxim always remains true."

Cora let the conversation hang in the air as she waited for him to continue past the recounting of baseline facts he always repeated.

"He's not yet a pacifist. We'll make one out of him yet. Cora, you know my steadfast belief in the cause of peace is fundamentally connected to my belief in racial harmony," he trailed off. He ran a thumb and forefinger over his mustache, clearly attempting to string together a thought in a way that would come off cleanest. Anticipating something awful, Cora felt a fist sit heavy within her stomach, pulling her down with it.

"Peace, Cora," he continued. "It can only be brought about by the coexistence of all the races. While I can't imagine a better pairing, you must understand that there is a dysgenic underpinning to this marriage. A horse and a donkey can only make a mule, and it must be clear to you that a world of mules is one that does not persist into the generations to come."

The father of her youth would always be present as a ghost, filling her world with stranger and stranger facsimiles.

Dawson took a breath. It was off-putting to see him act in this way, to see his fatherly confidence and resolute ideals put into practice in a space so personal. She knew he was a man of decision-making and power—he was the university's first president, after all—but she preferred the version of him that moderated debate rather than the sermonizer in the pulpit.

The unfortunate truth: he, like all people, did not meet change with change. Just because she had gone through some fundamental shift did not mean that he would recognize it as such. Indeed, it seemed to her that instead he could only become some ossified version of himself. Individuals could never find release from the prison of their own psychology and beliefs. As time went on, they retreated further down the cellar of their own self-assured thoughts and, when brought into the light, lashed out accordingly.

Even so, his point wasn't without cause. She had thought about it too, from the first moment she had kissed Indra. He had sent that letter, and she had gone looking for him at Suresh's house. There had been something irrevocable about their union. She had been right.

"You must know, Dr. Dawson," Cora replied, quick on her feet with the answer, "that I seek to never bear children. What was it that you said to me? 'The equality of women is the basis of suffrage, the basis of the soundness of all governance.' Well, I happen to believe that equality also can mean to hold the decision whether to bear children."

"Yes, the Sanger argument. Of course I'm familiar with it, Cora. Do you mean it?" He finally turned to look down at Cora with a piercing look.

Cora did not falter. "I do, Dr. Dawson."

And with that, his mood lightened, and he gave a small clap, pleased at her response. "Then you have my blessing. A fine man, Indra, and we'll make something new out of him yet."

SOMEWHERE NEAR TO THE CEREMONY, TWO MOURNING DOVES COOED A SOFT TUNE TO EACH other. There was a fundamental momentum to her life now that was in contradistinction to the dreadful and quotidian denouement that her father had hectored her about.

Scullion lit the spiritual joss sticks in front of them, opened a day of beauty to the holy fire. Cora tried not to hold her nose. The smell of sandalwood mixed with rose, camphor, and cinnamon made her feel a bit ill.

"May your consciousnesses commingle with this smoke so as to blend with the divine and holy light, the cosmic light, and may you both attune with the Divine Consciousness."

Cora smiled. It was a lovely sentiment, even though she had not asked Scullion to say anything.

"In this ceremony, we will join two souls as equals," he prattled on. "A balance of one and the other: man and woman, brought together to make something wholly new. We will begin with vows read by the bride, followed by vows read by the groom."

They had not discussed their vows prior to the ceremony, only that they would make their own. She had committed hers to memory, nervous she would trip over her own words at the worst possible time.

"Indra, you have brought me into your closest confidence and asked me to engage with the world around you, and that as an equal partner," she began. She had known him for only two months, and found that time had slowed down, revealing days that passed as weeks, moments when she not only fell in deeply with him but learned something of what she wanted for herself. Love felt like possibility. "I cannot imagine a life where I could ask for more. Your strong moral compass, your steadfastness in helping others, you inspire me. And with this inspiration, I vow to love you now and be the partner of our house together, whether in good health or sickness, until the day may come when we no longer breathe from the same air."

Indra looked so happy, the kind of effusive smile that brought out the little crow's-feet next to his eyes. They shouldn't have wasted money on a ring—this was the true gift they were giving each other, a chance to consecrate a marriage with joy.

"Cora, you bring the entire world to me. Every day. In this life, I can only hope I will bring the world to you as well, to show you every corner and protect you from the harm it may bring. You are both the world and the home." Cora, who had once thought it a bit maudlin that women cried at weddings, found herself beginning to well up. Life offered few moments of respite to look another in the eye and grant them the benefit of respect, admiration, and love. Every tear felt like a joyous victory. "A luck like this doesn't come twice in a lifetime. It rarely comes once. With you, I feel loved. You're the needed rest I've needed for years. I promise to always stay true to you, until our final days."

She wanted nothing more than to kiss him, and with this came a round of applause, leftover rice from Indra's trip to the store in San Mateo thrown upon them as a blessing.

She was no longer who she had been. Cora Trent Mukherjee stood at the side of her husband. She felt like she had lost nothing in this transformation, was instead growing into something larger than the sum of two disparate parts.

Only the world awaited them now.

CHAPTER FIFTEEN

The country was going to war.

They had other things to attend to. Indra and Cora had spent the night at the Mariposa Hotel on University, and when they woke up, for the first time in a bed that could actually fit them both (though they still remained close to each other, brought together by the muscle memory from smaller beds), he looked at her and realized that she was now his, and they would be together for all the days to come, and he said to her, "Good morning, wife," and she replied, "Why, hello there, husband," and they laughed like dreamers who didn't know if and when they would awaken.

Cora stayed behind while Indra went to tell his landlady that he had married and would be vacating his room as soon as he and his new wife found a place to live. He hoped that would be soon—they were going to spend the day visiting various apartments found in newspaper listings.

Indra met with his landlady in her kitchen, where it smelled faintly of cooking oil and rosemary, but the windows were all open, and there was a terrific lemon tree that framed the square window off the kitchen.

She was a weathered and small widow, an immigrant long since arrived from Italy, who walked with a small hunch in her back. She was one of the millions who entered this country with fistfuls of nothing, only to find themselves becoming little accumulators and collectors of capital, with enough saved up to the point where they, who once suffered in boardinghouses and cheaply rented rooms, took pleasure in meting out the same fate upon the newest boatload of arrivals.

She was nice enough. "Glad to hear you married that girl. I never like it when my boarders sneak around. Gives my home the feeling of a whorehouse. I was going to say something about it."

Indra was surprised to hear that, in their secrecy, they had been seen and noted. Cora had come over only when the landlady was echoing her sleep throughout the house, and he had rushed Cora out the door quickly at dawn. "Don't look so surprised," she added. "I know everything that goes on in my home. You remind me of my own sons. I raised two boys. They always thought they could sneak something around. A mother, if she runs a good household, and trust me, this is one of the best, knows exactly what's happening in every corner of her house."

Indra wondered if she knew about the drip in the faucet or the ants that traversed the baseboard in one corner of the room as if on a road to somewhere else. "Thank you," he said, unsure what else to say. "Once I know when and where we're moving, I will let you know."

"Good, good. By the way, there was a message for you on the telephone. Some foreign-sounding man. Accent like yours. Name was Go-wind or something."

Indra smiled at the thought. Probably an apology for not coming to the wedding. Some excuse as to what had happened. He was going to file away the thought to call him when the landlady added, "Said to call him as soon as you can."

She left the room. After he heard the front door of the house open and close, he picked up the heavy receiver to dial Govind.

"Brother, I have bad news. I wanted to tell you yesterday. I couldn't reach you. Couldn't get to you." Govind was speaking too fast, and Indra had to tell him to slow down.

"They arrested Anand and Singh in Berkeley," Govind said. "I fear I'm next. From what I've heard, they even took the bold step of arresting Bapp in the consulate. I'm giving you a warning, Indra. I think they'll be after you soon enough."

"Who arrested them? And after me for what? What happened to Anand and Singh?"

"The U.S. Attorney's office has a warrant out for every single Indian connected to the Ghadar. They're calling it a Hindu-German conspiracy. They say we're working together to fight the British, they say that we're in gross violation of some American law about neutrality."

"That doesn't make any sense. We haven't done much at all," Indra said, aghast at what Govind was saying. "We're vaguely associated with German officials! Nothing more!" No one had done anything beyond write a few tracts and stare at a swami from a distance. No one had successfully planned anything with the Germans in California.

"It doesn't matter. The Americans know that we want to fight the British, that sometimes we talk to the Germans about our mutual hatred for that country. We share a common enemy. That common enemy is now the ally of the Americans in the war."

"How did they come to think that we're trying to organize against an American ally?"

"With the war, Hopkins and the British CID probably have the Americans' ear now," Govind said. Indra grimaced at the mention of the law enforcement group. "We didn't exactly hide our intentions here. From our publications and communications, the British know that we talk in California. They've hated what we do here for some time. Don't you remember Lahore?"

Two years ago, the British had opened the Lahore Conspiracy trials. In the first case, they arrested eighty-two nationalists, forty-one of whom had just returned to India from the United States. They were charged with attempting to overthrow the government—Indra knew that desiring freedom was not a crime. The reports in the papers had emphasized how it was America, especially the Pacific Coast, that incubated the cause of revolution. Indian conspirators living in the United States were drafting revolutionary plans that, if brought to fruition, would lead to the downfall of the British Empire.

And oh, the heroes who had spoken, those martyrs for Mother India like Kartar Singh Sarabha, arguing before the judge with defiance that he had committed no crime, that it was the right of any and all slaves to revolt against their cruel masters. On the eve of his hanging, he had reportedly said, "If I had to live more lives than one, I would sacrifice each of them for my country's sake."

Twenty of them executed. Twenty-six of them were condemned to transportation for life in the Andamans.

In his heart of hearts, each revolutionary wished to be martyred like Nitin, but Indra had thought he would reach the firing line after committing some great act, not when he had been caught while waiting to plan for a first meeting that could lead to something more. "I have done nothing," Indra said, pleading with Govind as if he were the arresting officer.

"You've done enough. You were arrested and jailed for seditious activity in India. You slipped into the country under an illegal passport. You spoke with German consular officials about a plan to seek arms to fight an allied power. A conspiracy doesn't require actual things to happen. It simply requires the aspiration to do so."

Somewhere in the great heaving machine of world power, diplomats were convincing diplomats that America's entry into the war was a flimsy pretext to arrest and deport the Indians in California working toward freedom, to finally stamp out this small light (an easy debate: freedom was dangerous during wartime). America, for all her song and dance about freedom, would bend her knee before Britannia and her sword, punishing those who longed to be free.

"I'm sure I'm next," Govind added. "I'm surprised they didn't begin with the Ghadar offices. They'll be here soon."

"Why don't you try to slip away?"

"This has become my home, Indra. I have to accept its laws and its dictates as my own. I'll find a good lawyer for all of us. I have still friends at the papers. Maybe we can use them to drum up public support for us. The Britishers want to deport us. We'll find a way to stay. We'll be fine. I know not everyone shares my resolution. And I know this country isn't yours, Indra."

"How long do you think I have?"

"Yesterday was a good time to leave. That's when I first heard about this. That's why we couldn't come down to Palo Alto for your wedding. I'm sorry, Indra. If not yesterday, then today. Leave. Quickly."

"The Germans kept telling me that we'd have our meeting in early April. Something big would happen then. Even last week, Obermeier told me to keep the faith. Do you think they knew? Do you think this was all a ruse?"

"Seeing as they arrested the consular official himself, I doubt they knew a thing."

"My god," Indra said. "We've been damn fools. You warned me, brother. You told me that I'd be waiting for them forever."

"It doesn't matter if you waited for them or not. I wasn't waiting for them, and I seem to be in as much hot water as you. We all smell too much like foreign matter."

He was right. While creating an Enemy—the Germans—this nation had also conjured up an infinitely multiplying troop of foreigners infiltrating the body politic, simultaneously a singular criminal to be arrested, indicted, tried, and hanged, as well as an amorphous brigade of barbarians, each of them chipping away at the gates of civilization with crude axes made of hand-carved obsidian. And those barbarians would be dealt with swiftly, terribly.

"And anyway," Govind added, "you would have had to leave right when we spoke in Berkeley. And would you have?"

"No," Indra said with a hint of resignation. He knew why he'd stayed: his hope and her love. And nothing would have changed that.

"You know you must take her with you," Govind said. "Her fate is yours. And Suresh is the cleanest Indian on this continent. All he does is write poems. Maybe his brother is enough to lead to his own arrest. Give him the warning too. Good luck, brother."

"And same to you," Indra said.

There had been a dream. Hope was a terrible thing, a cockroach that would never die, content to constantly emerge and multiply no matter how many fists rained down to crush its body into a slick mess upon the counter. Even though all signs pointed to disaster, he remained steadfast in his dream that the Germans would come through at the last minute, and he could show them the revolutionary he had found to aid the cause. Not Govind, not Anand, not any of the men associated with the Ghadar. Not a man at all. He would introduce them to Cora, a woman at the intersection of life and love, idealism and talent, someone so brimming with capability that she would be an asset to any cause. And together they would travel across a country, an ocean, a world, moving from the platitudes of daily life into History, where together they would become part of a record of possibility and freedom.

Were they targeted because they were from the East and wanted to work with an enemy power, or because America had, with the righteous anger found only in war, arbitrarily decided what was wrong and what was right without any attention to reason and rationale? It didn't matter.

He had to tell Cora the truth of what was going to happen.

CHAPTER SIXTEEN

Outside the window, Cora saw the rhododendrons and azaleas beginning to bloom. Beyond the city, the hillsides were covered with a bright orange carpet of poppies—nothing like the soft blue bloom of columbine that filled the Aprils of her childhood, a pleasure second only to the soft red carpets of mountain mahogany. In springtime, an outdoor stage could be set up for plays that would be uninterrupted for months by any force of nature. Scullion's dinners moved into his backyard, Dawson's conversations into the quad near his office. April was supposed to be a time of ease.

Cora waited for Indra, passing the time with a coffee and the morning paper. Wilson was making his plea to Congress.

Americans were, by and large, simple people. War declared and the flags began to fly. Wilson was supposed to keep them out of war, but Wilson could do no wrong now. There was an enemy, and you were with us or against us.

While Indra was out talking to his landlady, Cora had placed their marriage certificate in the mail. That whole document had been built of lies, a way to avoid the punishments of a marriage outside of race and nation.

Legally, marrying Indra would make her a British subject. Indra, being born in a British colony, was automatically considered a subject of the British Empire. And because the law saw a woman as her husband's chattel, Cora would have to renounce her American citizenship and become British.

So they had lied. Suresh, of all people, had told them to. He had heard that it was as good a way as any to circumvent the law. On the documents accompanying their marriage certificate, Indra had listed his race as Caucasian, which he didn't see as a lie, for he was a proud descendant of the Aryans who once came to India, and as for his place of birth, he avoided writing down Calcutta or Bengal or any part of India.

"Put down Syracuse," Scullion had told them as their officiant. "Lived there for two years. Nothing of note happens there, and no one is from that damned city. No one will question it."

When Indra returned to their room, he looked haggard, beset by some great worry. "Something has gone wrong," he confessed, pacing back and forth in front of the bed. "I spoke with Govind on the telephone. Some of them have been arrested. I'm not sure what we can do." He was like a scared dog or a little boy.

"Why? What's happened?" Cora asked.

"They're saying we are in gross violation of the law. They're calling it a Hindu-German conspiracy against the British," Indra said.

"None of you have done any grand things against the British."

"They're saying that we *wanted* to do grand things against the British. They're policing desires, Cora."

She cringed, feeling the first intense pangs of fear. "Scullion invited us down to Halcyon. Maybe it's time to go down, wait for some of this to blow over?"

Hazel had been right all along. The British could never countenance the dissent of their inferior. It was time to hide away, to catch their breath as the world heaved itself into disaster. Everyone knew something was coming. It was as if some great fog had descended upon them, and this veil obscured any sense of communion and goodwill, and everyone was laid bare by paranoia and fear about what lay beyond in the mist.

"Yes. Halcyon. Of course," Indra said, never ceasing his pacing, wringing his hands behind his back, then in front, then behind, unable to keep still. "Let's go to Suresh's first. Govind told me to warn him. Before we go to Halcyon. He should know what to do. He'll have some advice for us."

Outside, Indra seemed allergic to the sun, a bit more rabid, looking over his shoulder, eyes searching the ground for some lost morsel.

"You had nothing to do with anything. This is all a misunderstanding," Cora said, nodding as if to agree with herself.

The cool edifice of logic had a mollifying effect upon her nervousness. In her world, men weren't arrested for spurious reasons. Though this too was a lie she was telling herself in the moment. She herself had explained to Indra how, a year ago, Mooney and Billings were arrested, scapegoated.

"They'll arrest me because of the guns. I know it."

"Guns? What guns? What are you talking about, Indra?" She felt like she had swallowed an anchor that was making it down into her gut.

"If they've arrested Anand and Singh based on the fact that they wrote articles and stared at a swami, they're definitely going to be after me." She barely followed what he was saying. He was muttering, talking to himself, not including her in a conversation she had every right to be part of.

"You didn't answer my question. What guns, Indra?"

"My meeting with the German consulate. We were going to talk about shipping a cache of weapons from California to India. They told me they were waiting for the money to come through but that it would happen," Indra said, looking weary, slouching as he walked. "I wanted to see it happen. I wanted to make sure they weren't going to lie to us again."

She felt like a small hand was pushing down on her shoulders, pressing her into the ground. He had never mentioned anything about weapons, she was sure of it. He had lied to her.

Not anger, not sadness, not fear—not yet. Only a sneaking sus-picion. "And you only found this all out today?"

"You think I'd keep this from you if I knew earlier?" he snapped.

She wanted to say: I don't know, you clearly didn't tell me that you wanted to get a boatload of guns and ship them off halfway around the world. She said nothing.

His trip to the United States had been paid for by the Germans, and the only money he had in California was from odd jobs. The money left his fingertips as soon as it was put in his palm. First to the landlady, then to the grocer, and then to their little flights of fancy. Had she known, she would have encouraged him to save, would have asked her father earlier for some money, and they would have left here for Berlin long ago.

They hovered around Suresh's kitchen—sitting, standing, pac-ing, crying, she could not stay still. The secret had been theirs, that he was going to Berlin, to India, that the revolutionary war would begin and freedom would be secured. Indra would be the leader, she by his side.

As the truth unfolded, any patience she once had was lost. "You lied to me, Indra," she said, filled with righteous anger. "You told me this wasn't dangerous. You said that in the Arizona Garden, right when we met."

"I didn't lie at all. I told you I was meeting with the Germans. I was honest with you, I promise."

"If this is honesty, I'm not sure I want to see what lying looks like to you. You hid the fact that you were shopping for guns with the Germans. You hid that fact, and you know it. And if you had been honest with me, I would have told you that you shouldn't do any of this."

Indra had a tic when he was losing his patience: his thumb would rub on the top of his ring finger on his right hand, gaining speed as he gained anger. She saw this, she could feel how failure tensed him, a failure unlike any other: no heroic arrest, no death in the line of fire. Abandonment and collapse.

"I can't believe this," she continued to rant. "I would have told you that it's a bad idea to associate with a goddamn hun at this time. Don't you read the blasted paper? Can't you think? Put one thought after the other?" She pointed right at Indra. "You've been blind. I can't believe this."

The tic reached its apogee when he flicked his thumb off his ring finger.

"What does it matter to you," Indra said. "You come to us, you learn, and you can leave. That's your right! If you're so impressed by our stupidity, why stay?"

"Tell me one thing," Cora said, seething, unable to stem the tide of feeling, of betrayal. "Why did you leave India?"

"What do you mean?" he said, stumbling over the question. "What does that have to do with anything?"

"Tell me, Indra, why did you leave India?"

"First I went to Batavia. The German connection told me to intercept a ship there. It was to be an arms shipment to India. It never came. I left after two nights. I was told to proceed to Shanghai. I was supposed to meet my handler there. He never showed up. I went to Kobe and onward to America."

"You really can't hear yourself speak—they stood you up in three countries. They sold you on a dream only you wanted more than anything else. And why? Don't you remember what happened to Nitin? Your friend died in the line of fire. I thought you were questioning whether guns or violence were worth the danger."

If love was softness, evasion for the sake of mutual preservation, a lover's quarrel—not a spat or the back-and-forth of a daily disagreement but a true blossoming of anger—was a great unveiling of all the blades unknowingly sharpened over the soft breaths of intimacy. A fight like this was not a dialogue, it was a search for the last knife lost in the wet and oozing silt of a life together, a resolution to pierce through the abdomen with the last word.

After Cora mentioned Nitin, Indra got up, furious, looking as if he could slap her across the face, and she cowered, wide-eyed, trembling.

"You go on about dreaming? I found you. You were a girl wandering and meandering through small rooms looking for something. You're a desperate barnacle. You were hoping for some ship to attach to."

Cora let out less a word and more of a sound, one of getting the wind knocked out of her. She tried to gather what remained of her energy.

"You think of yourself as a great ship? You and me both, flotsam—garbage, just waiting to wash to the shore. At least I'm honest with myself. I know what I want. My only mistake was trusting that you knew what you were doing.

"And you have the gall to ask me why I don't leave." She pointed to the ring on her finger. "What does this mean to you? This means that when you mess up, so do I. You understand that? Everything that you do happens to me too, Indra. You get that? They're coming after both of us."

"You want to know why I didn't say anything about the guns. It's because I knew I loved you from when we first met. I didn't want to scare you off," Indra said, and she saw how he was on the verge of tears.

She was losing steam, but she hated not to have the last word, and as such could have kept going, and Indra probably could have matched her one for one for the rest of the night, but Suresh came in to stop their scene. It was Suresh's idea to take a breath and think for a moment. He went to Indra, Hazel to Cora.

"You have to leave," Suresh said as Hazel sat down next to Cora. "We have no idea where the police are. It might even be too risky to return to your own homes."

"Halcyon," Cora said when she finally felt like she could speak without strangling Indra. "It was my original plan anyway. We'll get out of this pileup and go down to Halcyon, to San Luis Obispo, and wait for everything to blow over."

"Farther still. Leave the state," Suresh said sadly. "We might be doing the same. My brother probably makes me suspicious, even though I've done nothing. Indra, where do you know people?"

"I know a few brothers-in-arms in New York," Indra said.

"Oh, are they waiting for German guns too? You should talk to them about that," said Cora.

Indra shot her a look of anger and was about to open his mouth.

"Cora, please," Hazel interrupted. "I agree with Suresh, get as far away as you can. For all we know, no one has been arrested in New York. It's big enough to blend in, to lose whoever might be watching you. Suresh will go down to Los Angeles. I'll follow as soon as I can. We all need to be safe now."

"You should leave tonight," Suresh added.

It was settled. Hazel would go out to collect their belongings—Indra requested his one valise. Cora trusted Hazel to collect a few of her belongings. They would take the last train to Oakland that night.

When it came time to leave, Hazel and Suresh took them to the station. A hasty goodbye. Hazel pulled Cora aside while Suresh and Indra spoke in low, grave tones.

"I feel guilty," Hazel said to her, "like this is all my fault. I told you about that party. If I hadn't insisted that you meet Indra, then maybe," she trailed off.

"I chose to be there. I would have found Indra somehow in this small town even if I hadn't. It all would have happened the same way. None of it is your fault."

"I'll keep looking for your byline, Cora."

"Don't be so dramatic, we'll be back soon. I'll write to you once I can."

On the train to Oakland, the first leg of their trip, Indra was once again Pierre Thomas. He recommended that she take on a new identity as well.

"Don't you see?" Cora asked, too tired to be angry, only somewhat wry now. "Mine follows yours. I'm Mrs. Pierre Thomas. Done and done."

Indra smiled—a weary turn of the lips, exhaustion settling into the hollows just below his eyes, similar to the look she had seen when she first saw him in Suresh's living room. He rested his head on her shoulder and fell asleep, not waking until the train pulled into the rats' nest of tracks known as the Oakland Mole.

The train to Chicago wouldn't leave till the next morning, so Mr. and Mrs. Pierre Thomas stayed at a hotel on Ferry Street, just a few blocks away from the Mole. The noise—and occasional fights—from the bars on the street below kept them up, and when the night settled into the silence after last call, Cora could swear she heard the scampering of tiny feet (roaches, mice) along the floorboards. Indra seemed unaccosted, but she kept feeling something pinch her skin, and when she awoke, across her stomach were lines of bites—the bed had been infested with bedbugs.

Tired and without sleep, they left the hotel.

"Let's take a walk," Indra said when they arrived. "Stretch our legs before the journey."

They crossed the coal-fired bustle of the railroad yards to the marshes, and Cora had to resist the urge to scratch the bites on her midsection. They stood side by side, looking out to the mudflats and, beyond that, the constant ship traffic upon the estuary channel. Behind them, Oakland was no more than a wisp of factories and men, and across the bay was the city, a hair's breadth of buildings along the shore. In between sailed steamships, some of them ocean-bound, heading toward the Golden Gate.

"Did you mean all that you said yesterday?" Cora asked, tired, unsure what passed between them now. "Am I really just a barnacle?"

"I could ask you the same question," Indra said, his eyes following a small blue tug pulling a ship into the harbor, the gray-black smoke from its engine leaving a path that followed its wake. "Do you truly think so little of me?"

They had met, fallen in love, and married in two months. There was so much to learn about each other—she couldn't name any of his siblings, didn't know what he could recount about her family either. What had happened was not at all like courting or coming to a mutual understanding. Instead it had been some sort of chemical reaction, two molecules crashing into each other and then fused without care for the aftereffects of heat or energy or entropy. They had been brought together, and now came everything that should have preceded and everything else that would follow.

"I didn't see any of this," she said. "It's one thing to be scared of the police in the abstract, a whole other to have the threat of arrest right in front of you. It's happened so fast. I suppose it always does."

"We'll buy time for ourselves in New York. They won't be looking for us there. And we'll find something new. We can leave this world behind."

"I'm not sure if I want that." She turned to Indra. "We don't have a choice. This is you and me. And our life in front of us." She said this not to him but to herself, to remind herself that her father had been right when he chastised her for leaving behind her life in Sacramento for a flight of fancy. At twenty-four, her decisions carried weight, and this was what she had to bear. She was bound to Indra, by him. His choices were their choices, made for her whether she wanted them or not. There were women who seemed to move through this world without marriage, but no one had instructed her on how to be one of those, and no matter how much she loved Indra, she was left in the jaw of this institution. When he moved, so did she. It was her birthright, a lifetime spent being sent from city to city by various men.

They stood in silence for a while longer before turning back toward the Mole, to embark upon their honeymoon, the nine a.m.

train to Chicago. They'd get to New York from there. Get as far as they could from California. Nothing was left for them here anymore.

CHAPTER SEVENTEEN

The only thing that could distract him from the gravity of what had transpired was the America that passed like a moving picture in the windows of the train. As they left the state through the mountains, there were needle-green trees on the slopes of forests cast in a shadow from the east, the collection of them looking like stiff herons sitting upon a quay in judgment. When Indra looked out at the world in motion, he sometimes held his breath without realizing, and when he did so, the air around his body would go still, and the sound would drain from his ears. Without the wind, without the breath, without the air that constantly churned along the crest of the mountains, it felt as if time had stopped moving, as if these small changes in pressure moved the gears that turned the hands of all sense and semblance.

Even next to Cora, he was a singular figure, passing into emptier and emptier patches of the American west, thousands of miles from a home first departed, an ever increasing distance from the home that had just slipped away. Cora's love had done much to allay the loneliness he had felt after Nitin's death, but it was that same love that magnified his humiliation. An invitation—to intimacy, to dreaming—had instead brought forth the pressing weight of solitude, the great pneumatic machine that would flatten him until he was only a few molecules of flesh evaporating into the air.

Mountains eased into high desert. Tall evergreens growing out of patchwork snow were replaced by the orange, yellow, and tan of rock and plateau. The train crossed a salted sea surrounded by desert—the nation's landscape had the quality of a fever dream experienced behind a pane of glass. From time to time there would be a tree, a cottonwood or a scraggly pine, maybe, but each of these living things cast a long and emaciated shadow—all of them a portent, a pall.

In Wyoming, red striations of rock grew out of the hardscrabble earth like altars stained with centuries of blood sacrifice. From what he could gather, the train would not pass through Colorado, Cora's birthplace. Still, something about her seemed to be lost in memory at Cheyenne, as if she could sense a closeness to the past, and he wished he could leave her there, and in that parting, she would be given some vestige of life she could again pick up. She didn't need him, she could make it on her own.

They were meant to become something great. He had not only put his wife into danger, but he had been revealed to have been flirting with dalliances. California was to be the prelude to the world stage. She had been right. He had dreamed away solid ground into collapse.

He could hear Nitin chastising him. If you only had listened to me, brother. If you only weren't such a coward who needed a woman's love, neither of you would be here. She would be safe, you would be in Berlin.

This was to be his honeymoon: Indra purchased a deck of cards, and he and Cora played games of rummy where no one could remember who won, where only the sound of a shuffling deck and a new deal marked the passage of time. They ate their meals. He got a haircut and a shave. Simple routines and the passing of a flattened American landscape.

When they spoke, it was almost always about the immediacy of wants or needs: a meal, a break, a coffee, a hotel, a poor night's sleep. They didn't talk about the start of their marriage, didn't talk about where it was going. They surely didn't speak of the Berlin apartment they were going to share, only which seedy hotel in Chicago they could spend the night. It was a newfound shyness. The days of travel passed like that, idle chatter upon the constant clack-clack-clack. The train took them ever forward, into a new life, a new vision for what awaited them. And there was no stopping now.

He had a few contacts in New York—perhaps they could help. In Chicago he had sent a telegram to the last known address of his old comrade Benoy Chakravorty. The two had worked together in the same organization in India, though they had never been particularly close. Indra had always found him a bit too flashy, more interested in himself than the cause at hand, but he knew that Benoy was part of a cadre of Bengalis in New York, and even though they hadn't seen each other in years, his was the only help Indra could think of. In his message, he mentioned his forthcoming arrival, signed Pierre Thomas, and after his name included a code word they had used back in India (sujalam), something that could identify him. Benoy, as Samuel Jones, sent a reply to the train with a telephone number and the reply word (suphalam).

They finally arrived in New York's Pennsylvania Station, a temple made to worship the train, the god that made modern life possible. In that grand hall, steel columns rose into archways framed by windows on the wall and ceiling, and the constant movement made it seem like they had arrived at the center of something great. The city's millions of workers were spreading into every direction like so many columns of ants seeking out morsels of some discarded meal, sidewalks and trains filled cheek by jowl with those, Indra surmised, who had work to give them a sense of purpose. In contrast, he felt a stench escape from his every pore that filled him with the nausea of failure, a sickness that seemed to magnify whenever he was close to Cora. His sleep had been poor and intermittent since they left Palo Alto on a moment's notice. In Oakland, near the station, he had pretended to sleep, but had suffered through the very same bites throughout the night. Later, he forced himself to not complain, as if the bites were a hair shirt meant to punish him for his grand mistake, and he was driven mad by the need to scratch the line of red and inflamed welts along his back.

In their threadbare and dingy hotel in New York, Indra wanted to rest, but he denied himself the pleasure, felt that he needed to punish himself for bringing the two of them here: first came the work of finding money and a footing, a place to stay other than this rathole. Then he could grant himself idle pleasures.

The hotel had a telephone in the lobby, and Indra dialed the number Benoy had noted. Benoy sounded warm and inviting, and for the first time since the war broke out, Indra felt a measure of hope. He said to meet at Ceylon India restaurant and gave a scattershot set of directions that Indra had difficulty following the moment he left the hotel. Surrounded by buildings and people pressing in upon all sides, he didn't know which way was north or east. He didn't own an overcoat and felt the spring chill through his thin suit, though no one else seemed to be wearing one either. There was scant time to wonder at those around him—they had places to be and were walking to them with great purpose, and he, moving at half the pace, was merely an annoyance, a rock parting the flow of some great river. Someone would jostle him, and he would instinctively reach for his wallet to make sure no one had stolen it from him.

Life spilled out of every doorway and window in this city, people filling the sidewalks, hawkers selling their wares upon the precipice of the curb, motorcars vying with streetcars vying with people for space upon the road, all of it pressing upon Indra like two great hands upon his neck. He reached the gray stone building, its surface blackened by the city's soot. The restaurant was on the ground floor.

Perhaps there would be some respite, a meal or a cup of coffee to be had indoors. Outside the restaurant, he could smell past pleasures mixing with the city's stench, fried oil and a savory note of jeera, perhaps something more, and he was in Calcutta, sending someone off to buy a kochori or phuckhka, and there came the gnarling and terrible hunger for home, an exile made manifest by the denial of the simplest pleasures one could find on a plate.

Benoy was standing outside, a nervous look on his face, the brim of his hat bunched in his fist. The tangle of his curls had receded in the years since Indra had last seen him, and the expanse of forehead that remained was furrowed. He was just as thin as Indra now, as if the two had skipped an equal number of meals in the United States. Two dead cigarettes lay next to his scuffed shoes. He had been here for some time.

Indra reached out to embrace his onetime friend and found him stiffening upon contact. They exchanged pleasantries. Benoy seemed fidgety, biting his nails every so often.

"Indra-da, what an unexpected surprise to see you. So sad about your situation, and you see, I am happy to help," Benoy said. He had that overly formal tone of voice that so many of his countrymen reserved when they needed to make an ask of someone. "Of course, I myself am in need of help too," he continued, carefully avoiding the point.

"How much money do you need, Benoy?" Indra asked, trying to cut to the chase.

Indra listened as his former compatriot explained his situation, that his rent was due in a week and how the cause of freedom had siphoned his money. Indra wondered if Benoy had ever tried to work or if he was content to go door-to-door begging for alms when needed. Back in India, too many men treated Indra like an older brother, and in such a relationship, they couldn't see when he suffered and needed some help himself. It was the curse of competence.

Benoy had probably touched poverty for the first time in the United States and was desperate to reestablish a life at the top of the food chain like the one he'd had in India, but he was unwilling to put in the hours to make this so. It was why he was always a foot soldier, Indra the leader. Benoy tried to make it seem like his help amounted to some great sacrifice of time and effort. Indra was beginning to regret coming to him in the first place.

"I'm happy to help you, Indra-da, but this isn't India. In America, everything is so expensive. Ten dollars, that's all I ask for. I know they have a target on your head. I heard about the arrests. That's what happens when you trust the Punjabis in California. Out here, we keep to our own community. And look, we're safe. I can keep you safe too. Just need a little bit. I can help you and you can help me."

Indra smiled and said nothing. This ass wasn't going to budge until his wheels were greased. Dealing with a fellow Indian in this alien place, he could feel the hatred the British had felt about Indians, echoes of what that old bastard James Mill had written, that underneath the placid visage of any Indian were wellsprings of deceit, insincerity, perfidy. There was no echo of the brotherhood the two had shared in India, no reference to their accomplishments and low tides, only an open palm and a wicked smile.

"Five dollars?" Benoy asked, negotiating down in response to Indra's silent haggle.

"I'm always here to help a brother," Indra lied.

"I can help you find a place to stay, Indra-da. So many tricks to find an apartment. Someone's always trying to steal the shirt off your back. I'll make sure no one will lure you into a scam. I can help you find work."

Indra wanted to tell him off, but he also wanted to bring some good news to Cora, that a few hours into their stay here, he had already found help. What he found felt like a betrayal, that he had taken one step into the big city and been hustled. Wounded, Indra had no choice than to ask for help and hope for the best.

"Of course, brother," he said, handing over five dollars. He smiled, a trick to help hide the fear and seething anger.

Benoy told him where he lived and how to get there, that he should come over for dinner tonight, that he could meet some of

the fellows who had made it here from Bengal, that there would
be familiar faces all around. Indra agreed and wanted to leave the
conversation so quickly that he neglected to mention Cora would be
coming as well.

When he got back to the hotel, she wasn't there. She had left a
note saying she had gone out for a walk, but he had seen how tired
she was.

He was tired himself, weary, prone to catastrophizing the smallest vexation. If she wasn't there, it was probably because she had
left—none of the more reasonable answers came to him because he
had no energy for reason, only for worst-case-scenario anxiety.

She had fallen in love with an Indra who existed in a matrix of
possibility, not one on the run from the police, abandoned by his
contacts, with little money to his name, marooned in a country he
had never meant to end up in. He felt himself unworthy of her love.

He sat on the bed, running his fingers over the path of a stitched
diamond pattern on the duvet. The city hummed along to its rhythm
outside the window, uncaring of his existence. Somewhere in it,
Cora continued on, the brilliance of her life illuminating a path forward, while he was lost in a darkness of his own making. He toyed
with the idea of finding the nearest police station, simply turning
himself in. An arrest would allow her the dignity of an easy out.

There were no friends or comrades to check in on him, no family to create a home where he could hide. There was no love to which
he could return, no dream of something better on the horizon. It
was failure, one after another. Failure that ended in quiet defeat,
like all losses did.

CHAPTER EIGHTEEN

Cora had hoped that their hotel near Pennsylvania Station would be more hospitable than the ones in Oakland and Chicago. The welts on her stomach from their stay in Oakland had only now begun to heal, though lying down for rest gave her phantom feelings of small legs crawling over her skin—nothing had bitten her in Chicago, yet no sleep had come in that strange room smelling of oil soap and a musky dash of someone's once-spilled aftershave. The walls were painted a cerulean blue, and the entire time she felt like she was underwater, slowly drowning.

Mr. and Mrs. Thomas settled into yet another room, this one in New York City. Indra went out to meet his newfound Indian contact and let her sleep for the day. Her day of rest was soon cut short by the cacophony of men, women, train and tram jangles and steam whistles, the whinny of the occasional horse, the constant blare of automobile Klaxon horns and the wheeze of their asthmatic engines, men yelling, fights begun and made up in an instant, hawkers' cries—all of which seemed to float up four flights of stairs and hover right outside the window, which had to be kept open for want of any air in the room. Her room in Palo Alto had faced a verdant hillside, and she had often teased Indra about his room in the city, how conversations and the occasional automobile had rattled his windows. A paradise in comparison. Nothing could compete with this nightmare of sound.

How many times had she moved as a child? Enough to make it

easy for her to leave at a moment's notice as an adult. She had been born in Trinidad, Colorado, but when her father began to spend a little bit too much time on the vanning machine and too little time on the tasks meted out to a low-level mining engineer, he'd packed her up and the two of them had left for Butte, Montana, the land of the big sky.

People from places like San Francisco or New York took edges for granted. The buildings on all sides made one believe in the comfort that there was an end to all living things, that there could be a sense of safety in the animal pen, fences as a way to shield soft flesh and pink hands from the reflective tapestry of wide eyes hunting in the dark. There, big sky meant that the pull of the earth held no sway, that the ever expanding firmament could sweep anyone up into the heavens with the terrible and powerful chariot of the Lord—the one beheld by Ezekiel, wheels intersecting with wheels, all made up of unblinking eyes.

That copper town was filled with the desperate who first ran away from their past and then, once arrived, walked through the gates of hell, all the way down into tunnels that mazed miles under the surface. These men prayed, even though they must have known their prayers would reach their god as a muffled whisper from those depths. They prayed that they would strike a vein before the tunnel collapsed upon their heads, a death and a burial, all at once. And if they were lucky, they would rise again, only to find that outside the mines hulked the metal and the fire of the smelters, each of them pouring out a smoke so thick that the miners could still taste it in their rancid spit even after they made it to the shadowed comforts of a free lunch and a drink at a saloon.

At the turn of the century, Cora's father had left the Rockefeller mine to work for the Anaconda, which ended up part of the Rockefellers' grasping octopus of landholdings anyway. The managers didn't know him up there, didn't know that he was a man known to skirt work to tinker with his own project, and he was left in peace.

Butte was a town filled with copper men and the little women who made their meals and did their laundry, and lo, her father found one of those too, and it was upon her suggestion that he went to hang around the School of Mines. He needed another point of view to help him figure out the last steps in his quest to separate all that was of value from the slush of what came from the earth. Until his invention was perfected, he amounted to hardly more than a low-grade supervising engineer in the aboveground works. The constant failure of his invention wore hard on him, but he eventually found a partner who could mine the gold from his raw genius, and by the time Cora was twelve, there was no more big sky, or front range, or any of the joy and terror of the American west. Instead there was a coastal life of bleaching sun, and soon movie stars, a perfectly coiffed city known as Los Angeles, where she was sent to finish her schooling in a manner fit for a woman.

Leaving was never hard. Leaving was the easiest thing. Arriving wasn't too bad either. Talk to a few people, try on a few personalities, make pretend until pretend was real enough to be happy. It was like acting.

She left a note for Indra saying she had gone out for a walk, and went south on Eighth Avenue, and soon she chanced upon a commotion in front of a brick row house at the corner of Twenty-fifth Street. Brown-gray putrid smoke was pouring out of a few broken windows. Here, she could already see how law and order prevailed: three police officers swung their nightsticks at the crowd without caution or care to make room around the building for the fire engine to spray its jets of water. People would be beaten, property would be saved. Cora stood, mouth slightly agape, watching the scene at its edges, and caught a few bits of conversation from the crowd.

"A goddamn Italian cooking God knows what. Fire started in the kitchen," one man said. He was thin and streetwise, in a bowler and his shirtsleeves, with a sallow face and sunken-in eyes, self-assured in his analysis of the world.

"Naw, that ain't it. I heard it was a firebug setting fires here, there," said another, a baby-faced boy just on the threshold of becoming a man, standing, holding his bicycle handlebars in his threadbare telegraph boy's outfit, the logo patch on the chest so old it must have been a hand-me-down from the previous century. His excitement at the scene was countervailed by his world-weary sailor's voice.

"You idiots don't know shit," said a third, not turning to face the other two. All Cora could see was the back of his frayed and patched tweed. "Landlord wants to collect on insurance."

"Insurance? Never considered you can get some damn cash from a fire." the boy said.

"Why light the fire in the middle of the fucking day?" the thin man asked. "Wouldn't you want the whole goddamn thing to burn to the ground? Light it in the middle of the night."

The third man turned around, and Cora was alarmed to see a diagonal scar running from his forehead to his nose, sealing one eye shut in scar tissue. San Francisco had been a union town filled with workers standing shoulder to shoulder, but this was a city filled with workers maimed by business. "He wants to burn the building, not kill every last resident sleeping there, come on, don't you know somethin' from nothin'?"

The dance of water and smoke continued even as she left to walk south. There was a lunch counter on the first floor of the hotel where they were staying. A kitchen fire could always be a possibility. Death hung heavy upon her mind—if a fire consumed her hotel, would the crowds speak of the insurance payout, or would they talk of how she and Indra were asleep in each other's arms?

No one within three thousand miles knew she was in New York City. And no one within the city limits, save Indra, knew she existed. The rush of feeling as she walked was not unlike the dalliances with panic she'd felt in her childhood, when each thought seemed to spill so quickly from her, and she would feel dizzy from how it felt like everything could overflow from within her head, and when those moments came to pass, what helped was movement, and she would wander at the far reaches of the mine encampment, walk alongside the scrub in the shadow of the mesas, and if she passed a night without sleep, she would leave her bed to wander at dawn, when those altars of rock and stone were bathed in the light of a new day, and when the thoughts that raced finally took rest, there was the feeling that no one knew where she was or what she was doing, and inside that fear was a touch of excitement, a rush to the head.

The feeling came back to her now, save one difference. No one knew, but one knew, and she was reliant upon that one in a profoundly banal way—she was his wife, and in that role, she had to maintain a sense of duty toward him, though she tried to reason with herself that she would have maintained that loyalty whether or not they had married.

Her first walk in the city was to nowhere in particular, from grand apartment buildings transitioning without warning to cramped tenements and again to offices with clerks running here and there, and after a while, she doubled back to the hotel and found him waiting inside their room. There was a plaintive look on his face when she opened the door, and the smile he tried to put on broke her heart more than the sadness that preceded it.

He had returned, and she had not been there, and even though she had left a note, he probably had not believed a single word on the page and must have sat there for hours, wondering if she would ever come back.

She had spent so many of the days since their departure silently stoking the embers of a smoldering anger, repeating arguments in her mind—oh, the things she could say to him, would say to him, if she had the chance.

She sat down next to him and put her hand upon his. She drew him into an embrace and soon felt her shoulder wet from his tears, and she drew him close, but when that did not stop his crying, she tried to move her hand up and down his back, some form of reassurance that would tell him she had never left, that she was here, right here, and she wasn't going anywhere.

"I'm sorry," he whispered. She almost didn't hear him—the awful noises continued to filter through the window. "This wasn't how it was supposed to be."

SHE WAS AGHAST THAT HE'D GIVEN BENOY FIVE DOLLARS, AND HE TRIED TO MAKE A POINT that they needed his help, and he was never a man to say no to an Indian in need. She tried to argue that *he* was the Indian in need, but he seemed fragile and she decided not to push it, just let out that sigh so common to women exasperated with their husbands, and she was surprised how this little facet of her personality had come on so quickly.

They would meet Benoy at his apartment on Twenty-third Street, not too far from where they were staying. As complete novices to the New York City grid, they did not know the difference between a numbered street and a numbered avenue, and what Cora thought would be a five-minute walk to West Twenty-third stretched to thirty as they went east. Cora had thought that Indians seemed to have a loose relationship to punctuality, although being forty minutes late would stretch anyone's patience.

The moment the two of them entered the cramped sitting room, lit only by an unadorned electric bulb hanging from the ceiling, four men sharing a small bottle of whiskey, the smell of grease in the air from eggs that had been fried hours earlier, the party seemed to slow down from whatever pace of conversation had gripped it prior to their entrance. There were small smiles of recognition at Indra. Quickly, they turned to her, and their up-and-down eyes were not of flirtation. Disgust, maybe. Possibly confusion too.

At first she checked her clothing for some stain, some unbuttoned button, touching her hair to see if it had come loose on the walk, wiping her nose and brow: there had to be some detail missed.

One of them posed a question in Bengali. She had the feeling that it was a basic: who's this, they wanted to know. Not a single man seemed to be looking at her anymore.

Maybe, then, it was something else. She was willing to give them the benefit of the doubt. Cora had read about women kept in purdah in India, women kept behind the veil, away from the prying eyes of men, a life lived in total seclusion from unknown members of the other sex. Indra had told her that this India had already passed into memory, that they weren't living in some Tagore story set in the 1880s. Maybe these men were. Perhaps these New York Indians were quite a bit more conservative than the men out west, and perhaps they were angry at Indra for bringing a woman so they would have to change their behavior to adapt to her presence.

A man who seemed to be a leader among them (perhaps Benoy— she had yet to be introduced to anyone) launched into some tirade, and the other men nodded. He was speaking on their behalf. His soliloquy was in Bengali, and she picked up only a few words she had learned in California: desh, bhai, inkalaab. Then the man began pointing right at her. And when he did that, something seemed to break in Indra, and he pointed right back, began to yell in Bengali, and soon the room was a mess of two men seemingly fighting over her, but she couldn't pick up a word of what was being said.

When Indra and Cora left, Indra muttered something about a disagreement back in India that had crossed borders with them. When she pressed as to what it was and asked why they were pointing at her, he demurred, and they walked in silence as the streetlights began to flicker on, and she realized only then that neither of them knew where they were going and under this mutual incomprehension had wandered underneath the overhead spur of an elevated train line, the rumble of a train shaking them down to their bones when it passed overhead, both of them oblivious to the cacophony of poverty that surrounded them, filled with the naive understanding of the new arrival that not all neighborhoods were to be entered freely under the cover of darkness, and yet no one seemed to bother them because they amounted to no more than a spectral presence floating upon the sidewalks. They reached the end of their walk, a slip where they watched the comings and goings of the steamboat ferries making their way between Queens and Manhattan, the lights of those boats seeming like rippled islands of light upon a plain of darkness.

"It's you," Indra finally said. "And me. It's both of us."

Her heart sank, but there was a self-effacing desire to know more, the selfsame feeling that encouraged one to press deeply upon a bruise, some part of her that wanted to luxuriate in the pain to come. She was already miserable in New York, might as well add on some more.

"They think I've betrayed the cause of revolution," he explained, "that I've abandoned our country and our ideals, by marrying a woman outside of our race. I've become a traitor, and I'm no longer useful to the cause. I've gone outside our beloved country, and they don't think I can think straight anymore. I'm impaired."

She turned from the river and saw that he was crying again. She wanted to slap him. To hell with them! He could make his own life.

It was always going to be her words in his mouth. She didn't know what to say anymore. Some of this felt like her fault, like she had built him up at the party at Scullion's in her attempt to amplify his importance and in doing so had sent him teetering upon the edge of self-destruction. Or maybe she just suffered from the misplaced belief, common to many women upon seeing a broken man, that she alone could fix him, make him anew.

When she was a child, her father would threaten to send her to the orphanage whenever she was filled with the solipsistic and rambunctious energy common to children. Most of the time she did nothing at all. Maybe he was in one of his moods, angry because he embodied, in those years, an inventor as an anti-Midas: all that he touched turned to dust. In the plume of that kind of repeated failure, a child-without-mother had no place, was caught in the fit, was thrown aside.

"It is because of you I fail!" he would exclaim, all maudlin and full of the wrath of a man forced to be a caretaker. In his world, it was a punishment for a man to do a woman's work, to busy himself with the boring and useless task of raising a child. Cora didn't know if he hated her in those moments because she had taken away his wife or if he hated his wife because she had died, and he was merely taking this anger out on her. "I'd be better off if I sent you to the orphanage once and for all!"

Of course, when the rage simmered off into the air and the wretched look on Cora's face finally made it through to him, his heart would begin to break, and he would ask for her forgiveness in a warm embrace, and indeed, he seemed so saddened by his own capacity for anger that she would begin to pity him, and what began as her own consolation would turn into his. From a young age, she was made to do a woman's work: to soothe a man beset by his own emotional capacity.

To mend even though she was the one who was made broken: perhaps that was why she felt like she had to stick with Indra through his own failure. He had hurt her deeply with an omission that, by his own admission, was because he had loved her, but as soon as she saw the hurt doubled back to him, that old instinct kicked in again, and she felt for him, and the memory made her love what had only moments ago singed all her frayed edges.

To love a man was to give. If she, as a woman, wanted something more from this small and pitiable life for herself, maybe she had to guide him through whatever darkness stood before them while letting him feel as if he were the one to discover the path. She didn't know if she wanted to. A growing part of her, one that she was taking effort to silence, longed to have herself in the singular once again. There was no guarantee that any of this would be worth it.

CHAPTER NINETEEN

He who had been so central to the revolutionary cause of the nation had betrayed it by marrying a white woman. Indra could no longer be loyal because he was now bound to the white world. These were concerns that never once came up in California, other than the mutterings of the angry Singh. Only in departure could he see that he had been living in the comforts of a dream world. Back to reality, back to small-minded men squabbling into the early hours of the morning. And he, for the first time, was no longer welcome in the underground, had been kicked up to the street.

Maybe he knew in his heart of hearts that Vivekananda was right, that in the end, the reaction would be swift and terrible.

When he and Cora left Benoy's apartment that evening, he could not turn to face her, could not bear to speak to her. One failure after another. He wanted to be a man of the world, dazzling at the center, but now he was just another man left limp in its cold and hollow embrace.

They spent the next few days at the hotel, trying to get their bearings, busying themselves with finding a place to live, figuring out who else they knew in the city, trying to ascertain how they could secure some meager amount of money to pay for day-to-day life (for now they were living off of Cora's father's wedding present), wondering if they knew anyone who could provide actual help. Indra left one evening, lying to Cora by saying he was going to the Ceylon India restaurant. He told her that he was thinking of working there, a place to keep his head down and make a few dollars for them without attracting much attention from the law. He didn't know if the arrests were to be coming for them in New York. He couldn't tell if she believed him.

He slipped on one of his nice jackets from Shanghai, still at the bottom of his suitcase, its inner pocket heavy with steel and lead. He had never worn this jacket. He had worn the other tailored suit on his wedding day. It was fitting that this one was for the end. He kissed her before he left and told her that he loved her. He couldn't bring himself to look at her face, didn't want to be reminded of what he was leaving behind. If she wasn't going out on her own now, he would force her hand.

He wanted to return to where he and Cora had watched the ferries, but he didn't know exactly where to go. He passed the glory of Fifth Avenue, the romance of crowds with shoulders lined with fur, figures in the shadow of a fading light entering taxicabs going north, gregarious laughter and conversation rising from open windows, the movement of all those more important than he, each of them enmeshed in a world of capital and culture, and his heart sank deeper into his own mumbled loneliness. He preferred the darkness under the elevated lines on Third and Second avenues, dank, seedy, crumbling tenements with open windows letting slip foreign tongues, proof of poverty seen in half-naked children playing in the streets, scrawny bellies hungry for a meal yet to be made. Onward he walked, zigzagging so he could go north too, until he was in the shadow of smokestacks pouring out putrid coal-fired smoke, the constant hum and crash of power being generated filling his ears. He made his way to the water's edge, trash and rock and debris lining the shore, no one in sight willing to bear the stench of industry's refuse.

The day had been overcast, and at its close, the waters of the East River were becoming a great expanse of darkening, its choppiness heard as a sloshing against the garbage washed along the shore, the sky undifferentiated from the great clouds of smoke that pumped out above his head. The day had eased into night, the sun had slipped behind the city's great buildings, and he was left in cold shadow. The ferries continued to come and go.

He had been a fool. There were small conspiracies around every corner, men believing themselves to be heroes, but they were all dupes, small-time casualties of empires jockeying for power. Germany didn't care for any one of them, only its own position as a world power. And such power did not care for the lives of men. It was what came from the electric outlet, always flowing through the wires, always needing more coal to burn at the generation station next to him. He amounted to nothing beyond a lump of potential energy mined from some foreign hollow, and they would burn him when they needed it.

He could not outrun the heat and the pain that emerged from this fire.

He had constructed a narrative of events, a dramatized life of heroism, one in which he would flirt with danger yet always emerge as a success.

Success—he wanted it, of course, but couldn't define what it entailed. Nitin had been a success. A hero too. And now he was dead, successful inasmuch as he had bent the line of his life so that its final point intersected with its middle.

Wholly focused upon the sureness of his self, he had forgotten the truth: life was tedium and boredom punctuated often by a multitude of failures, made enjoyable by the smallest of joys—making love to Cora by the open window, a breeze coming in as a tickle along his back, walking through the city, seeing a fat black-and-white cat sitting on a fire escape, meowing in a fit of anger at a bird sitting idly in a tree branch just out of reach, the satisfaction of a payday, money exchanging hands, an evening spent in good company, wiling away dollars hard earned.

And though he could recognize this, to accept this small tedium felt like a failure (if not success, only failure for him, and nothing in between). He was not one for a quiet life. He did not know when or where the desire came to him to transcend what he saw as the smallness of his birth, but once it entered him, nothing would be satisfying save its fruition. At first he would be the revolutionary, then, across an ocean, something more. *Cosmopolitan.*

He had had the vision, the capability, the intelligence, the voice, the capacity. It had been his.

Now all he had was that he loathed himself. Loathed his stupidity. Loathed his naïveté. Loathed his belief that he could be something great. She was right. He was just a dreamer. A damned fool. And an exile too. The road to Berlin was going to take him back to India. Now he was cut off from the land that he fought for—perhaps permanently.

A darkness dimmed his vision. He reached into his pocket. The gun felt so cold, real in a way that nothing else was anymore. It had all given way—anger, guilt, sadness, fear—all of it once so solid, simply melted into air. He was firmly ensconced in the orbit of grief for a life lost, stuck in a shadow where no light could reach him.

He looked around him. He was far enough away from a dock so that here, there was no one to bother him. Motorcars hummed far behind him, interspersed every now and then with the clip-clop of a horse drawing a cart. The gun was out now, in his hands. He checked the chamber. It was loaded. He hadn't touched it in months. Wasn't sure if it would jam.

The passion he had felt with Cora had constituted a kind of delirium, a hallucination of possibility where the future kept opening wider and wider, and this opening was filled with every kind of place and location for both of them: Berlin, Halcyon, Palo Alto, India, Europe. And when the war broke out and the papers confirmed what Govind had said, that the Americans had arrested most of the Indians associated with the Ghadar Party as part of the Hindu-German conspiracy, his imaginary time line shook itself out like

an earthquake and collapsed in an instant, leaving only the emptiness of failed potential. The frenzy had passed, but the loss of this
sensation did not return Indra to reality. The humiliation had been
twofold, first what happened in California, second to be cast out by
the very men he had once led. He loved her as he loved the idea of
himself with her, and even though her closeness had never ceased,
everything now was at a remove.

The steel felt colder from the sweat in his hands, trembling ever
so slightly at what lay ahead. On the other side of the bullet, his
soul would find new life, a chance to begin again. There would be
some punishment for this act of destruction—perhaps Indranath
Mukherjee was the pinnacle of the arc of transmigration, and what
came next would be some denouement, some minor life. Maybe he
would be happy there with the smallness given to him, maybe he
would find peace, and from that peace would come the great release,
liberation from this endless cycle of death and rebirth.

He would miss Cora's face. He would miss the wild tangle of
her hair. The way she looked so serious in the middle of pleasure,
focused upon feeling. He would miss the softness of her skin, especially along her shoulders and down her back, how he loved to kiss
her shoulders, her small mole. He would miss her conversation. Her
voice. Her hands.

He pressed down on the trigger, and there came the sound, the
ringing in his ears. The burnt smell of gunpowder in the air.

Yes, the one truth of life was that it was small, and confronted
with the magnitude of this smallness, suicide was the only way one
could express any sort of agency. To decide right then and there that
this was where the story ended.

The myth of suicide was that this life could continue on after
death: that before his soul moved on, he would be able to see Cora's
tears, that he would laugh when he saw Benoy and the New York
Indians rue their own callousness, that he would hear the mournful
wails of those back home.

That was the myth. The reality was an end, a full stop to a rambling sentence.

In this formulation, hope was the enemy of agency. Hope again, that disgusting and wretched shackle that had kept him in Palo Alto until it was too late. Hope was both stupidity and possibility, was an all-encompassing force that led him to believe that the through line of action in his life's narrative could still splinter into directions yet unseen. Hope was the outlandish and strange wellspring of daydream and fantasy. Hope was that which kept man forever locked inside this small life, forever checking the peephole in the door for the unexpected visitor who could gift him something new.

Hope was Cora. Hope was the love he felt for her, the goodbye he owed her if he was truly going to stake his claim upon the world with his small action of a gun and a bullet.

When he had shot, he had shot into the water.

Another steamboat ferry passed close along its way to the docks north of him. It sounded its foghorn as it reached close to shore, and he threw the gun in the river. That gun had seen him through every fight and battle in Bengal but had remained unused for his entire time in America, stuffed into a suitcase until today. And here it would be left to rust and gradually dissolve into the atoms and particles from which it was forged.

In his ears thumped the pulse of his own heart, and an unforeseen anger took hold, something primal, something he couldn't put into words as to why it had emerged in the first place. He squatted down to slap his hands against some cast-off piece of man's making, concrete disguised as half-buried rock, the only proof of its fabrication a rusty piece of rebar emerging, like some frightened serpent, from its side. His hands made no noise against the roughness of its surface, but the skin upon his right palm broke open. He licked the blood from a hand so salty and warm, like drinking from a rusty nail, and he was dizzy, everything seemed to be moving now, a new delirium to fill him.

His mind moved like a broken compass, lurching through cardinal points, from anger to a laugh: something that began as a chuckle gained momentum until the whole-body convulsion he experienced forced small tears out of his eyes, and he was lucky no one was there to see him because he had all the marks of a man who had completely lost his mind. He laughed the laugh of the creator of the world who knew that when he died, the world he created would cease to exist alongside him. He laughed until there was nothing funny to laugh about, and he was left with the heat of tears on his face, all mixed in with the rushing euphoria of a man coming out of a firefight without a bullet anywhere in his body.

CHAPTER TWENTY

All hope had not been lost, Indra had explained to her. There was another in New York, an elder statesmen of the nationalist cause: Kesari.

Indra had learned of his presence from some small conversation at the Ceylon India restaurant. He had met Benoy there on their first day, and gone back later to inquire about a job opportunity. The errand had taken the entire evening, and Cora was annoyed when he got back, but he was so loving, so happy, with such a wide smile on his face, something she hadn't seen from him since the wedding. His hand was bandaged, and when she asked what happened, he murmured something about an accident in the kitchen at Ceylon. He seemed filled with a great relief, and there was nothing she could do except meet joy with joy, even though little had changed in their circumstances.

Kesari was also the reason behind a small fight.

"Don't you think we should be staying away from Indian revolutionaries while we're here?" Cora asked Indra. "We're here to hide. The Ghadar in California was all arrested. Your so-called comrade Benoy cursed us out. I don't think this is a good idea."

"He's not some small-time fighter," Indra replied, in a voice both pleading and annoyed. "Kesariji isn't his real name. It's a nickname. Kesari means 'lion with a great mane.' 'Ji' is what we say to elders out of respect. He's been a father to the nationalist movement for years."

"What's he doing in New York?" Cora asked.

"He's been stuck here for a year. The British threatened that if he ever returned to India, his arrest would be swift and severe."

"You're joking, right?" Cora said mockingly. "Here's another wanted man, and you want to openly associate with him?"

"Nothing needs to be out in the open, we can simply say hello."

"You're not thinking, Indra, and I need you to think. We have enough money for a couple weeks. You're working at that restaurant, right? All we need to do is find an apartment, and all I need to do is find some small job, and we'll be good. Nowhere in that plan is associating with more revolutionaries."

"He's nothing of a revolutionary anymore," Indra said. He sounded like a child trying to convince a parent to give in to a demand to buy yet another toy. "He's more of an old man. And from what I've heard, a generous old man. If we ask just the right way, we can probably borrow some money, which can either buy us more time or help us secure that apartment off the Main Stem that we saw."

"How can he be stuck here and have so much money to give out?" Cora asked.

"He was a barrister. Most of his money came from an investment he made thirty years ago. Some sort of insurance company."

She was curious—a man who had found wealth and, unlike her father, used the proceeds to further a cause rather than retreat to club luncheons. Besides, she wanted that apartment, airy and open compared to others they had seen, complete with a price a bit out of their budget. Apartments seemed to go quickly in this city. They just needed a little more cash.

"One quick meeting with him, that's all," Cora said. "If he doesn't give us any money, that's it. I don't want you to see him ever again."

He looked so self-satisfied, and seeing that, Cora wished she hadn't given in, but she didn't say anything after they left for the old man's small apartment, north of Central Park. Descending into the earth on the IRT, Cora marveled at how the trains ran underground in New York as subways—they had taken the principle of the mines, that life could continue to pulsate belowground, and applied it to the simple movement of people. Sure, San Francisco was building a tunnel through Twin Peaks, but this city had managed to tunnel its entire length and width. She told Indra this with the kind of giddiness marked by nostalgia, an attempt to move their conversation past the annoyance from before they left. He seemed uninterested, nervous.

Her gaze wandered around the train car, though now she knew better than to meet the eyes of another. If she showed Indra any affection, something as simple as a hand in his, the looks of judgment would shoot from around the car right at her. The relief and joy from the night he returned from Ceylon India had turned out to be a brief intermission from an unabating lassitude—no matter how much rest he took, he was made quiet by the burden he carried. In truth, she missed the company of her husband, even though he had never left her side. She missed the man he had been before Wilson dragged this country into the damned war, before the center fell right out from underneath them, carrying them away into eddies of misery.

And even if she wanted to return to a sense of levity, the public did not countenance her gestures of warmth and love. The first time she held his hand, she felt that sense of being stared at, and the look of an old woman, wrinkled and weathered into hatred by the passing of each day, made her feel like everything was a mistake, that she had no right to be in that seat with him. She'd slowly gotten used to it, let them look, let them judge, the two of them had places to be, they had money that was running out—bigger worries occupied her mind.

But the day before, it had escalated from simple dirty looks from old ladies. Cora had rested her head upon his shoulder as Indra's hand hung from the strap on a densely crowded train. The grunting sounds of revulsion came first, but people were always making strange sounds on the train, and she didn't move.

"Disgusting," a man hissed.

She lifted her head and turned to look and met his blue eyes. A doughboy, soft-faced and in uniform, probably off to Forty-second Street to have his first experience at a whorehouse before he left to die across the Atlantic. He was probably only a few years older than her half brother—thank God he was only sixteen and couldn't yet ship out.

Like the rest of them filled with their race hatred, he only looked at Cora, couldn't bring himself to look Indra in the eye, only had a nauseated scowl on his baby face, like he had bitten into a just-bought loaf of bread and found it eaten alive by mold. From where had he learned such hate? That was a dumb question, the hate was suffused through and through in the most quotidian of ways—kill the Germans, smash the hun, liberty steaks forever.

"Do you fuck him," he growled. It was not a question. She couldn't tell if he was drunk. The once crowded train seemed emptier, suddenly space was made, and in this widened margin were the three of them. Indra, taller than the doughboy by about half a foot, looked down and cleared his throat, but Cora placed a hand on his shoulder. Public castration. There was nothing he could do. Punch a doughboy and see how fast they'd throw him off a moving train, probably in front of one passing in the opposite direction.

"Yeah, you do, don't you. Disgusting."

Cora couldn't stop looking at him—there was something gravitational about this hate—and at the same time, nothing could come out of her mouth, nor could she swallow.

"Next stop, Forty-second Street," the conductor called out. The soldier moved to get off the train. An argument wasn't worth losing his pre-departure appointment.

"Next time find a real man, you dumb bitch." And he was gone.

Don't look at anyone. That was the rule. Her eyes moved only between the red floor to the advertisements along the top of the car: the importance of eating Grape-Nuts every morning, the need to support the war and enlist, white and pure Fairy soap only five cents, buy a Liberty Bond lest freedom perish.

When they reached Kesari's apartment, Cora was somewhat astonished by the man on the other side of the threshold. There were certain men whose bodies began to assume the stature to which they had risen through their life. Kesari fit this perfectly: his hair, thin and wispy, hung loosely around his ears (later, she would learn that he left the house always wearing a stark-white turban), and he was tall, quite thin. His face was severe, heavyset and full, though his body was lean, with a large mouth set under a bushy mustache. He was without a doubt an ugly man, but when he spoke, it was as if his body disappeared into nothingness, and all that remained was the timbre of his voice.

She learned more of the story that Indra had mentioned. Kesari too was a castaway in New York. He had completed his grand tour of the United States, taking notes on the lives of Indians in America while also trying to glean some understanding of America's mixture of races and peoples. He had written a book out of the experience and then sailed off for London with every intention of returning to India to fight for the cause of freedom. Upon his arrival in England, he learned that he had been marked as a German sympathizer. Again, to be against the British meant to be for the enemy Germans, and officials in India threatened arrest and imprisonment if he were to step foot onto his native soil.

And so he returned to America, where he found that those who had bankrolled his tour supported him no longer—the curse of wartime patriotism meant that they questioned his loyalties.

He was stuck in this apartment, which, from want of furnishings, had a feeling of openness. Unlike their hotel room, which allowed only one person to move around the room while the other sat on the bed, Kesari's apartment had actual rooms: a long narrow hallway, off which branched a small kitchen, a study, a bedroom, and an area to sit.

"Have you met up with some of the other Bengalis here in New York?" Kesari asked. "There are quite a few of you settled in the city. In fact, Benoy Chakravorty was recently here." Cora stiffened at the reference and felt again that this had been a bad idea, but saw that Indra kept his composure. "These awful men, they always come in and out, they even cook here in my kitchen, they think they have free rein over my home. They never make me anything. Indra, do you know how to make rasgulla? I miss the taste of our sweets. Cakes, awful pies, none of it compares to the perfect sweetness of a rasgulla."

Cora appreciated the small insult lobbed against Benoy.

"There is a grocer just at the corner of the block. Go, Indra, get a bit of milk. I have plenty of sugar. Let's eat rasgulla today, Indra."

Kesari told her to stay, to speak with him. "What has brought you two to New York?" he asked. If they were here to try to get the man to lend them some money, she might as well channel her husband's way of speaking: Indra had a way of answering a question, of centering a narrative around himself. There could be no simple recounting of facts, only a story, with character and action. In her best attempt to imitate, she did not demur in her answer. And perhaps because no one had asked her that question since their departure from California, everything came out: their marriage, the arrests, a hasty departure, and finally, arriving in New York and immediately being rejected by the very people they'd believed would save them in their time of need.

Kesariji had gotten up and walked to the window while she spoke, hands clasped behind his back. When she finished, he turned around, and there was such a grave look upon his face, as if he were truly moved by their plight.

"You have my sympathies, my sincerest apologies, for this.

Fools, the lot of them, each believing he is the savior of the cause, and that to stand tall, one must live and die by the struggle. Any deviation from their notions of what this life is to look like is cause for mistrust and disdain. It's an insult to intelligence to think in such a way."

At that moment, Indra returned with a bottle of milk and a few lemons.

"You see, Cora," Kesari said, "there's no chhena here to purchase from a grocer, no pure milk fat to make the perfect rasgulla. Go, let's see if your husband can make it." He sent her off to the kitchen with a wink and a smile.

In the small kitchen, a darkened window looked into the center courtyard of the building. Only a weak light filtered down into the airshaft. Cora could see the lives of others continue inside apartments across the way. They lived on top of one another in this city, and she wondered why anyone at all would choose to live here over the open expanse of almost anywhere else.

"Do you know what you're doing?" she asked Indra.

"Not at all. You don't say no to Kesariji when he asks you to do something. I've never met him. This is my chance to get something for us."

"So what do we do?" she asked, wondering why he thought their future hung upon his cooking rather than her conversation with Kesari. He hadn't even asked her how their conversation had gone.

"I watched my mother make rosogolla around Durga Puja. Heat up the milk, but don't let it scorch on the bottom. Keep stirring. Then add the lemon juice to make the chhana. Hang it from some cloth to separate and let the water run out. Roll it into balls with some flour, then cook it in hot sugar water."

Their time in the kitchen was punctuated by laughter, a lightness as they worked, bumping into each other with every step, stirring the milk constantly, shouting when it threatened to boil over, gently chiding when stirring was left unattended for a minute. Life had been grave since they had left California, the color of their life together gray and dull, tepid bathwater providing little comfort.

Here was Indra, next to her, and all the energy that one spent in the beginning of a relationship talking, trying to seem smarter or wittier or more astute than one actually was, had given way to a conversation between two physical bodies: bumping into each other and making an exaggerated face could be as funny as a spoken joke.

Kesari came in, laughing and smiling along with them, and when he took a bite of the rasgulla, his natural look of severity melted into that doubled look of present melted onto past, the simple lightness of a memory made real. He took a few bites, chewing slowly, and after he finished one of their misshapen creations, he closed his eyes and didn't quite smile—a smile rarely came to him—but the look of satisfaction was enough. He turned to Cora, and before he said anything, Cora knew that her plea had moved him, and she had done it, she had found someone who could love them like a father, someone who could see them through their time in New York.

CHAPTER TWENTY-ONE

Kesari immediately gave them fifty dollars, enough to move out of the hotel and get the apartment she wanted. It was in the Main Stem, just off Eighth Avenue, and they rented as the Thomases. He was no longer the Catholic priest, instead becoming a French teacher stranded in New York because of the war, and that generated enough pity for both of them that the landlord overlooked his countenance and his accent. A good lie could still get them far, and it could keep them safe.

There had been no word of arrests or manhunts in New York. The government seemed content to arrest and indict those back in California, though for how long this détente would last, Cora couldn't be certain.

Even though she loved the apartment for its spaciousness, it was that very quality that made it feel as empty as Kesari's. Their belongings were spartan, so this place, the first home they had ever shared, was barely more than a place to eat and sleep, and that not quite—they had purchased only two spoons secondhand, and it became clear that one was far superior to the other (a bigger bowl, a comfortable handle), and so whoever got to the breakfast table first got the good spoon, and the other would either have to use the one that was far too small—or wait for the other to finish.

There were domestic tasks to get done. The making of a home with its comforts and its cares was of course an important job for a woman—and one that Cora had no interest in completing. Indra wasn't doing much. Cora wanted him to take an interest in the task. The assumption was that the job was hers, as a dutiful household manager, to complete. He was still chastised enough not to mention his dissatisfaction. Nothing got done. They made do with two spoons.

Kesari had offered Cora a job. He had asked her if she knew how to type, and she'd told him about her job at the *Union*. He said that the editor of the editorial section had been quite kind to him when he came through California. It was enough to ask her to help him with his correspondence. It was somewhat clear that the job was pretense, that they weren't just mooching, they were working their way into something new, and Cora wasn't one to complain when handed a gift.

Their life entered a routine. There was their spoon wait in the morning, and there were often evenings taken up with Indra's shifts at the restaurant. She missed the man she had fallen in love with, missed the man who had a vision and the acuity to take him to his destination.

He had taken a job at Ceylon India, and he seemed so needy about it, like he wanted her to pity him for taking work that was beneath him. He said it was different now after she reminded him that he had done the same thing in Palo Alto. Which, of course, it was. What was before done as a way to bide time before a life began was now done as life itself.

Maybe he could be a bit more manly about it. Maybe he could take it on the chin and move on. Yes, she loved him, but it had been weeks since she'd seen him crying in their hotel room, and she no longer knew what to do or how to rescue him from his self-loathing and despair. Perhaps she had been wrong. She couldn't guide him through his own feelings. He had to figure it out on his own.

Last night he had come home late from his shift and slid into bed just as she was falling asleep. He had sidled up next to her, clearly looking for her attention. He smelled so strongly of cooking grease and spice. A pinch of Indian spice made for a good meal. A whole kitchen's worth of it soaked into his skin made her queasy.

"If you would like that, could you bathe?" she asked him, curt from her own sleepiness. She thought it wasn't a big deal to ask him. It was, after all, what he had done almost every time back in California.

Instead, he grunted, turned away from her. After a few moments he stomped out of bed and went to the washroom, but she fell asleep before he came back.

In the morning, as she ate her oatmeal, he hovered behind her before finally putting an envelope on the table.

"What's this?" Cora asked.

"Two tickets. I was reading the paper and saw that Rachel Crothers has a play down at the 39th Street Theater. They're not great," he said apologetically. "Standing room. You devoted so much of your life to her. I wanted to surprise you with these."

Rachel seemed like a lifetime ago.

Cora smiled, got up, and wrapped her arms around him. He still smelled like soap from the bath she made him take. She kissed him. He still had a surprise or two in him.

AT CEYLON INDIA, INDRA WAS STILL SURROUNDED BY INDIANS, BUT THE CAUSE OF FREE-dom was at a distance. On the other hand, Cora felt like she hadn't left the cause at all. Indeed, by working for Kesari, she was closer to it. And now, with a figure not too far from a guru, she had insight into its inner workings, its personalities and figures.

"They're provincial," he'd explained to her once. "Each and every one of those Bengalis can't get over their provincialism."

Cora learned that her teacher hated being interrupted, even if it was for a clarifying question. It would derail his train of thought and rendered him annoyed at the failure of his once-keen memory. She would look up at him quizzically, and if he chose to notice, he would explain what he truly meant.

"Haven't you noticed, Cora, that the Bengalis seek each other out? They can never be too far away from each other. There's a joke. One Bengali is a nationalist, two is a political party, and three make two political parties. When they're with each other, they debate fiercely. That's only among themselves. They'll always close themselves off to outsiders. It's why I have so much respect for Indra. He's one of the few who will meet a Punjabi or a Marathi as a fellow man."

Given a framework, Cora found it easier to understand the way those men in the apartment had turned against Indra. There too was the larger context: no one knew whom to trust anymore. The arrests on the West Coast had rattled them all. And the meeting places were becoming fewer and fewer: the restaurant and Kesari's apartment were two of the few trusted locations.

Benoy came to Kesari's apartment often, and she couldn't stand how he would hum, off-key, some tune she couldn't place, and how he never had anything to do but while away an afternoon reading some text that sat on one of Kesari's shelves. She figured that was why he had tried to fleece them for money, for unlike Indra, he didn't seem able to hold an odd job to support himself, so he had to take from those who were vulnerable. She was content that he ignored her and she him, but his presence hammered away at the concentration she needed at the typewriter, plenty of correspondence for Kesari that required typing, and she needed the time and silence to decipher his unreadable scribble.

Two weeks into the job, Benoy finally asked her something. "You were in California with Indra?" he asked, standing next to one of Kesari's bookshelves, open book in hand.

A polite nod.

"I see," he replied. He went back to reading. She rolled her eyes.

The next time he saw her: "You were in California. You met Indra there. That means you're familiar with the Ghadar?"

Another polite nod. She thought of them often, wondered if Anand had been arrested, if he could handle life in a jail cell, if any of them were ready for the punishment that could be handed down to them.

And finally, a real question: "You must be aware that I am the founder of an organization in New York, the Friends of Freedom for India," he said with an imperious air. "We're seeking a wide membership, people who can fight for the cause. What's impressed me about the Ghadar in California was how they were able to gather their numbers from among the workingmen. What we have here are far too many intellectuals and far too few men who actually work."

Cora thought about it for a moment. She thought of insulting his manhood, saying he was too weak to get his hands dirty with work, that he took donations from the unwilling. Mouthing off about actual work—she could show him. Out of deference to Kesari, she held her tongue.

It was difficult to speak with Benoy—she remembered the night after coming to his apartment, the walk to the ferry, the crackling of Indra's voice. What outcompeted this memory was a preternatural need to be heard, to be truly useful. From that evening walk with her husband, she recalled the ferries and barges on the East River.

Of course, the ferries, the barges, the waterways, and again she could not resist the temptation of being able to hand over a correct answer.

"There are many factories in this city and across the state, if you're willing to travel to some place as remote and cold and dreary as Buffalo to set up an operation," she said casually. "What we also have in New York are the docks—there must be a number of lascars here. Indra once mentioned to me that they spend time at the Ceylon. And in a lascar, you have someone who can take an idea further than any one worker. Give him a pamphlet, and who knows how many destinations it will find."

"Of course! And the Americans are monitoring the mails now,

I've heard of three newspapers today who've had their right to mail revoked. What better way to smuggle our cause overseas than in the hands of a seaman? Do you know Aziz? He runs a laundry near Thirty-seventh Street. I remember him saying something about men from the docks."

Benoy did not thank her when he left, did not acknowledge the beauty of her idea. For all she knew, he would take it to his people as his own. Even so, she was made light from the interaction, warmed through by the work.

Kesari was unimpressed.

"He speaks of needing workers. Damned if he can ever lead a man into anything except ruin," he said, shaking his head with the gravity of a king seated upon a throne. "He's not a leader. Thinks of himself as one. Never will be. Men like him read too much Nietzsche. They all think they're supermen. You see how many Indians pass through my home and every one of them thinks that the cause for freedom rests upon their shoulders alone. The worst part is they want it that way. They want to be the hero. They want to be the one to liberate their nation. I think if India were given to them, they would bypass democracy and go straight to an enlightened monarchy. They want to be a kind despot, nothing more."

Cora nodded in agreement and, for a moment, thought of her husband as some would-be king trying to lead his people.

As the days went on, Kesari's correspondence grew thinner, though he kept asking if she had other plans for work—he said he would be more than happy to supply any money she or Indra needed, hinting that there was more to the world than typing the letters of an old man. She ignored him. When he persisted, she jokingly asked him: "Tired of me already?"

"Tired!" he roared. One word to reprimand, and she felt in his presence the teacher with a switch, her knuckles anxiously waiting for the stinging pain.

"Cora, I think you have some talent. You told me you wrote

for the *Union*. You were finishing graduate school at Stanford. I've heard your conversations with Benoy. And I think you can take all that talent outside this small apartment. Do you know the Goldings? Jude and Penelope? Jude is an actor and a poet, Penelope is a journalist and writer—they're both leaders in the Irish Progressive League. Strong proponents of Home Rule."

Cora was flummoxed as to why Kesari would send her to the Irish.

"The fight for freedom is not limited to one nation or one race. We act in tandem. The Easter Rebellion was just as important for Delhi as it was for Dublin. Or take women's suffrage. The right to vote is part of the fight for the freedom of men denied the ballot box in the colonies. We live in the thicket of connections, Cora, and you need to see both the forest and the trees at the same time. I'll send an introduction. You should consider speaking with them."

HER MIND CHURNED LIKE A STEAM ENGINE, PIECES ALL HEAVING ALONG GEARS AND COGS in tandem, propelling her ever forward. She hadn't been some dilettante, flitting from meeting to meeting. She had been living in that very thicket of connections, and now she could see all the pieces moving as one great heaving machine. She'd gone from meetings for women's suffrage to socialist readings to tutoring the poor to Indian nationalism because some part of her knew none of these things worked alone.

She couldn't wait to tell Indra about the Goldings.

She met with Indra at the theater at Thirty-ninth and Broadway, not too far from where they lived. It was a beautiful monument to the dramatic arts, a handsome Italian renaissance style of golden sandstone with terra-cotta acanthus reliefs underneath tall arched windows. When they went inside, Cora was surprised to learn that Indra had never taken an elevator before, that he was unsure of stepping across his threshold, and after the operator closed the cage door, she saw how his eyes shifted with the walls outside. So worldly and yet still so inexperienced in many ways.

The two crowded into the standing-room section of the third-floor balcony and took in the beauty of the playhouse, all red velvet, golden lights upon the wall. Even in its grandeur, it retained a sense of intimacy—the stage didn't seem too far away, and if not for the well-placed bald head of a rather tall man seated six rows away in the balcony, she would have had a clear view.

The play was *Old Lady 31*, one of Crothers's comedies, light and domestic, versus the plays that Cora had been more interested in, those that grappled with women in a fractured society. In this play, an old couple, Angie and Captain Abe, married for many years, fell upon hard times, causing the wife to go live in an old ladies' home while the husband had to be sent to the poor farm. But the two couldn't be separated, and the women of the home were so affected by the pathos of their parting that they agreed to hide him in the ladies' home as the disguised Old Lady 31. Humor and hijinks ensued.

By the time the play ended, they were filled with the lightness of good entertainment, and on the walk home, Indra seemed happy to have experienced what he had seen. "So that's who you were studying!"

Cora had given years of her life to the study of Crothers's plays, and yet leaving California had fundamentally cleaved her from her past with the finality of a butcher's knife. Crothers, the playhouse, the characters upon the stage: she had given years to their study and review. And now it was over, her master's probably reduced to an incomplete in every remaining course. There wasn't anything she could do about it—it wasn't like anyone at the school, save Hazel, knew why she had left and where she had gone.

"That was definitely more frivolous than what I studied. Nothing like where she was asking questions about what it means to be a woman. That was more dramatic. Incredible stuff."

They were walking up Broadway past the wrought-iron entrance to the IRT, where the garish electric light from the hotels and
theaters cast eerie shadows upon the faces in the billboard advertisements above. The street was filled with as many people as there
would be in the daytime, streaming out of the Astor Theatre, coming in and out of the Hotel Albany, piling into the back of motorcars
to continue the night, and amid all the activity, she and Indra had
to stay close lest the unceasing rill of people pull them apart. In the
conversations that passed, Cora could hear the pedestrian criticism
of all other plays just seen.

Indra looked worried. "So did you like it?"

Cora didn't want to mention that it was plays like this one that
had a part in dulling her studies. Crothers seemed to have turned
away from the daring heroines of her early work, the plays that
featured women seriously negotiating their own freedom in a world
built by men. A few years ago Crothers had written *The Heart of
Paddy Whack*, and it was as if she had discovered how lucrative banal comedy could be. *Old Lady 31* seemed to continue that trend.
Gone were the plays suffused with suffragist and feminist ideas.
In their place came something conventional: shallow pieces of entertainment where women stood by their men through hard times.
And worse, these plays were all supremely well received. Large audi-
ences always enjoyed the most vapid stories. What surprised her the
most was how someone could give up an idea they had once been
wed to and change abruptly to something else. She had wondered
what the mechanics of that could entail.

"Oh, it was enjoyable enough," Cora said. "Emma Dunn was
marvelous." She was stretching her legs as a former critic. Old habits died hard. "She played the idea of plaintive woman with such
tenderness. Reginald Barlow was this great salt of a man, and done
with an earnestness, you know? Those two young lovers—I can't
remember their names anymore—they didn't belong. They seemed
too out of place."

"I agree," Indra said. "It made old love seem beautiful. What was it that Angie said? 'Sometimes I think the dreaming is more important than the facts.'"

"Oh yes, Crothers has a marvelous way with dialogue. But Indra, listen, there's something I want to tell you," she said, changing the subject as they stepped into the street to make their way around the crowd in front of Cohan's Theatre. They were passing Forty-seventh Street and had only a few blocks left to get home. "Kesariji wants me to meet this couple, the Goldings, up in the north of Manhattan. He says they run know some people who run a newspaper, that I can write for them, maybe."

To her surprise, Indra stopped at the corner of Forty-eighth and Broadway. He seemed apprehensive—fearful, even. "Are you sure this is a good idea? You told me before we went to meet Kesariji, we're here to lay low. Drawing attention to ourselves probably isn't the best idea."

And with that, the gaiety of the evening was lost. Cora felt defensive of her own dreams, desires for something more. "I seriously doubt this draws much attention to us. We're just meeting up."

"If you meet up, I imagine they'll see how you can write, and if they see that, they'll want you to write for them. And that, to me, feels dangerous. Are you sure you want to do this?"

"I don't think it's dangerous at all," she replied rather quickly. "And in any case, what's the matter if I do write something? You were at risk because you're from India and you were working with the Germans. This would be an American working for Americans. Totally different. They're not arresting many Americans, as far as I know."

"They're arresting Americans left and right," he said in an indictment against her ambition. "Besides, I know we listed my place of birth as Syracuse, but that's only if they believe it."

"Let's just sleep on it, okay?" she said, not wanting to press the matter forward. It was too late to think about how much of herself she was going to sacrifice to keep him safe. She led the way into their apartment, and later, they went to bed, not having said a word to the other.

CHAPTER TWENTY-TWO

The Ceylon India on Eighth Avenue was a beacon at the edge of a seedy neighborhood of brothels. The restaurant was owned by a sprightly man named Yaman, a Buddhist from Ceylon who had come to the United States as a traditional Ceylonese dancer and had toured the country for five years. He was short and stout, like he was some compressed spring full of potential energy. His face was full and square, with a droopy mustache and a receding hairline. One of his eyes was permanently fixed upon some random point in the distance. It was difficult to think of him as someone who could move to a rhythm, but that was the trick that art played—always a possibility of sublime transformation.

Still, Indra wanted to know how a man of such refined art could end up owning an eatery in the center of Manhattan. Before one of his shifts, he had struck up a light conversation with the proprietor and learned that he had met a woman named Elizabeth from southern Germany. Yaman was dancing with the Barnum & Bailey circus up in Connecticut. Elizabeth was a singer in the chorus and somewhere under the big top, they met and fell in love. Here, Yaman glossed over the details of their story, though Indra wanted more, wondering, in a way that doubled back to his own story, how the two had courted, or if all love followed the same pattern of desire, anticipation, and giddiness followed by the long repose of comfort. Yaman soon gave up on the opportunity to tour the United States indefinitely. Years of dancing had taken a toll on his body—no day began without joints aching for rest. When Indra asked why he had started a restaurant, Yaman casually replied that he simply missed the food from his homeland. He used his savings to buy the restaurant. Word spread quickly among the lascars who would come for a hot meal after arriving in harbor.

There were so many more things Indra wanted to ask. He wanted to ask Yaman how he managed to live with Elizabeth in a city (a state, a country) that hated any love that crossed the invisible lines seemingly set everywhere like trip wires. Indra had returned from the East River tired—the initial elation he felt had faded, and the world, even as it burst with the bright green of May's maple leaves and the yellow, pink, and white of tulip blossoms under a warm spring sun, seemed to fade to an exilic gray, and he was left listening to the edges of conversations, wondering what he had to add, and when he could think of nothing, he simply said nothing. Only a bit of his pride had come back after the experience with Kesari, a belief that he had impressed the old man with a random ability to make rosogulla, that he'd been able to capitalize on a fellow outcast's taste of nostalgia for a country left behind, and pleased that it had led to the infusion of money he and Cora had used to get their apartment.

His job at Ceylon India was mainly washing dishes (scrape, wash, rinse, dry—an experience made valuable beyond the recommendation for where to buy some rice). The restaurant functioned as a meeting place for the Indians in New York, mostly old lascars tired of sailing, looking for some land to settle down on, eager to give up the limitless horizon of drudgery and calloused toil. The first sailor must have picked New York at random, his final port of call, ready for a life on shore. He was like the piling of a pier around which each subsequent lascar was a mussel sticking to a surface, agglomerating until they became a small community.

Indra listened to scraps of their conversations, of the roughness of their lives, mostly spent twenty, thirty feet underneath the surface, toiling belowdecks. Many of them were Bengali, mostly Mussalman.

"Didn't see the sun for three weeks," one muttered.

"Fresh air? What's fresh air?" another asked with a sneer, the one Indra knew as the man with the throaty, persistent cough. He often came in blue denim coveralls unbuttoned at the neck, streaks of grease staining the fabric throughout. Indra assumed he either left for or arrived from a shift at some waterside factory. "Breathed in the dust of the coal all day, every day. I spit on the streets here, and I still taste the black coal on my tongue."

Another time, Indra cleared a table of what perhaps was its thousandth cup of coffee, taking his time so he could hear their stories. "The heat, the fire. Felt like hell on earth." If Indra could remember correctly, this short, often charming man was a bellhop at a nearby hotel. Indra didn't expect his story from behind that dazzling smile. "Standing at the door of the furnace, stoking the fire. If there is a moment of less than perfect heat to get power to the engine, they come from above deck, calling me lazy, ungrateful. Bastard should try standing in front of the engine furnace for twelve hours and then tell me how to shovel."

"No white sailor is ever in the engine room. Who will work the oil and grease down there? The sons of Bengal. Who gets paid the most? British bastards." When Indra heard this, he was reminded of the farmworkers back in California. The group of men who worked the earth, the mass who could give an idea its true power and force. He felt his heart pine for a time when he believed he would be giving speeches of inspiration to those men.

Each of these sailors had seen men die, driven mad by the work and the heat. The cool respite of a final dive into the sea was the only escape from shifts in the fire. Indra wanted to say that he too had seen the final breath of a brother, of someone crushed by a power so great that it seemed like any rebellion was impossible but still necessary. He lacked the language, the nuance, the capability to thread the metaphor.

There were so many things he wanted to ask. He wanted to know why they had taken the job, why they had subjected themselves to the pain and torture of such work, and the answer was always the same, debts to be paid in their home villages, the sleight of hand of moneylenders whose interest bonded the next generation into ceaseless labor far from home.

And the guilt, of course: where they had nothing, he had been given plenty. Indra was descended from a long line of proud kulin folk. The land had always been theirs. Those in his community who found themselves bound to the money lender had been let loose by the chain of vice. Others were damned by nature: one mistake following excessive rainfall, or maybe a monsoon that didn't arrive, or maybe everything was too perfect and the price of indigo plummeted. The evil eye had never passed over his land, his family.

Here, in this foreign place, he served them. He cleared their tables, washed their plates, ensured that the ceramic mugs for their never-ending cups of coffee remained spotless. The old world could turn upon its head in an instant.

They knew the pain of colonial rule. The wealth that the British drained from Mother India was theirs in the first place. They could be sympathetic to the cause of revolution and nation.

He could meet them, man among man, and fight for them. He didn't yet know how to speak, unable to move past pleasantries and hellos. They constituted a group unto themselves—even if they spoke Bengali, they seemed to have their own language, turns of phrase that Indra could never decipher. Ceylon India was the only place in the city that he knew of where he could connect with a true mass of men, but he remained distant, as if there were some chain of thought missing that could bridge the gap between class, upbringing, and position.

It was Benoy who first brought them into the fold. He came in one day and sat down at a table among them. Indra did not get close enough to hear what he had to say, but it was clear he held their attention, they listened closely to his words, grunted in appreciation at his jokes, nodded at whatever he was planning. When he was done, seemingly filled with the confidence of having won their approval, he came up to Indra, who had watched from the door that separated the dining room from the kitchen.

"I'm sure you heard some of our conversation," Benoy said, sly and full of pride, none of the beggar left in him.

"I heard a little bit here and there. I was focused on my job. I work to earn, Benoy, you should try it," Indra said, uninterested in this man, wanting to be as far as possible from whatever toxicity he was about to spout.

"Who has time to work? We're planning something. Everything is falling into place. We could use you, Indra-da. You led us in India. I think you did something in California. Can you do it here?" Benoy asked. Indra could feel this ass trying to goad him into joining with them, trying to speak to a boastful past in order to raise Indra to the moment. Underneath were the words of Obermeier, exhorting him to keep the faith. A good god always knew a man's step before he took it.

"They indicted me out west, Benoy, and you're asking me to join in here?" Indra said, not wanting to give Obermeier, or any of the Germans, or any of the rotten Bengalis, more of his time. "I must seem like a fool to you. I'm not going to risk arrest."

"That woman has cowed you, hasn't she! You should know that this idea is hers too. I asked her at Kesariji's if the lascars could fuel a revolution, and she agreed. Come on, trust me, your woman won't mind. We need you." Benoy smiled a little fox smile of someone who could sell a person upriver to save his own hide.

It stung that Cora was helping this stingy and small man—she was living her own life. Even so, Indra wished to tell Benoy to buzz right off, to get out of the restaurant. He couldn't. This wasn't his space to make a command to anyone.

"I'm keeping my head down for now, Benoy. Maybe once this

all blows over, maybe then, maybe I'll join you."

"Indra-da, if you keep your head down for too long, you'll become a mole. You'll lose your eyes, and then what? You'll be like Yaman, selling food to lascars on ship leave."

"I appreciate your concern," Indra replied, biting the tip of his tongue between his teeth as a distraction from the shame of conversing with someone who once was his subordinate and now lorded over him with glee.

These games of chance and making war on someone else's dime were nothing but a past life. And at least what Yaman did, what Tokutaro did, was honest work. Hard work. Nothing wrong with it.

Indra had to figure out what came next, what world would open up for him. When listening to the stories of these men in the restaurant, he wanted Cora there to think and listen with him. That's what she'd done so well in California—they had thought and dreamed and envisioned new worlds together. Cora had a wonderful ability to complete his thoughts, like when they left the protest in San Francisco and she brought him down to Palo Alto to see and hear from everyone new. When he looked at her then, he saw someone who could erase herself and become part of his own needs and life—and he wanted that back.

At the end of each day, Indra's hands would end up wrinkled and ashen from the constant exposure to hot water and soap in the kitchen. Yaman had offered him a pair of rubber gloves, but the damned dishes kept slipping from his grasp under the stream, and he had been lucky so far that none of them had broken. Without the gloves, the backs of his hands began to burn red and peel. As he nursed a cup of coffee after one of his shifts, one of the lascars took notice.

"Go to a chemist," he said in Bengali, knowing exactly what part of India Indra had come from. "Get some petrolatum and mix it with beeswax. Half and half. You can melt it in a pot and pour it into an old jar. Cover your hands with that, and it'll clear right up."

Indra thanked the man, who held out his hand and introduced himself as Faisal. Indra replied with his name, and the man gave a grunt of assent, a recognition that he was a man, a fellow worker, a body that could be made frail by work. It wasn't much of a conversation, but Indra was thankful. He went and bought both ingredients from a corner chemist and soon ended each day with hands so greasy he had difficulty turning the knobs on doors.

Still, he was grateful to have regular work.

He was keeping his head down. He was listening.

CHAPTER TWENTY-THREE

Kesari had written to the Goldings. Jude had replied enthusiastically that they both wished to meet Cora, and maybe it would be best if she could take the IRT up to Dyckman to meet—the weather was so fine, and Penelope, expecting their first child, could benefit from fresh air and new conversation.

Kesari had told Cora that Jude immigrated from his birthplace in County Cork to act on the stage in New York, while Penelope was from some small village far upstate, near the St. Lawrence River and the border with Canada. Her parents had been owners of a large timber estate, and she grew up among the spruce and pine and softwood used for the manufacture of paper. She gave up the life of an heiress for the passions of the freedom struggle.

Cora's mind buzzed with excitement—an immigrant man and a woman who was born and raised in a wilderness destitute of polite society. It didn't seem possible that two people could mirror her own life experience as much as Jude and Penelope. She wanted to love them. She wanted to be them. She *was* them. Or perhaps they were some slightly older version of Cora and Indra, and speaking with them would be like gazing into her own future. Minus the pregnancy, of course. Though she wondered if that could be possible, if marriage always meant that one day she would have to give up her resolution and would be asking some young upstart to come visit her uptown so she could get some air.

Cora had never been that far up into the reaches of Manhattan.

Her thoughts raced with such speed that she barely noticed the train emerged from its subterranean depths to reach quite a height near 125th Street only to dive back into the earth. By the time the train reached 155th Street, she'd grown antsy. The journey lumbered on until finally, after what seemed like thirty minutes too long, she reached her destination at Manhattan's northern tip.

They had given her an address on Sherman Avenue, but when she left the station, she found the streets running upon their own volition, the comforts of an understandable grid gone. She walked along a familiar street—Broadway—following it to 207th Street, and was left wondering where four streets had gone when she hit 211th Street. On a lark, she turned down 211th and somehow found herself on Sherman, and from there she walked, hoping it was the correct direction. The neighborhood was one country atop another, Jewish immigrants lived in buildings next to Irish immigrants who lived next to Italians—a tangle of languages growing out of every window like untamed ivy.

She saw Jude and Penelope hand in hand, sitting on a slat-wood bench front of their building. Jude got up to meet her. His face looked a little sad when at rest, though ever the actor, it lit up into kind joy the moment he saw her walking over.

"Are you Cora? It's lovely to meet you," he said, holding out his hand. "Thank you for coming all the way here. We used to live down in Greenwich Village, right in the middle of all of it. We need more space for the child."

Penelope strained to get up to stand by his side, very pregnant, almost every part of her swollen, her dress loose at the shoulders and legs, but tight from the protuberance at her stomach. Despite that, she had the somewhat lazy and happy look common to women just about to give birth. A hand reflexively rested upon her future child.

Jude, with bits of white speckling his swept-back reddish-blond hair, couldn't have been more than ten years older than Indra. Penelope was maybe five or six years older than Cora.

Cora felt a deep ache of emptiness that Indra was not there to share in this moment, wishing he were there to greet their mirrors. In the end, it was better that he was not there. The conversation was left for her alone to reap the benefit. In a marriage, one person's life would always take precedence over the other's. And perhaps he would have assumed Cora to be content to be shunted into conversation solely with Penelope.

The three exchanged pleasantries. "Kesariji said you had lived out west and went to Stanford. You didn't happen to know John Scullion, did you?"

Cora was delighted to hear that name again. "It's hard to live in Palo Alto without knowing him. He was a good friend. How do you know him?"

"Wonderful to hear. Ireland is a small island. Not many others combining the stage with the freedom struggle. Say, did you ever read his play *The Children of the Dagda*? He's the only person I know who can take something as grand as mythology and find a way to fit it in a small space."

Never say no, never say die, my dear, Scullion had told her. "I know the play well. I acted in it," Cora said, lying. She had been so pleased with the connection to Scullion that she wanted to impress Jude immediately, one of those white lies that could be used to build herself up with a stranger.

"Acted? That old bastard told me he would write if he ever staged it in its entirety."

"Oh, it was just a reading," Cora said, trying to hide her mistake.

"He's such a micromanager that you must've felt like it was a staging. Well, any friend of John is a friend of ours," Jude said, and Cora was relieved that he didn't seem to care about her misstep. "Shall we?" The three of them walked down Sherman until they reached a wall of maple filled with the bright green leaves of early

May. The trees blocked any path up the hill of wild land.

"Rockefeller's bought it all up," Jude spat. "Says he wants to build a park. Easiest way to dodge paying taxes. Buy some land, conduct a few improvements, get the city to write it all off."

"Rockefeller," Cora trailed off, wondering how much of her past she could reveal to impress upon them her seriousness. "I grew up on a mine owned by that awful name. In Trinidad, Colorado."

"The Ludlow Massacre was only a few years ago, and you're telling me you lived there?" Jude asked.

"Even back then, Rockefeller was starving his miners," she said, eliding the fact that her father's position meant they'd lived in relative comfort. "I miss the west. I've never found anything else that can compare to the terrible beauty of that desolate and cursed place."

As they walked along the outskirts of Rockefeller's property, Cora felt compelled to share the arc of her past.

"The physicists say now that the world is made up of atoms," Cora continued, remembering some soliloquy she endured from a scientist at one of Scullion's parties, "and every atom has this small core, and around that core floats these even smaller things that can never touch the center. They rotate around in some sort of cloud. Sometimes I feel as if I'm in that cloud, and I'm looking for the core. I can never touch it. I'm always going to be bound to it. I can't escape its pull."

Jude and Penelope nodded vigorously and looked at each other, a glance that anyone from the outside could read as one of the quirks of being together for a long time, where the gestures of thought of one slowly meld into one the other.

"Are you familiar with what's happening in Russia, Cora?" Penelope asked with great emphasis, as if it were what she had wanted to ask the moment the name Rockefeller was mentioned, but she'd had to contend with Jude's dancing around. "A great upheaval. They're burning down the old world. What do you think of it?"

"I think it's just and necessary," Cora said, adding a few embellished details regarding her attendance at socialist meetings back in California.

"I know Kesariji wanted you to work with us on the Irish cause, and we'd love to have you with us," Jude said, "I know an editor at the *Clarion* who I think you should meet. You read the *Clarion*?"

"Of course," Cora lied. She knew of the socialist newspaper. A few of its articles had been shared at the meetings in Palo Alto.

"There's the *Clarion*, there's *The Jewish Daily Forward*. There's the Irish press too. I'm friends with the editor over at *The Gaelic American*. They're sympathetic to the radical cause. I don't trust *The Irish World*, sycophants to the bourgeoisie, but there's plenty of places where you can write. What you just said, the atoms and the cloud, it's beautiful. You're smart, quick on your feet. Any publication would be lucky to have you. Damn, we could use you."

There was something about his effusiveness that made Cora feel guilty, as if she should fess up before she was found out. "I had heard the comment about the atoms from some scientist at a party," she confessed.

"Of course you did," Penelope said. "I don't think he made the metaphor, right? That's the point of a good journalist. You hear things, and you keep them, you sit down to write, bringing a little bit of yourself into the information. The best of the lot can make the voices of others more beautiful when written out. I agree with Jude. You've got talent."

"Would you want me to write about India?"

"India? Who cares. Why don't you write a few things for me, and I'll pass them along to *The Gaelic American*. Then we'll get some of your clips over to the *Clarion*." Jude said this with a confidence in her that she had never felt about herself.

"That's incredible, Jude. This is so kind," Cora stammered.

"Kindness? You're the one doing us a favor. There are those of us born in these rooms, and we spend our lives fighting to say that this room is our own. Then there are people like you, people who move from room to room, bringing news from one to another, leaving behind the comforts of one bed for the hard and rough floor of another. As much as we need our own people to rise up and fight, we need you, we need the ones who move so freely."

"There's a word, you know that, Cora," Penelope added, completing Jude's thought. "They call it cosmopolitan. You're at home in every part of the world. That's the most useful trait anyone can have."

WHEN CORA GOT HOME THAT EVENING, ALL SHE WANTED TO DO WAS SHARE THE DAY WITH INDRA, TO LET HIM KNOW of everything that had happened, of the possibilities that were coming out of their time in New York. They had left California, and the news in the papers of the arrests was absolutely dreadful. The papers reported all the salacious (and mostly fabricated) details of a Hindu-German conspiracy, a global attempt by seedy rebels to undermine the allied powers. If the men back in California were capable of half of what the papers claimed, they would have brought down the empire, and the entire known world, ages ago.

Alongside these falsehoods, the papers had published a list of names lifted straight from the court documents, and from these reports, they learned that Indra had been named as a fellow conspirator and indicted even though he wasn't present. It seemed to be a conspiracy limited to California. As far as she knew, no one in New York had been targeted, giving any danger a supremely distant feeling.

She decided she wouldn't tell Indra about the Goldings or the *Clarion*. Not yet. She didn't want to revisit what they had said after the Crothers play. She knew he was being too serious. No one would question articles written by some American woman. And for all she knew, she was still American. She was certain that what she was doing was far less dangerous than trying to meet up with members of the German consulate.

Yes, she told herself. This was fine.

The truth was that the moments leading up to their marriage had been ones of great possibility, of a meandering path that switch-backed into the unseen, and they would go into it, machetes in hand. The moment they married, the word "compromise" entered her vocabulary, and it did so with such momentum that she hadn't even begun to comprehend the sheer rearranging capacity that compromise with another human being could entail. The singular *her* was lost. She was permanently entangled with a him—maybe she could resist the pull of that synthesis for just a moment longer.

He was Pierre in this city, and for all she knew, that identity could keep them safe—for now. Maybe they would be here for a few more weeks, or maybe they would stay for a few months, she couldn't be certain.

No, rather than tell him about this, she would be content with imagining what they would talk about. In these daydreams, she would ask him to join her as she became a version of herself made anew by novel challenges, a whole world of make-believe similar to the play of a lonely child. She learned much about herself from conversations with those who existed nowhere in particular, allusive foils against which she could understand a true measure of who she wanted to be.

Even if they were in New York for the briefest of moments, doors were opening for her, and she wished to share everything she saw with the person she loved, but she feared that these experiences could become a pretext to the possibility of more arguments between them. She would refuse to compromise. She wasn't ready to have this life force subjugate her to the dull task of considering someone else at all moments. She was so convinced of her own rightness that she denied herself all possibility of empathy, of reason.

She wouldn't keep a secret from him, but she didn't have to tell him everything.

Maybe that lie of omission would even keep him safe.

CHAPTER TWENTY-FOUR

Cora was expanding her world—she didn't talk about her articles, but Indra knew she was writing them, and he wished she weren't. There was one about the upcoming Irish Convention in Dublin. Another one talking to Irish American doughboys. She was traversing the city, putting her name out there, writing all that she saw.

He honestly felt a great fear for both of them, that she was putting them both at risk, except who was he to deny her dreams? And when he attempted to argue with himself from her point of view, he allowed that perhaps she could be right, that by virtue of being a white American woman, she could move through the world in a way entirely different than he. Then again, she was the one who had pointed to her ring in Suresh's kitchen.

How he could thread that needle of her wants and their needs, he couldn't be certain. What she was doing was beyond money. She didn't need to work at all, they weren't hard up for cash, there was enough for both of them to eat and live from a combination of his income from the restaurant, the remainder of what she had earned with Kesari, and the remnants of her father's gift. They didn't feel the pressing needs of want and deprivation.

He wanted her to be happy. He wanted them to be safe. Maybe he also wanted her to return to the person she'd been in California because that was the version of her who made him feel important.

More than anything, he wanted this damn war to be over so

they could get on with their lives. It seemed like neither of them knew how to find the fine balance between him and her, and without that, their marriage was beginning to lack a fundamental focus, a place for both of them. And without that thing on the horizon to walk toward, she was beginning to go her own way.

He went few places these days.

Mostly, he walked the same well-trodden route between their small apartment and the restaurant, the once overwhelming sense of New York's infinite expanse of bodies now delimited to seeing the same men walk down the street, the greengrocers setting up baskets of produce in front of their shops, the shoe shiners sitting upon the corners, the newsboys hawking papers. For a city reputed to be as dynamic as the world itself, it seemed to turn upon the same day-in-day-out routines as anywhere else.

He was listening, not only to the men at Ceylon, but also to the world around him. And even if she told him little, he heard how she was circulating now. She was working for Kesari, she was impressing Benoy with her knowledge, she was meeting with editors, and now it seemed like she was going to write for the socialists. She had a meeting downtown.

What were they all talking about? If it wasn't the war, the choice word on everyone's lips was socialism. The February Revolution in Russia had toppled the czar, brought hundreds of thousands into the streets. This was the revolutionary power Indra had dreamed about, the ability to bring everyone united into one cause to displace a power that once had been known as entrenched. At Ceylon India, he would listen to the tirades of socialists, anarchists, and syndicalists, most of them against a war that pitted one workingman against another. And he would go home and see his wife preparing for a meeting with the editor of a socialist weekly. She was at the heart of a movement gaining momentum, sweeping across the world.

Of course Indra knew a bit about socialism—who didn't these days—but he wished for Cora's knowledge. He knew that before she had met him, she had attended countless meetings, learned the ins and outs of what Marx had said. And that she had grown up in the mines, among workingmen, mines now famous for their labor uprisings. She had knowledge he could only hope for.

Indra would meet up with Kesari after a shift at the restaurant, and the two, washed ashore in New York, would share a little misery together. Kesari, barred from returning to India, longed to see his country one last time, to address a meeting of like-minded nationalists before his death, his last wish for his life. In return, he knew that Indra wanted to somehow make his way to Berlin, though the dream felt so deferred, so far off, that Indra offered it up only because it seemed a fair trade: one confession for another, both longing to cross the ocean to find what they wanted.

Kesari was scheduled to speak at a small socialist meeting at the YMCA near Columbia University, and Indra decided to tag along to listen to the old orator work up a crowd. Indeed, it was a speech that denounced capitalism as an absurd enterprise, beginning with the fact that the political economy of one nation could subjugate a great and ancient civilization was a vulgar precept, and he went on about how Indians struggled in poverty. Indra could close his eyes and pretend he was in India, hear the growing murmur of approval at the end of some anti-British tirade.

The whole evening ended in disappointment. Some socialist in the back raised his hand to ask a question, a wiry streetwise type with a nasally voice: "What you say is very moving. You've spoken at length about how the British have driven the Indian workingman into poverty. How will you nationalists end their plight? How will you help the masses of Indians needing uplift?"

Kesari seemed annoyed at the question and tried to brush it off. "Before we lift every last man out of the poverty you speak of, we must control the levers of government." Indra nodded. It was a belabored point because a movement that represented everyone could do both at the same time. Still, it was the kind of answer Indra himself would have given just a few months ago.

The man in the back let out a sarcastic laugh. "Control the government! Well, what difference would it make to the average Indian if he suffers under the boot of a native-born capitalist instead of a foreigner?"

Kesari's eyes flared with anger, and it seemed to Indra that he was about to jump down off the small stage of the meeting hall to stomp over and punch the rabble-rouser in the nose. "What difference does it make?" he roared. "It makes quite a difference if a man is kicked by his own brother or beaten by a stranger in a highway robbery! I assure you, the fights among family leave fewer bruises than the brutality of strangers."

Indra almost choked on his own spit and covered it up with a slight cough. The audience, who had been so willing to voice agreement with loud grunts or spontaneous bursts of applause, remained completely silent. The stunned blankness was filled only when a socialist leader came up to the stage to conclude the night and ask those gathered for one last round of applause for the speaker. A halfhearted series of claps, mostly fingers grazing against palms, sputtered forth from the audience, who murmured as they got up to leave.

Indra walked up to Kesari. "These hoboes," Kesari said to him, shaking his head, using the denigrating term for left-wing troublemakers. When Indra heard it come out of Kesari's mouth, he felt that this mentor, this fatherlike figure for him, was an old man, one bound to feelings quickly becoming outdated as the tide turned faster than anyone had predicted. "They always think they're the smartest people in the room. They're always looking for a way to catch an honest man in the web of some supposed fault in logic. They know nothing. Right, Indra?"

Indra smiled and voiced a desultory sound of agreement, though inwardly the gears began to turn, a great machinery sputtering into life, and Indra did not want to lose this forward motion. When Kes-

ari asked if Indra wished to return to his apartment to share dinner,
Indra made some excuse about work at the restaurant.

"You know, I'm always happy to lend a dollar to any one of my
countrymen who asks, but it's also important to earn your keep. I
can have respect for that. Listen, Indra, speaking of lending money
reminds me, there's something quite important I need to tell you."

Indra nodded, impatient to leave.

"A messenger from the Military Intelligence Bureau arrived at
my apartment yesterday morning. He had a few questions."

"What kind of questions?" Indra asked, trying to hide his sinking feeling of being followed across the country.

"I have nothing to hide. They asked mostly about my money.
I think it has something to do with that rascal Benoy. You know I
never say no to an Indian in need. They wanted a list of everyone I
lent money to. They seemed to have followed his money back to me,
I'm not sure how they can do it. They knew quite a bit."

"What did you tell them?" Indra asked. The question came out
with more venom than Indra intended, but he had no patience for
a man who spoke with the police, even if it was the elder statesman
who stood before him.

"You must know these days deportation can only mean death.
The bastards who'll receive me at the port of Bombay will grant me
the luxury of a trip to the gallows. They already knew who had my
money. They said, 'Here's Benoy Chakravorty, you lent him one
hundred and fifty dollars on February sixth. Why?' And I would
explain to them that the fellow asked for the money for rent or to
settle some debt. I told them I had no control over what they did
with the money after I lent it out."

That grifter Benoy. Borrowing one hundred fifty in scratch
from Kesari and still hounding Indra like a welcher for an extra five
bucks. "Did they make any inquiries about me?" Indra asked, his
fingers fidgeting a coin in his pocket.

"Nothing. Know that if they can trace my money from Benoy,

they can do the same for you and Cora. I didn't like his tone. He seemed like he knew too much. I see Cora's writing more widely now. She's written for Golding, for that Irish paper. That's my fault. She has such great talent. I should have known that the Goldings would take her further. There must be CID here in the city. Keep yourself safe—these are dangerous times. Americans can only think in simple ways: for or against."

Indra went out into the night feeling like he had lost a key to a locked door, and he was searching all his pockets, retracing all his steps, coming up with nothing. The past was reappearing, with all of its dangers and considerations, and he had no idea how he could he convince someone who had chipped away at the hard granite of her own life to carve something new that this very act was one of mutual destruction.

He climbed up the steps along 120th Street onto the far end of the Columbia campus and wandered south upon the redbrick path, the green copper roofs looming as silhouettes in the darkness. And yet the possibility of her intelligence as a crime only made him surer of its correctness.

Kesari had been a fool: to be robbed by one's own brother was worse than being robbed by a stranger. All men deserved the dignity of a life free from the burden of poverty. Complete freedom was freedom from foreign rule and native exploitation. Indra needed more than these pithy truisms. He wanted to devote himself to understanding what all of this could actually mean.

In front of him, the large dome of the campus library loomed, lit from below by pale orange electric lamps along the pathway. He walked around the library, seeing through its windows the frenzy of activity within, students cheek by jowl in the reading room. Late May probably meant that they were preparing for their final exams.

He tried to go inside but was denied entry at the door. The library was for use only by university faculty, students, and affiliates. If he wanted a public library, the guard at the door sneered, the New

York Public Library was free to use.

THEIR MARRIAGE WAS ONE OF HABITS AND WAYS, OF MORNINGS AND EVENINGS, OF TIME spent around waking and sleeping, with the majority of the days spent apart. And when they made love, far less frequently now, it was quick, mechanical, and always in the dark, less of a representative act of love and more of a relief of some deep bodily need.

In the mornings, after their little spoon wait, she would leave first. The way the silence after her departure echoed through the apartment (the sound of overbearing footfalls from the apartment above, doors closing with an impatient crack from the outer hallway, the ghostly sound of a cough of some other resident) was so strangely lonely that he went quickly to Ceylon, even if his shift wasn't for hours.

The morning after Kesari's talk, he caught Cora as she was finishing her breakfast. Indra sat at the table they had purchased at a neighborhood flea market. Cora, frightened by the possibility of bedbugs (the itch from their time in the hotel had taken so long to abate), had doused the table in kerosene to kill anything that may have lived in it. Whenever he sat at it now, he would smell the fumes from this erstwhile act of extermination, and the faintest tap of a headache would announce itself.

After he sat down, Cora promised from across the table that this would be the day she would finally buy another spoon, that she would stop by the secondhand store on the way home from her meeting at the *Clarion*.

"Listen," Indra said, "I talked to Kesariji. They're here, in the city." When she asked who, he explained how Military Intelligence had questioned Kesari, asking about the money he had loaned out.

"Sounds like they're not watching us. Good. They're looking for Benoy," she replied, rapid-fire, as if trying to sidestep Indra's point. She continued before he could respond, looking not at Indra but into their kitchen, avoiding any eye contact. "They might be looking for you too. You need to stay away from him. Maybe don't work your shift today. Call in sick."

He was stunned how she had turned what was going to be his reproach to her back at him. Indra was surprised how, given one little chance to achieve something, she had become bold, reckless. *It means that when you mess up, so do I.*

"Maybe you should stay away from all this too. Do you need to take this meeting with the *Clarion*?"

"As far as I know, I haven't committed any crimes," Cora said curtly. "I wouldn't think too much of it. I've heard that every writer in the city has a file three inches thick over at Military Intelligence. But they're not going to arrest an American woman. Could you imagine what the press would say?"

"But they could," Indra argued. "That's the endgame here. It's the same thing that happened out west."

"Arrest me for what? Speaking truth to power?"

"Arrest you for whatever they want. You see it happening all the time back in India. You think the men back in California were guilty of anything? All it takes is a whiff of wrongdoing."

"This isn't imperial India. Your cohort in California were fools for working with a foreign adversary of the United States. I assure you, this is still a free country with a free press. And as far as I know, I am still a citizen of this nation. I have rights."

"We don't know that. Having the spotlight on you sheds some light upon me too, which puts us at risk. I want you to be safe—I want to leave this city one day. I want us to have a life together. I want us to have that little apartment in Berlin that we talked about."

"Is that what this is all about? You still want to go to Germany?"

"It was just an example. It doesn't have to be in Berlin. All I want is for us to make it out of here."

"I've worked too hard to simply give it all up. I hustled to get three articles written for Jude about everything Irish. I've got a good portfolio now, between that and what I wrote at the *Union*. I wish I still had the Balance Sheet from back in Berkeley. No way Govind's publishing that now."

Indra was amazed. Here he was talking about danger, and she replied with a list of her recently published works.

"How about this," Cora continued. "First, you stay away from Ceylon. I'll stay away from Kesariji. That'll keep some distance between us and Benoy. Second, I'll write under a pen name. That way, no one will know it's me publishing anything." She pushed her chair back and moved to get up. She was ending the conversation, but truthfully, Indra hadn't expected her to be so hostile to his concern. He gave meek assent to her plan before she said she was leaving, that she was going to be late.

She left, her bowl of oatmeal half eaten.

He was shocked at her recklessness. She wanted to make a living by writing, and here she was, the opportunity presenting itself. Did she really have to make it in such a way? Her talent wasn't going anywhere. Surely she could put aside some of her own ambition until the whole thing blew over.

He'd heard that curt voice before. That defiant tone. Nitin and Govind both, at different times, had told him that following the Germans was a fool's errand, that the fight was more important at home than abroad. He'd denied it, refused to believe in the very possibility of everything falling apart. When one felt high and mighty, failure could only be the realm of the inexperienced, or the unlucky, or the doomed—until it came to pass.

Maybe she was right. Maybe she knew this country better than he. She was smart, capable. She would know. He would keep his distance from everyone today.

Instead of going to the restaurant, he walked across town to the New York Public Library, and before he entered, he stood in awe of the monumentality of the building. Something this beautiful in

India would be reserved for British use, some sort of government building like Lutyens was building with the Central Secretariat, architecture as a testament of victory of one nation over another. Here, the beauty was meant to house books, and the knowledge contained therein was free for all. If anything, Indra felt, this building and everything it represented should be something his own nation aspired to.

The awe he felt at the building's exterior did not diminish once he entered. Great halls of marble, walls covered with art. He followed the crowd of people up staircases that seemed to float upward without support, and into a grand rotunda framed by murals, each one depicting some history of learning and knowledge throughout the ages, and upon carved benches in front of these works of arts, everyday men and women sat and talked, some snacking on an apple or some other fruit, all seeming oblivious, or perhaps just accustomed to and expecting the great beauty that surrounded them.

Indra passed through the catalog room into the great reading room, rows upon rows of tables in that cavernous hall, elegant chandeliers hanging from the ceiling. He had brought a small pad of paper and a few pencils and placed them at an open seat before he went into the catalog room to requisition his first book.

Where he began was simple. If all the debates, from Moscow to New York, had in their origins some of Marx's writing, it was with Marx that he would begin. He asked for *The Communist Manifesto* and was surprised to be told that all the copies were currently in use, so he asked for *Capital*, gave his seat number, and was delivered a tome.

It all began, he noted down , with money. From money, he moved into surplus value and from surplus value into primitive accumulation. He didn't know if he understood all of what he was reading. Indeed, at times the language and the concepts passed in front of his glazed eyes like celluloid from a silent film. What did manage to stick was like a grammar, unforgettable, right up against his bones, a generative force that pushed through his understanding of the rest of his world.

The plan was this—he would read for as long as he could. And if he could convince Cora to leave sooner, he'd finish his reading in the library of the city that awaited them. He would read and read and read until he could hum "The Internationale" by heart under his breath. And then there would come that moment when there would be nothing left to do but to write, to coalesce around some thought, and he'd put something together, and this would be his rebirth, this would be how he could rise from his own wretchedness into the sun of a new world.

CHAPTER TWENTY-FIVE

Before she had met Indra, Cora had wanted to finish her degree and try to make a living by writing. The former wasn't possible anymore, and whether she liked it or not, it was perhaps because of meeting Indra that she now had the consistent opportunity to write. It was the strange and circuitous path of chance: a party, a meeting, a wedding, a departure, and this, an opening. Jude had made good on his promise to introduce Cora to the editor at the *Clarion*.

As she went to the meeting, she thought that Indra was probably right to be frightened of Military Intelligence, but every time she thought of the dangers of writing against the grain of a society at war, she convinced herself that she was a white American woman—she was safe.

And if she wasn't, she just had to make this meeting, get something written under a pen name. Then she and Indra could figure out what came next. Let her have what was hers first.

Rose Talley was a woman who talked so fast that she seemed like some sort of grand auctioneer constantly out of place. Slightly taller than Cora, she was beautifully severe, cheekbones hollow from overwork, hair combed into a Castle bob in the front and tied into a messy bun in the back. Supposedly, she was married to—and estranged from—some rich son of a railroad magnate. She used his money freely among the socialists.

Talley oversaw the paper's Women's Department at the cramped offices downtown and, as a result, was well connected with both the socialists and the suffragists. She asked Cora what she could write about. Imperial exploitation was capitalist oppression, so Cora told her about the Ghadar back in California and how their arrest after doing nothing wrong, despite what the papers said, could be a great write-up.

"Let me tell you, we can write about whatever we want in the Women's Department. First, let me reprint your piece on the Irish Convention. Next, give me five hundred words on your Indians. An introduction to the whole struggle. If it goes well, there's more to write," Talley said, all at a clip so fast that Cora had to repeat everything to herself to make sure she had accurately grasped the general contours of the assignment. She asked if she could write under a pen name, and Talley said that most of the articles in the paper lacked a byline anyway, to protect their writers.

Talley gave her a week to complete the task. She wrote it in two days, longhand, and brought it to the office, where she typed it among the click-clack of activity around her. Talley accepted the article on the spot, gave her eight dollars and fifty cents for the work, and immediately asked if there was anything else she could publish. Talley wanted something light to fill a page, wondered if Cora could write something related to arts or culture. On the spot, Cora made a pitch around reviewing *Old Lady 31*, taking the playwright to task for abandoning suffragist themes in her work: out with the old, in with the new.

When they talked, they did so in the hallway of the building. It wasn't an office where the journalists were chatty at work, that was for sure, and when someone stopped typing, the sounds of creaking floorboards and footsteps from the floor above filled the room. When someone needed to talk, there was a rule: conversations were conducted away from others.

"It's a matter of respect," Talley explained. "We took a vote, and everyone opted for a quiet office. Some place they could think.

Not like those hoosegow places where workers are made to endure the pain of constant small talk." Cora had never worked in an office like this, remembered how the *Union* was anything but a sanctuary. She agreed as if Talley were repeating some essential truth. It was a civilized place to work, where gravity of thought was given sanctuary.

It was a civilized place that opposed the war.

The paper's staff was constantly on the defensive—no, they were not pacifists, they believed in the cause of force. They did not shy away from bombs to make a change. No, they were not German sympathizers. They had been a voice against the kaiser when American businessmen were frothing at the mouth over the efficiency of his government. The spirit of the Second International lived on at the *Clarion*. They didn't believe that this war would do anything to improve the cause of workingmen. They weren't militarists. What was happening in Europe was an imperialist war, capitalists rubbing their hands with glee as their pockets were lined with the fat proceeds of military and industry. This could not be their fight. To sacrifice young men to the altar of a war of capital was not something they could stomach.

Maybe it was too nuanced of a position for an American population hungry for blood. By early June, when the paper was due to be published, there was nothing to be sent out. As Rose put it: "Anything that had the faintest whiff of supporting the Germans was doomed."

By that logic, so were the Indians.

So were the Irish.

So were the socialists.

Cora had an inkling that she might have been wrong going on to Indra about being safe.

The *Clarion* had its second-class mailing privileges revoked. It wasn't just the *Clarion* either: *The American Socialist*, the *New York Call*, *The Milwaukee Leader*, *The Jewish Daily Forward*,

The Masses, *The National Rip-Saw*, the *International Socialist Review*—all of them could no longer be distributed through the mail.

Talley was livid. "The war may be overseas, but we are at war inside our own country," she roared. "And you know what they've done? They've assassinated free speech!"

For now, the paper would be hand-sold at newsstands in Manhattan and not many other places. Cora was deflated.

It only ever took one.

She was surprised to receive a note the day after her first article was published. It was from Emma Higgins, inviting her to talk about the possibility of writing for *The Birth Control Review*.

"Rose gave me a copy of both your articles. And then I went and read what you had published over at *The Gaelic American*. I want you to write something for me about Japan," Emma said. She was at the forefront of the birth control movement, someone who was spoken of often (Cora once attempted to get her to speak on campus for the NWP and never received a reply), whose stature and eloquence had even impressed Dawson, and yet she was a simply dressed woman, her hair done in a quick and messy low pompadour, a preternatural look of calm on her pale face. They met in her office on Fifth Avenue near Union Square on one of those clear and sunny days of early summer in New York, days when it felt like the world could open up to a person, that possibility flitted upon every street corner in the city. Cora was immediately at ease with Emma, conversing with her as if the woman had been a mentor to her for years.

When Cora asked why Japan, Emma laughed. "I'm betting you weren't born in India or Ireland, were you?" she asked. "You seem to be a quick learner, able to grasp what's essential, and present it in a way that a readership can understand. There's been a few fellows visiting this office. Government officials from Japan. Never actually say what they do. They're interested in birth control. Interested in the idea of curtailing the birth rate. They're the only free country in Asia, and now they want more. They want to be better than the West. They know women can't have thirteen children anymore. It's a noble cause, to look toward your own race and say less is more."

"Can I use my pen name?" Cora asked, trying to allay her worries.

"Oh yes, Rose mentioned that when she told me about you. You're worried about something with the Indians. Of course. Your name is safe here."

Cora was relieved.

Socialism, freedom, even birth control. Everything that was once studied was turning into something real, something she could hold. Emma gave her a list of names and citations for her research. And in this joy, she missed Hazel dearly. How long had they worked to invite figures like Higgins to campus? And now here she was, meeting across Higgins's desk, working for her organization. Hazel would thrive here, but Cora didn't know if she could send a letter under her pen name without drawing suspicion to them both, so she and her friend would have to remain two buoys, separated by miles of empty expanse, floating on a desolate sea. Time was weakening memory and she struggled to remember what her friend's voice sounded like. She resolved not to let this sadness take her, not now. Cora took the book list to the New York Public Library and passed beyond the stately lions flanking its entrance. She requisitioned her books and magazines from the stacks and went to sit in the grand Rose Reading Room.

In that splendid space that smelled faintly of sweet baking bread, Cora was surprised to see Indra, stunned by the ferocity of feeling when she saw this handsome man sitting by himself, a few books spread in front of him. It was as if she were looking at some ex-lover from across a room—her heart quickened, and she had a desire to leave.

They weren't ex-lovers, not yet. What had passed between them was a divergent ambition, not quite a wedge but, rather, the sensation that they were two magnets slowly sliding to separate poles, and if not acted upon by some outside force, they would one day see each other at a distance, from opposite ends of the earth. And perhaps then, and only then, having turned from lovers back into strangers, the space between them would never again yield, and from that vantage she would give him a forlorn wave, the sad hello of two people who saw in each other a death, for the life of a lover could only ever end with a kind of death, the loss of a personhood found only at the side of the other. To be his wife or to be herself, that was the choice, but all love is drunkenness, and like the drunk unable to walk a straight line, there arose in her some uncontrollable bodily urge to go between both, to stumble between fidelity and solitude, to reveal herself at dinner as the (always unnamed) half of Mr. and Mrs. Indra Mukherjee after living a day on her own as Cora Trent.

She sidled up in the seat next to him, pulling her chair close to his, and he looked up with an impression of innocent surprise.

"Fancy seeing you here," she said with a wry smile, the weak acid returned.

He gave a sheepish look in return, like a boy caught doing wrong. "I didn't expect to run into you," he whispered.

"I haven't caught you much at all outside our small mornings," Cora replied.

They had become awkward with each other since making rosgolla in Kesari's kitchen.

"What are you reading?" she asked, trying to break the ice with her own husband.

"I've been reading up on the cause of socialism," Indra replied.

She was surprised, hurt. She had been frequenting the offices of the *Clarion* for a few weeks. He could have asked her.

He motioned for her to come out into the hallway. They were already attracting the annoyed stares of those around them.

"It was you. You inspired me to start reading," he said in the hallway outside the reading room. "You were just about to meet with the editor at the *Clarion*. I was interested in the idea. The night he told me about the police, Kesariji was giving a speech in the city, and some fellow in the back row asked whether freedom was freedom if they were going to replace one class of capitalists with another. Kesariji said it made quite the difference whether a man was being kicked by his own brother."

Cora laughed. "Did he really say that?"

"Almost exactly those words! I was stunned. He's of another generation. He's older. He's set in his ways. I thought, What would Cora have said to such a comment? What would your editors and friends have said? I immediately began to come here, to read. I needed to know more about the equality among men, the revolution in Russia, everything."

Cora kissed him, quick and decisive. He was surprised but soon eased into the embrace. "I've missed you," she said.

"After you told me about the Goldings, you seemed like you didn't need to hear what I had to say. You were going to do what you were going to do. I wasn't sure if you wanted to listen to me anymore."

"Shut up," she said. "I love you." What he said was true. He had seen directly into her heart. She did not want to listen to him. She wanted what she wanted for herself. "I didn't know what to say. I'm here now."

"I'm only in this library because I thought, What would you think about this? What would you do?"

"You can ask me right now," she said, inviting a spirit of collaboration over compromise. To be his collaborator also meant becoming invisible. She would have to figure out some way to stake her claim, to evade any sense of erasure.

She held his hand and squeezed it just a little bit, the kind of unspoken gesture that said she too was sorry for everything that had passed, that there was something new in front of them now, that the past could burn itself in the great trash heap upon which it accumulated.

For the rest of the day, they worked side by side in silence with a renewed love that passed between them that needed no reassurance of its existence: no conversation, no discovery, just that feeling of sitting next to each other, the heat of his body filling a void she hadn't known she had felt in the city until that moment.

By the end of the day, she had made good progress on her article and would have something for Higgins soon. As they left, Indra had the same expression of failure as he had on that day he'd told her about what would send them out of Palo Alto and into New York.

"I've thought about this a lot," he said. "I know you want to continue writing, and you can. You just have to do it far from here. You can keep writing for all these publications after we arrive somewhere safe." He was unable to look her in the eye.

She still desperately wanted the life that was just forming. New York was opening wide to her at the same time forces well beyond her control were beating that world small with heaves from a billy club.

"Where do we go next?" she asked with a sigh.

"Mexico," Indra said. "We need to go to Mexico, like everyone else."

Everyone seemed to be going down to Mexico. At first it was the pacifists and the draft dodgers. Now it was the socialists, the anarchists, even the artists and writers, they were all leaving for the revolutionary land to the south.

"You don't have any more contacts, do you?" Cora asked. "We need someone who could get us papers to move freely down there. We could cross ourselves, but that could be risky too. Nothing's guaranteed. You got here as Pierre Thomas. Any Germans willing to help you get there?"

"Nothing," Indra mumbled. "We need someone who knows

people of importance. How about you? Scullion? Dawson?"

Dawson. He had to have a connection to someone in Mexico. Or he had to know someone who knew someone who could help them. If he couldn't help them, no one could.

She would write to him and ask him for something. It would take a few weeks. They'd be here until then. They could pass the time in the Rose Reading Room.

They got to the train.

"Where are you going?" she asked.

"Ceylon India," he said. "Should I go to my shift?"

"Oh, to hell with that job. If we're going to Mexico, you have to quit anyway. Things are swell with money for now. Come with me," she said. She wanted him to know that all she wished for in that moment was to have him once more. He had a light in him again, and from that light she drew close to his body. She didn't want to lose what was hers.

CHAPTER TWENTY-SIX

Although they had met near and around Stanford, it was in New York where they felt like students, whiling away their days at the library. Cora wrote about the birth control movement in Japan, spending her time reading on the history and politics of the only country in Asia to have resisted foreign rule. She could not find anyone to interview on short notice, so she played the trick, the sleight of hand, common to journalists—she found quotes from other periodicals that she pulled and inserted into her own essay.

Indra watched Cora hum with the possibilities that work could allow, and he saw how she twirled her pencil in her hand, or how she leaned back and her fingers slowly traced down one of her curls when she silently reached some conclusion, or how she slouched close to a book when engrossed, as if, in this position of prayer, she could absorb the knowledge contained therein. And the summation of these mundane idiosyncrasies created a kind of reverberation that jostled him backward in time to the nights in his room in Palo Alto (their last night there was more than two months at a remove, a lifetime), how he would watch her body as if reading a book, his eyes scanning over every inch (the whorls formed by the parts of her hair, the lightness of her fingers gripping a pen, freckles across her arms), finding all that he loved and now longed to love again.

When they came home in the evenings, they stayed. There were no meetings, no errands, nothing to keep them. They made love with the window open, the weather outside so fine, and the cool

evening breeze tickling the thin sheen of sweat upon them. To watch
her close her eyes in focus, so quiet until everything that built up
found its release—this was the sound, the sensation he had missed,
and oh, to have it again, every time the dance of pleasure and desire
felt anew.

On one of those nights, the sounds of a band playing in the
streets came up to their room. There was some street fair going on,
some bit of summer revelry. She got up and hastily put on her dress
and invited him to join her. He pulled on his trousers and stood
awkwardly shirtless next to her.

"Remember when we were going up to San Francisco?" Cora
asked. "On the streetcar, I told you I would teach you the Texas
Tommy. Here we go, let's get it done."

Indra smiled but didn't move. Even though they were alone, he
felt stiff. He smiled and shook his head.

"Wrong answer," Cora said, laughing. "You don't have to worry
about not being able to dance. The beat's not right. Who cares? The
music's here, and it's just us."

He got up to join her. She led and he followed. The dance required a looseness, a rhapsodic skip, and he felt wooden, keenly
aware of how feet did not connect to ears, did not connect to the
beat, did not find the swing of the music. Step, kick, step, kick, run,
run, run. That's what she said, that's what he tried.

It didn't matter if he couldn't do it perfectly. Being near her
again reminded him why he loved her, how she brought out the version of him he wanted to be. They danced, and he saw her close her
eyes and let her body take flight, and he could see the faint outline
of her breasts move under her dress, and they danced with a heat of
passion and desire, but also a true lightness, and they danced until
they laughed in a heap upon the bed, joyous spirits once again.

To love was to endure a continual act of humility. He had entered the United States thinking it only a small sojourn on some longer journey, at the end of which would be some cosmopolitan form

of himself, adored by the world for his greatness. To love Cora was to realize that he could become himself only with her.

There was no need to embark upon careless risk anymore. She had sent the letter to Dawson, explaining how New York seemed like it was closing itself up, that her opposition to the war had put them in danger of arrest. Indra asked her to play up the pacifism element, thinking that would perhaps get Dawson to take pity upon them—surely someone of his stature had some connection to Mexico and would be able to help them escape. Mexico, where the socialists and pacifists were all settling, where a glorious revolution had continued, the beautiful 1917 constitution, rights for the people enshrined in a new document.

In the meantime, they were slowly wrapping up the lives they had started in New York. He continued to read in the library, absorbing every last tenet Marx had to offer, the voices of Dawson and Scullion ringing in his head.

He began to write an essay organically from this reading. National liberation from imperialism was the only durable path to peace, and participating in a war to end all wars was only a diversion from this goal. One had to denounce a war of capitalists and instead examine how colonialism was a process of starvation. National identity, anti-imperialism, pacifism, socialism, everything that swam in his head now had an outlet.

He wrote in parallel with Cora, admiring anew her steady work ethic, separate projects written with the deadline of departure looming, and when he finished, he showed it to her, and her face lit up with the same look of possibility she had given him early on, when he had initially confessed the Obermeier connection and she'd thought he towered upon the world stage. She said she would show it to her editor, Rose Talley over at the *Clarion*. Indra had always assumed her editor was a man.

Talley replied enthusiastically and wanted it published as soon as possible, and she hoped Indra didn't mind that they had no wide means of distribution anymore. Cora seemed pleased at the new development, and in her pride, he felt sure-footed once again. Indra had been welcomed into a new community of radical intellectuals: the first, he surmised, from India. He had escaped two suicides: the second had been along the river, and the first was a journey with the Germans that could have ended only in catastrophe. If to love meant to invite the specter of humiliation, it also surely meant inviting the possibility of reinvention.

There had been a failure, a great emptiness that swallowed everything he once held as true. There was no Berlin, no German transport, and his friends had been arrested in one fell swoop—he had been only a half step ahead of those arrests. Had none of that come to pass, he probably would have remained dedicated to the cause, would have loaded his gun and shot, and would have ended up as dead as Nitin. Nitin, he said, I found it, the cause that can take your spirit and move us toward freedom. And for the first time, there was no echo reply, and in this, Indra too felt joy. Joy that he had found footing in new beliefs, joy that he was alive to learn them.

CHAPTER TWENTY-SEVEN

Her period did not come as it should have. At first she denied this. There had been times when she was harried or ill and it would come a few days late, and hadn't she felt a touch of a sore throat just a week ago? So she waited for the day to come when she would feel the signs: the bloating and the fullness, maybe a little cramping, and then it would be all over.

But that day never came.

There was an irony to this, that she was working for Higgins, writing for *The Birth Control Review*, yet she had not gone to the clinic sponsored by her organization to get fitted with a pessary. It was an appointment she'd kept putting off, for until that day, the tablespoon of Lysol mixed with cold water had done the trick just fine.

Until it hadn't. The one thing she learned about the early weeks of pregnancy was its blusters of nausea. Her insides twisted and heaved with a painful retching. Her senses were tuned too far, past breaking. Any small and unwelcome smell could turn on her and send whatever scant leftovers in her stomach out into the world once again. Foods she once loved now brought neither sustenance nor pleasure, only the waves upon waves of sickness that could not abate. The only thing she could eat—and soon began to crave in a ravenous, animal way—were summer strawberries purchased from a corner greengrocer, big red things that she ate in a single bite, throwing each hull out the kitchen window before grabbing the next one.

And between bouts of throwing up, she felt a different kind of fear, of a caged life, of the routine of daily chores that would keep her from the very act of being herself. She had told Indra she didn't want a child, but she didn't know how he'd react to her pregnancy. For now, she could only hope he remembered his promise. Motherhood was a gun pointed at every woman: if it did not kill her, like it had her own mother following Cora's birth, it would kill any intelligence and talent by confining her into the petty limitations demarcated by the care for another. And then in some cruel metamorphosis, she-as-mother would become the assassin. She had seen it in her friends' mothers: the domineering attitude, on one hand filled with selfless servitude, and on the other, manipulative without realizing it, forcing daughters to become gargoyle versions of themselves. Easier to kill the child and its infinite possibilities than to face the fact that she, as a grown woman, had wasted her own life.

Growing up in that desiccated mining town surrounded by the wild and undulating west, she had wandered, and in those wanderings had been able to discern the way in which nature took its course. She'd watched the animals raised by the company for slaughter to feed the workers scraping by on company scrip. And the way it worked was this: the male existed for only a brief moment, to quench the crippling heat felt by the female, to take advantage of her single and debilitating moment of weakness, and then moved on. Then came the burden, and then came the wet, sticky yowls of becoming into a world that, unknown to both mother and child, was circumscribed by the fence and the abattoir. The young would grow, as they always did, under the protection of their mothers before moving on to be killed or to give birth, and when they suckled no more, the heat again grew wild—a cycle unending until the butcher himself lent the grace of a knife to a spent womb. Maybe she would keep this whole ordeal from Indra—if he didn't know, he couldn't refuse.

She needed help, needed to figure out her next steps. Higgins could be of little assistance: in public writings, she had said that legalized birth control would mean no need for abortion, would rid the world of that scourge. So Cora went out on her own. Every drugstore across the city had its collection of pills, tinctures, potions. When she walked along Broadway, there was a chemist who openly advertised more than thirty-five different balms for what he advertised as "female trouble," emmenagogues that ranged from pennyroyal pills to quinine to slippery elm. It was a transaction like any other—a vial of tincture of ergot for a little over a dollar. The pharmacist, a chatty balding man with hair spilling out of his ears, gave her instructions on when to take it. ("Twice a day, nothing more than that. For two days. I've heard of girls taking it all at once. Unless you have a death wish, I'd strongly recommend following my instructions, my dear.")

She took the bitter liquid by the spoonful and noticed no change. She continued to vomit every morning. The putrid piss-and-rotting-flesh smell of the city's transition to midsummer still drove her to nausea every time she walked out of their apartment.

She asked Penelope. It seemed cruel to ask a woman who had just given birth, but Penelope knew the city better than she. It wasn't like she could ask Rose Talley—though she was probably sympathetic, if the men at the *Clarion* heard anything, their opinion of her would be transformed. Cora was a comrade, a writer. The moment they caught the faintest whiff of anything related to the body she wore under her clothes, the elixir would wear off, and the spell would fail, leaving her not as a journalist, only as a woman among them.

Penelope was gentle. "You can't use those pills. If any one of them worked at all, why would they sell so many different kinds? You need an operation," she said up in her apartment as her new baby napped in his cot. Jude was out somewhere, continuing his work as an actor as his wife started upon her new life bound by the home. She was able to focus on two things at once, with one hand upon the edge of the baby's cot to keep it rocking, the other upon Cora's knee.

"I saw that doctor once," Penelope said. "It was all very easy. He's down in Greenwich Village, not too far from where we lived, just on Sheridan Square. He doesn't haggle like all the other doctors. Not like the ones where you have to bring your own bottle of Lugol's iodine, or the ones with dirt under the fingernails, blood on the apron. Gansevoort Street butchers, the lot of them."

It was a relief to know that someone else had gone down this path, was right in front of her and seemed to be fine for it. Asking around to find an abortionist was an act of secrecy, but abortion was hardly a secret itself, just another part of a woman's life that slid into whisper networks of who-knows-whom and who-can-do-what. Men, haughty and dismissive, made their laws and, as was usual, turned their backs to the details of what women actually did among and for themselves.

"Are you going to tell your husband?" Penelope asked.

Cora said she wasn't sure.

"I never told Jude. I didn't want to worry him. Sometimes it's best if they don't know."

But to keep a secret of this magnitude was tantamount to giving up the rhythm she and Indra had just found again. They were on the precipice of a new life—she had to trust him, had to believe that he would remember his word. That evening she would tell Indra about both the pregnancy and her decision. She thought he must know something. They were together so often now, and she had told him she was unwell, but he seemed suspicious about her excuses.

"Is this what you want?" he asked her when she told him. A feeling of relief flooded through her—she loved him for the fact that he was a man who would keep his word, that he knew who she was and loved her for that.

They were sitting side by side on their bed. His eyes were warm, and he rubbed the top of her back. Just a few weeks ago they had danced here, and from their joy had come this anxiety. Thankfully, he seemed calm, and she was grateful that he would not draw this into some argument that could end only in her sharing this space with a baby.

Her answer was without hesitation, without fear, a commanding response, as clear as a full stop.

Indra nodded. She added one more thing, and she said it in a small voice, as if this were the ask that would throw the two into disarray. For Cora, even now, even after they'd found each other again, equality could retain a sense of balance only if they were not joined together but kept apart, two weights on either side of the scale measuring her possibility against his.

"I will pay for the operation myself. I have saved enough from my work with Kesariji and the articles I've written."

"What do you mean? We can pay for this together. There's no money that belongs to you or me anymore, only what's ours."

She hardened her face into cold resolve, and she tried to control every emotion that came out of her by making her mouth some small thing, every muscle focused. "There remains me, and there remains you. We are not one and the same."

"You want to keep accounts, run a tab for what is owed to you and what to me? This is madness, Cora, simply madness."

"Do you remember how Scullion said we were joined together as equals? I don't think of it as some frivolous thing taken from the theosophists. We are equals as a union of two separates, weights on either side of a scale, I as me and you as you."

"You're saying as much nonsense as Scullion would," Indra scolded, but she knew she had the upper hand. He was losing steam, no tic between his fingers to be seen. "Is it because you don't trust me?"

Only now did Cora feel the pinpricks of rage cross her face. She could slap him. She controlled herself instead. "Indranath Mukherjee, I trust you. I trust you to treat me like you would treat yourself. Grant me that."

THEY HAD CALLED THE DOCTOR WHOM PENELOPE MENTIONED, AND HE ADVISED THEM TO come down to Greenwich Village together.

From the train, they walked by the Will o' the Wisp tearoom on Sheridan Square, passing a group of shabbily dressed men and willowy women dressed in flared black skirts who were talking about avoiding the draft around happenstance tables—barrels topped with planks of wood. Next to that was the headquarters of a little magazine, *The Ink Pot*, a William Morris–inspired publication that Penelope had spoken fondly of.

The doctor lived on the second floor of a three-story brick building just beyond the magazine. His apartment was wide and spacious, taking up most of the second floor. Cora did not know if he always practiced out of his own home or did so for these kinds of appointments—she found it strange that such a man would live in a neighborhood of bohemians.

There must have been a woman or a wife. The apartment had the air of being decorated by a feminine hand, small prints framed on the wall, plush cushions of maroon on the settee, a high-back chair for reading, all unified by a single Arts and Crafts style. Maybe she was an artist. Maybe she'd been the one to convince him to provide this service. But if there was a wife, or a child, or any hint of a domestic life, they had been sent out and away from that home. It was just her, Indra, and the doctor.

The doctor himself was reminiscent of Dr. Freud—the same round spectacles and close-cut beard. He had a neat appearance, and Cora saw that his fingernails were trimmed down, clean.

He led them to the kitchen, which looked at first like any other, except for one oddity that drove it apart: flanking the kitchen table was a small surgical chair, tall with emerald green leather. Cora assumed that the procedure would be done there, though for a moment, she imagined that if the surgical chair weren't there, the table itself was big enough for her to lie upon. For Cora, a kitchen table had long ago ceased is connotations as a place to gather over a meal and instead had become a site of raucous debate, of politicking and the creation of pamphlets, of consensus and consequence.

The kitchen table, for most women, was far more than where dinner could be served. The men of capital had their desks, and women had the table from which the tasks of domestic servitude could be completed, uncompensated toiling to make sense of sums required to sustain life across a household.

It felt fitting that it was here where the kitchen table could surpass its status as either something domestic or someplace political and become anew in both, for what could be more political than for her to decide the future contours of her own life, to decide to quell and contain the mother that, alongside the child, grew inside of her?

"Twenty-six dollars for the procedure," the doctor said. "You can pay half now and half after. Forgive me. I tell this to everyone, I don't like to haggle. There are men, so-called doctors, who haggle over the price, as if this were some meat market. And trust me, they are no worse than butchers. They know nothing about cleanliness and modern medicine. I don't like to mention this," he said in a low voice, as if sharing a secret, "there are still others who use this as a chance to further their own sin. I can't control any of that noise."

Though Cora looked around the tidy kitchen and was thankful, she remembered Penelope's comment about many practitioners being no better than butchers—it was a curious comparison, woman as meat. If the metaphor expanded, perhaps it was: woman was raised by a man, fleshed by a man, sold by a man, yet cooked, more often than not, by a woman.

"Maybe if the service I offer is ever granted the grace of legality, you both can help me to clean these stables of the monstrous fifth that has accumulated. For now I keep my head down. I can be clean, efficient, no-nonsense."

She hadn't told him about her line of work, but based upon his pitch, he seemed to think of her of some kind of Upton Sinclair, ready to reform an entire industry from her articles. She didn't want to write it—she just wanted the abortion, not a new line of work. From her purse, she handed him thirteen bills.

"Thank you, I do appreciate it. You'd be surprised by those who come to see me. Last week, there was a woman, mother of many, and herself of quite a bit of wealth. She just called upon me yesterday, and I went to check in on her. I forgot to mention that. If you need me for whatever reason following the procedure, simply telephone me and I will come to you. Only three dollars for that service."

She knew he was trying to put her at ease, but there was something about the comparison that bothered her. He had taken one look at her, sized her up, and placed her in a hierarchy of class. "What about those girls who work?" she asked.

The doctor nodded and looked at her as if she were just a dumb little girl. "I doubt they could afford my services. Perhaps they would be better served by the Florence Crittenton Mission down on Bleecker." He laughed, a little cruelly.

Desperation could keep people locked into situations they otherwise would have avoided by dint of their own morals, so she held her tongue and laughed nervously with him. They agreed upon a date later in the week for her to come back. "One last thing," the doctor said, turning to Indra, who had been oddly silent throughout the entire meeting. "On the day of the procedure, I ask you to remain outside. There are plenty of tearooms in the neighborhood to pass the time. I used to allow husbands here. They would often grow queasy and anxious at the sight. It's best to wait outside."

Indra nodded gravely. The doctor turned to Cora. "Be sure to stay quiet and not say anything more about this. It will be over soon, and that will be that."

THE LETTER FROM DAWSON ARRIVED A DAY BEFORE CORA'S PROCEDURE. DAWSON SAID that he was happy to help anyone against the damned war in Europe, especially his favorite student, and it was a pity that officials were tracing the steps of Indra, whose cause of anti-imperialism was both necessary and just. He enclosed a letter of introduction to General Alvadaro, the governor of Yucatán state. Dawson explained in a lengthy aside that they had come into regular contact when he was the director of the World Peace Foundation. Dawson praised Alvarado's program of education for laborers and his campaign against the hacienda system. He was a good man, and Indra and Cora should make their way through Mexico to its southern and eastern reaches as soon as possible.

All Dawson could offer them was a name, a piece of paper with an introduction, and with that, a hope for an audience in another city in a foreign land. Their shared world was filled with those individuals whom they could charm or ask a favor from, like Kesari and Dawson, or alternatively, those who would cut them open for a dime, like Benoy.

It was settled: Indra and Cora would leave for Mexico. Before then, back to the doctor's apartment. Indra kissed her before she went in.

"I love you," she replied, squeezing his hand. And when she went in, she thought that she could truly lose him—a fear made more real by the fact that the door was closing behind her, and they were separated by a scalpel or something else: Cora realized that she had no idea how the procedure would work.

The only proof of life in the sitting room was a pillow that had fallen from the high-back chair onto the floor, but otherwise it was as still and empty as it had been earlier in the week.

The kitchen was warm from a pot of water boiling on the stove. As Cora stood in the doorway, the doctor removed something from a small leather case filled with his medical tools. It was thin, almost twelve inches long, and had a nickel-plated sheen to it. At one end was a handle, demarcated by two eyelet loops of metal to form a grip. At the other end, the device curved upward.

"This is called a catheter. We'll use it to open the womb," the doctor said.

"Is the water to boil it? I was told to ask if you were going to boil it. I've heard it prevents the sepsis."

"No, the water is for my tea," the doctor said flatly.

"Really?" Cora asked, incredulous.

"Of course I will be boiling it," the doctor said. "What do I look like, a midwife? I'm not here performing cheap procedures for little immigrant women. I'm a member of the American Medical Association." He had an impatient side, as if he wanted to get this over with more than Cora.

The doctor flattened the surgical chair with a creak of well-used hinges and instructed her to hike up her dress and remove her underwear. A doctor could take a person and turn her into a scientific object, a specimen in a glass jar, and to be handled as such, all human touch was replaced with the cool metallic grip. He looked into her, and one hand was cold and the other was warm, and everything that said this body was hers fell away, for what was once hers was now his, and she hoped that he knew exactly what he was doing. She tried to breathe, but it came out all shallow. This was like an illness, and to be ill was to be vulnerable, and to be vulnerable was to be like a child, hoping that an adult in the room could be a bridge to safety.

The doctor removed the catheter from the boiling pot with a pair of tongs and placed it upon the kitchen table. "After the procedure, I want you to stay upright for as long as you can, and when you can stand no longer, you can go to bed. If you need to, call upon me after, and I can come to you."

He inserted the catheter, and at first she felt its warmth from the stove, and as it went farther into her, the pain was immense, searing, as if a fist were suddenly inside her gut, grabbing and pulling and twisting inside her.

"Stay still and be quiet so I may complete this," he said without a hint of compassion. He turned to get something from his medical kit. "Bite down on this." He handed her a tongue depressor. "And be still."

She crunched down on the depressor and heard it cracking from her teeth's grip, and then it broke into two, and she tongued its parts to either side of her mouth and bit down again. She could not see straight, felt as if she would pass out. Then it was over. She felt herself flowing fast.

He took something else out of the pot and grabbed some cotton gauze from his medical kit. He used something that looked like scissors to pack it inside of her. The scissors were warm from the water.

"No different from a miscarriage," he said matter-of-factly. "That's all that's happened. Remove the gauze in twenty-four hours and no later."

She spat out the two parts of the tongue depressor and was now desperate for air, as if she had unwittingly stopped breathing at some point during the procedure. Her bangs were pressed against her scalp, damp with sweat.

As the doctor moved the surgical chair back to its upright position, he placed a hand on her back to steady her. In his hand, he held a small towel. "Put this underneath you," he said. "The bleeding will be at its worst now." He left the room, to do what, Cora wasn't sure. It was typical for doctors to leave at the most human moment, when scientific knowledge would not suffice, when all that was required was tender care.

She was still dizzy and looked around to find some source of stability, some real thing that could straighten out her vision. To the left of her was the kitchen table and to the right a stove, the steel saucepan of water in which he had sterilized the catheter and scissors still steaming. Somewhere in the house, a clock ticked. It was done. Outside were the tearoom and *The Ink Pot* and somewhere in between would be Indra, and they could finally go home.

She sat, and though the vertigo began to abate, the nausea did not. She wanted to vomit. The doctor reentered the kitchen and told her to get up, and when she did, she saw the dark red splotch, its shape bulbous and undefined, on the towel. Again she felt sickness arise from the knots in her stomach.

Could she ask the house mother in Los Angeles about this? Was this normal too?

"Remember, stay upright until you can't," he said. "Preferably at least three hours. Call on me if anything occurs: fever, malaise, anything out of the ordinary." She handed him the final thirteen bills. When they left New York, they would do so with razor-thin savings.

The doctor helped her down the stairs. Each step felt like learning to walk again, as if her body had lost some fundamental weight and she was learning how to balance, but with that loss came a feeling of relief. It was over. It was done. Indra was waiting outside.

"Next time, don't wait by the door," the doctor said, scowling at Indra. Next time—Cora couldn't believe the implication that women saw him more than once. "Loitering draws attention. Take her and leave."

She held tight to her husband. The day's exhaustion grew with every step, even though she felt the lightness of a burden removed. By the time they went underground, the relief she felt was interlaced with a need to sleep. He propped her up with his arm and whispered under his breath, "Steady, steady."

On the train, there were plenty of seats, though none for her. Standing upright felt like a task she could not complete, for the cramping was immense, every muscle squeezing itself into a tight ball that would not release. She let out little moans of pain, and he held her closer.

She stood until she could not, but by then they were home, and she could go to lie in their bed. Indra decided to sleep on the floor to let her have as much room as she needed. The sleep she so wanted was kept away from her by what she soon realized weren't cramps. This was some form of birthing, perhaps less so than an actual delivery, but enough to let her know she never wanted it again. She lurched her way to the bathroom while Indra slept. The spasms of pain were every muscle pushing something out of her body and into the world. Each time her stomach contracted into a knot, she held her breath. It was soon over, done without complication, and what came out was not a child. Her motherhood had bled outward and away from her in clots the size of summer strawberries.

CHAPTER TWENTY-EIGHT

Indra couldn't wait to leave this godforsaken country. He was sick of the danger, of the potential for disaster. He was sick of waiting for something bigger. He was sick of its society too, of the text and the subtext of race, how it suffused every interaction, every part of life, how the doughboys on the subway could seethe with anger, how the country could label him and his ilk traitors, taking their cue from the British. Suresh was right. Damned if Indra knew why that man didn't leave this country at once.

Mexico would be a welcome change. It was a three-night journey down to the border.

"Rest now," he had told her on the IRT back to their apartment. She had looked so pale, struggling to keep her eyes open. "We're leaving in just a few days." He was angry that he hadn't been inside the apartment to hold her hand as the doctor cut her open—or whatever he had to do to perform the procedure. While she was in there, her suffering moved him beyond pity to fear. He didn't know much about abortion. Widows sometimes went to Kashi, as they said, and sometimes astrologers said the pregnancy was inauspicious, and it wasn't uncommon that the woman was struck by fever soon after the task was complete.

Now wasn't the time to die. They were going to leave. And when he saw her after the procedure, exhausted but fundamentally okay, he thought he could weep from joy. He steeled himself to betray no emotion. He had to be steadfast for her, had to hold her up when she needed him.

In truth, he had known that she was pregnant well before she told him about it. He'd suspected something was wrong when she began to seem sick, especially when the symptoms continued for a week without her countenance getting better or worse. His suspicions were confirmed when he found the druggist's pills, which, of course, did nothing but perhaps make her sicker, and he, who had heard stories about pills like these, worried that she would be racked with convulsion—or worse.

Even though the silence had been thick enough to muffle the lightness they'd felt over the past few weeks, he had been surprised to feel delighted by the possibility of a child, a happiness he tried to keep a secret, for he would not speak about the child until she did. Still, the fantasy kept pulling at him, even as he tried to focus on the revisions for the essay he had written. Perhaps a son, perhaps someone who would take on the mantle of Indra's life struggle and push it further. Like father, like son. The endless bounty of progeny.

Maybe they would leave New York before the pregnancy became cumbersome, and the son would be born among the radicals and artists and pacifists down in Mexico, a place that existed to Indra now only as a dream transposed onto a map. He knew no Spanish, nothing of the culture. The boy would learn alongside his father, and together they would take on the sound of a new tongue, and he would be strong for it.

Curious, in these fantasies, that Cora was nowhere to be seen. When he attempted to will her into this future, he could only see her nursing the boy, holding him close in a sling, preparing his meals. At the end of *Devi Chaudhurani*, one of the novels he had read over and over when he was just entering the nationalist movement, the heroine made her choice: she could have been so much more. She could have actually picked up the sword to fight instead of remaining ensconced in the world of her own purity. She could have taken those men and led the fight for freedom, and yet she never wavered from her desire to return to her husband, to have a home and build her life as a mother and wife in the household that once so violently rejected her. A woman could lead a revolution, but home was home.

Whose ending and why—the questions he had never asked himself, lost in the fancies of possibility. That fantasy had never been his right: the first thing Cora did when confronted with this newfound burden was to buy the pills. He knew about her mother. He knew about the life Cora wanted. Her choice about children had always and already been made, and yet he sent himself on the fool's errand of dreaming about some boy yet to be born. From the first time he spoke with her, through their courtship, and even onward into his failures and slow discovery of new ideas, Cora had tempered his own feelings of lack, making her little more than a statue cast from his own desires. There had been some real Cora always there, filled with her own absences and erasures that made her whole.

When she told him, he knew he had no say as to what came out of her mouth next. He had already agreed to this future: that night at Scullion's party, the disgust at the child, the confession he had comforted. In that small interaction was a documentation of a debt, and one day that debt would be called upon.

A fantasy ended abruptly, as fantasies tended to do: the clap of thunder to rouse the sleeper into the waking world.

Cora would not give up the dreams that centered herself as an individual in the world. They had fallen in love so quickly that they hadn't stopped to consider basic precepts. If he were to love her, he'd have to do so knowing full well who she was, which was a person just as ambitious as he, a person just as wanting of the attention of the world. Whatever they would do, they would do together.

He told her that she could take the time she needed to recuperate, and in the meantime, he would pack their few belongings, try to sell back their meager furniture to the secondhand dealer, make her the salty chicken soup she had taught him to make. And then they would be off on the three-day journey: the evening train to San

Antonio, a train to Laredo, and then they would cross the border on foot. Indra had heard stories about the south, and, truth be told, suffered from pangs of race anxiety when he thought about taking the southern route, but that was a worry for later.

Her recovery was easier than Indra had thought it would be. There had been more fears, left unspoken again, of fever, of sepsis, of an emergency, of death. But she was fine, and it seemed like they could save three dollars by not having to call upon the doctor to see her again. After the first day of rest and little paroxysms of pain, she slept a bit and was awake to eat the soup he'd made for dinner. They debated whether they should leave the next morning. Instead, they decided to play it safe and not overexert her. They'd wait a few more days, as planned.

The next day, Indra went to pick up a few cold cuts for lunch from the Italian butcher up the street. He returned, and the door to their building was ajar.

He walked up three flights of stairs.

The door to their apartment was wide open.

A neighbor, someone he had never talked to, peeked out from behind her door in her apron and reading glasses, and stood still, only her eyes moving to watch him cross his threshold, and he knew that her eyes were the ones of evil, that the worst fortune had fallen upon his house. He entered his apartment knowing everything was falling away.

The entryway had been muddied with footprints of four feet. She was gone.

CHAPTER TWENTY-NINE

From the apartment, the two burly and thick-necked officers took her on a train downtown. Her thoughts bounced between two questions: whether Indra was safe and whether the blood from her spotting would soak through her dress. Beyond those questions, she recounted the shock of their entrance, the anger at the way they dragged her outside, and finally, the settling nervousness about her own fate. Indra had warned her, but she had courted this fate by ignoring him. And now maybe she would lose it all, rendering everything she had experienced over the past few months as some sort of hallucination or fever dream.

When they got downtown, the arresting officers didn't book her, didn't bring her into the general population of the jail, instead took her down the stairs and farther still. She couldn't tell if this was some sort of isolation cell or merely a holding pen as she awaited transfer to somewhere else. Underground, the single electric bulb never ceased its garish illumination of the toilet, of the steel cot, of the vermin that crawled at the base of the sweating stone walls, but she was able to keep time through the sound, the low murmur and the rumble of the city above, ears tuned to tremble with the sensation that the world continued on as always, uncaring of the suffering of others, while she—locked in some underground cell four steps wide by six steps long, where the stagnant air was suffused with damp (a night spent like the miners of her childhood), where she could stretch her arms to touch both walls in a cellar storage—

was kept awake in the darkness by shivers of cold even as the city above was blanketed by the humid summer's heat. She was thirsty and her mouth felt cottony, as rough as the coarse and itchy blanket they had given her, though even if it were soft and downy, sleep came hard in a place like this. She felt filthy, needed to change her cloth for sure now. There was nothing to do here, no one to ask. The exhaustion pressed in upon her from all sides, and it surprised her that this body made frail by fear and isolation had ever felt vigor at all.

Indra once recounted that freedom's weight was too much for any one person. That's where the danger came from. She didn't listen. She was in love, not only with him but with the romanticism of it all: she, Cora Trent, could fight for the freedom of people across the world—no, why lie to herself in here of all places, she, Cora Trent, could love and be loved, and from that love, she could become the person she wanted to be on the world stage, and all could finally see the mettle from which she was made.

Another guard, some urchin who had been scooped up and given a uniform and a baton and a sense of ownership over others, opened the door to her cell. Somehow a whole night had passed. He led her out into the blinding light of day, where he hustled her down what she thought was Lafayette, and they soon went into some nondescript building ten stories high, another edifice dotted with windows, where inside clerks pushed their papers left and right, and the two took a lift up (the operator stared forward the entire time) to a room from whose windows could be seen the trusses and cables of the Manhattan Bridge. The unremarkable everyday was always the best place to hide little scenes of violence. The guard sat her down at a table and left, the click of the deadbolt on the door following his departure. She put her head down on the table and promptly fell asleep.

She was awakened by the sound of the door opening, and a man walked in like some totemic figure from a recurring nightmare.

He looked scarcely different from the office clerks who scurried about the building, with his tortoiseshell glasses and a white shirt starched to the stiffest possible collar, his hair combed to the side with a sticky slick of pomade. He seemed vaguely familiar, like one of those men she saw on the train—men she assumed made much more money than she did—and then promptly forgot about. He sat down in front of her and slid across an onionskin piece of paper, and from his hands she caught the strong smell of Pears soap. Typed across the paper was a list of names:

INDRANATH MUKHERJEE, ALIAS "PIERRE"
BENOY CHAKRAVORTY, ALIAS "SAMUEL"

And below that, more names she could not place to faces.

The man introduced himself. British. CID, stationed in Calcutta, working here with Military Intelligence. The type of man Kesari and Indra both feared.

"Your husband is a terrorist and an anarchist," he began, with an accent that sounded how Cora imagined Wodehouse's Reginald Jeeves would sound. "You must know this. His liaisons with the Germans make him a traitor too. He is dangerous and has committed atrocious crimes—"

It was here that Cora interrupted him. In the face of opposition, she felt a great wellspring of courage buttressed by a fundamental belief that this well-kept goon could never tell her what to do. "What crimes are those? He hasn't done much in New York. He washes dishes and reads books in the public library."

"We know about California. We know about his proposed venture with the German consulate in San Francisco."

"California?" She laughed. "He washed dishes there too. Read a lot fewer books, though."

"No matter what he did in your presence, you married a fiction. He's a wanted man from here back to India. He associates with other terrorists, like Benoy Chakravorty."

"I didn't know Benoy was capable of doing anything at all. How fascinating," she said.

"Is this a joke to you, Mrs. Mukherjee?"

"I don't lick the boot of an Englishman. I thought we fought a war back in 1776 to be rid of you."

"That's very funny," he said with a flattened affect. "Here's the truth. You'll be tried for obstruction of justice, espionage, treason. And let me remind you that by marrying Mr. Mukherjee, you're well on your way to losing your citizenship. That makes you subject to the laws of our king." He paused. "Oh, don't look so surprised— you must know the laws of your own country, right?"

Cora felt like a fool. She had placed so much trust in the lie they had scribbled on their marriage document, but beyond that, she had faith in her own Americanness, a belief that even if she had married a foreigner, she still was who she was. Only now, upon questioning and imprisonment, could she see how naive she had been, that it didn't matter if she was American or British, and it surely didn't matter that she was white—what mattered was that she was a woman, subject to the laws of men.

"We've already been in contact with the authorities to expedite that process. Once you see the light of day, we will deport you alongside your husband. Or you can give us the last known address of these two men, and we'll wipe the slate clean. You won't have to lose your country. We'll nullify your marriage. Maybe you were kidnapped. Maybe you were coerced into marriage by a greasy foreigner. You had been such a good girl until you met him, and now you're associated with awful types like Rose Talley."

Cora tried to keep herself from betraying her shock. She must have done a poor job hiding it.

"The Americans have been keeping track of her for ages," he said with a smile. "It was relatively easy to pick up your scent once you began associating with her."

Behind those glasses were eyes so hollow. This was the empire, this was the West. Beautiful words and ideas woven into fine cloth that hid the horrid and disfigured. The fool didn't know that her mind had barred itself from him, was deep somewhere else, inside the protective cocoon of possibility. It didn't matter that she was going to lose her country. There would be somewhere else waiting for there when she got out.

She wished to be done with the man. To self-servingly give this officer of a foreign nation (or her new nation—whatever it was now) what he wanted would not only betray Indra and his cohort but would be too a betrayal of the trust given to her knowingly and lovingly, of the invitation by many into something new. She had been looking for so long. She owed them.

The transit of the sun passed through her. From the window of that room came a light so clear, she strained at its brightness, and an electric pain shot through her eyes, and she fought her body's sense of self-preservation to look it dead on, to feel it course through her— she didn't know when that light would return to her. She needed it as some meager spoonful of nourishment.

The light—there had been a lesson taught to her about the light. Scullion had taught her. To greet it, to worship it, to treat it as the god that it was. Scullion was at such a distance from here, and from this range, he no longer felt like the guiding figure he once was, but instead like his vim flattened until he was only in two dimensions, leaving him as a character in a book prattling off precepts that Cora could call upon for the remainder of her days. Life had toddled on until that evening in Suresh's home, whereupon it had accelerated, and the world spun faster and faster, taking her with it at a speed so great that the story seemed to have a hallucinatory quality to it.

"You're a coward," Cora said. "And so are those Americans who are willing to betray this country to serve yours. You can feel what's coming, and you know you can't stop it. You're watching the revolution in Russia, and you know on the horizon are more revolutions, more wars, a great upheaval. The future will forget you quicker than you can imagine. Where is my lawyer? I demand my lawyer."

"You can demand whatever you want, Mrs. Mukherjee. It doesn't mean I have to give it to you. Rights like that don't extend to non-citizens. We will get the information we need from His Majesty's newest subject. We do not falter in the face of petty opposition. Your cellar room last night was a taste of what we can do to you. We can put you in a room like that for the rest of your life, you know that? And not in a city like this. We can put you on an island so far from humanity, you'll wish for that underground cell.

"You all think you are important, ambling around, parroting ideas on freedom, falling in and out of love with each other. You're a bunch of feckless bohemians and Bolsheviks, unaware that there is one real power in this world. It is ours. And you will remain in this prison until we have the information we seek, among women so far beneath you that you will wonder how you have fallen so deep."

The man got up to leave. Cora noticed that his cheeks looked a bit red from his soliloquy, and she couldn't help what came out of her mouth next. "Wait," she said. "There's something I want to ask of you."

He stood impatiently waiting for her to speak.

"In the women's prison, they must have cloth, right? Women's cloth. I need something for my blood," she said matter-of-factly.

"All women disgust me," he said, sneering. "You have the special position of disappointing me too. You had your chance, Mrs. Mukherjee, and now you can await your future. You'll find what you need when you're booked into the Tombs."

CHAPTER THIRTY

Indra sat in their apartment, at the table yet to be resold, staring at the bed he had left her in. The sheets were thrown off to the side. When he walked over to touch them, they were still warm.

Where they had taken her, he didn't know. He couldn't go to the local police station and ask where his wife had been arrested and imprisoned. It was an easy way to get himself stuck in the mire.

In the end, the names of her angels were Higgins, Talley, Golding, Kesari, Scullion, and Dawson, names as waypoints through a city, across a nation, back to where it all began. Indra packed a small suitcase with whatever he could, grabbing a few dresses for Cora—she would need them when he saw her again—and left, not knowing if anyone was watching or following, and made his way uptown to Kesari's, who met him at the door and could not hide a look of wide-eyed panic when Indra recounted how Cora had been arrested. Kesari thought it too risky for Indra to stay with him, but he promised to take the message onward, that they would find where Cora was, they would get her out. He scribbled a note for Indra and told him to go uptown, to the Goldings, they would let him stay there. They would help.

Indra got uptown and met with the Goldings and was surprised to find a child only weeks old with them, its mewling cries emerging at a cadence that paid no heed to time of day, only to a persistent hunger experienced constantly. They first offered Indra a corner of their living room. Jude said he would send a telegram to a few con-

tacts, and they would find her, but meanwhile, did Indra know anyone else he could get in touch with?, to which Indra recommended
the editor of the *Clarion*, and Jude said that Talley was already on
the list. Indra offered up Higgins, and Jude replied that she was a
great choice, that she had a lot of pull. "Who else?" Jude asked, impatient. He wanted to know family, friends, important connections,
people who could be counted on in a crisis.

Dawson, Scullion.

"I like John Scullion as much as the next man, 'cept he's not the
one we need now. The president of a university? That's exactly who
we need. She sure knew a lot of powerful people, didn't she? I met
her, what, once, twice? I'd fight for her. She was not a person you
can forget."

Indra noticed that Jude had already switched to the past tense,
and the anxiety that gripped him must have been obvious, for Jude
immediately began to soothe: "We'll get her out, don't you worry,
we'll get her out."

In the meantime, it was time to let them handle everything. Indra had to lay low, and a quiet baby's cry emerged from another
room, and Jude wondered out loud if it would be better if he went
where no one could find him. Jude said this in the same light and
caring voice he reserved for his infant.

"I'm not leaving this city without Cora—" Indra began.

"Of course, of course, no one said you would. Just until we get
her out. But where,"" Jude trailed off.

Penelope emerged from a back bedroom, their small baby in a
sling, its face half hidden in her breast. Seeing her, Indra felt a pang
of nostalgia for the fantasy life of him and Cora in Mexico, and
this desire for something that never came to pass was so strong that
Indra, for a moment, forgot that it had never actually occurred, that
it was something he had conjured in his spare moments.

"How about James?" Penelope said. "No one would look for
him there."

"James? His neighborhood is squalid, disgusting, fetid," Jude went on, leaving Indra feeling like a child being discussed between two parents. "It's crowded too. Who wants to live there?"

"Perfect place to hide, dear. We're not talking about anyone living there."

"I've got a friend," Jude said, turning to Indra. "Irish, name's James. Lives down in Williamsburg. Fifth floor in a walk-up filled with every single human being on the planet stuffed into three bedrooms. He's a shop steward at a foundry on the waterfront. Wrote a couple things for us. You should stay with him. No one's looking for anyone in Williamsburg. Beautiful idea, P."

"I suppose I don't have a choice," Indra said, feeling as if he were being carried out to sea by a riptide, helpless in the currents, bound to die somewhere far from shore.

"Don't look so grave. It'll be a couple days. We'll get her out. This country is going to hell, but she still has her rights. I'll make sure to keep you informed of everything. I'll get messages down to you. We'll use a runner, no letters, nothing that can be traced, nothing, you'll be fine." Jude patted him on the back with all the assurance of a man who knew nothing of what would come ahead.

A FEW DAYS, IT TURNED OUT, WAS INCORRECT. A WEEK PASSED. THE PEOPLE OF IMPORtance had been rallied: Dawson sent a note of support, as did Scullion. Kesari knew that he would only cause issue, as he was probably being trailed by the same folks who'd arrested Cora. In the end, it was Higgins and Talley who led the cause, finding a lawyer who could ask all the right questions.

From time to time, Indra would be beset with such a furious anger—at himself. He wished he had been more forceful, had shaken his wife by the shoulders and told her to stop. It was his right to do so. It was his duty to keep her safe. And he had failed her there. He had been right, but correctness was little pleasure—want of love had a way of forgiving even the most egregious of trespass. He just wanted her back.

What they could learn was that Cora had been arrested by the Office of Naval Intelligence, probably related to the same folks who detained and questioned Kesari, all most likely working in tandem with CID from India.

No one could find out anything about her for the first days, and it was only after the lawyer threatened to go to the press— "All-American girl detained mistakenly by feds"—did they find out that she was being held at the Tombs downtown. The threat backfired. The lawyer was shaken up by some detective who said if they blabbed to the press, every paper in New York would be talking about how an American woman was taken in by dark and oily revolutionaries, that she was arrested because she was about to betray her nation. They had found a warehouse full of guns and ammo downtown. They knew that Indra was part of the plot.

Indra was surprised to hear this. He had nothing to do with the cache, of course, but the only other person he could think of who could pull off a project like that was Benoy. Perhaps he wasn't as useless as he seemed. The damn miser needed the money after all. Guns and ammo, that's what money could be used for in their little world. Obermeier, in his final missive, had said to keep the faith. Here was the cache. Even upon the precipice of success, this plot too had met its end in doom.

In the meantime, Indra was living in Williamsburg. James, generous and ruddy-faced, missing half his right pinky and a quarter of his left thumb ("Cost of the job," he said), told Indra he could stay for as long as he needed in his small spare room ("It's all I got"). The room was in actuality a pantry: a small mattress on the floor surrounded by sacks of flour and other sundry items, where at night Indra could hear the small squeaks and pitter-patter of movement as mice took their fair share.

The building was mostly Irish, with a smattering of Italian immigrants, but James took Indra across the street to meet a man who worked at his factory, the one Indian he knew. And after that introduction, Indra saw little of James ("I got lotsa shit to do, sorry. I hope you're not arrested. Goddamn stupid cops. Rat bastards, every single one of them").

"I go by Frank Hanson here. It makes things easy," the Indian across the street told Indra. "The name given to me when I was born was Fayaz Haqq." When Indra repeated it, Haqq closed his eyes for a moment and smiled. "You never realize when the time passes. It's been years since I've heard the sound of my birth name spoken by someone else."

Haqq had come to New York from St. Vincent, where he had worked the sugar fields, worked as a lascar for a few years, going up and down the Atlantic coast before he tired of a life at sea. He had worked as a nickel plater for a few years at the foundry, and had the deep cough to prove it. Indra was pleased to learn that Haqq originally came from Bengal, not too far from where Indra had grown up.

Indra soon came to crave their conversations—a pity because Haqq worked nine-hour shifts six days a week at the foundry—as they were the only respite that truly passed the time. Otherwise, Indra would play game after game of solitaire in James's apartment, listening to the sounds of families waking, fighting, lovemaking (alternating harried, lackadaisical, everyday), doors and windows always open, the apartment sweltering. Indra never liked the looks he got when he went to the neighborhood staples along the block, looks he could stomach when with Haqq, who knew everyone not only by first name but, further, by some nickname known to those who lived in the neighborhood.

The sweaty games of solitaire were all Indra could do while waiting for some crumb, some morsel, of news about Cora, only to be confronted with more and more waiting. It was within these long hours that Indra cursed every single step he had made. He had made the same mistake in New York that he had in California. Comfort opened up the possibility of destruction. They should have left for San Antonio as soon as they could, or he should have taken her with him to buy the cold cuts (the fresh air would have helped her), or they should have changed apartments when he heard Kesari's warning. If she wasn't going to listen to him, he should have said to hell with equality, and he should have been a man, a proper husband, and acted for the two of them.

When he wasn't cursing himself, he was always remembering, craving, dreaming of her, a lover driven to insanity without the beloved—empty time was a curse, was a drag, was a feeling that the clock served solely to taunt him. And so when Haqq got home, they would play cards together and maybe share a drink, which Haqq, who prayed five times a day and went all the way to the kosher butcher because it was close enough to halal, was more than happy to imbibe.

Indra asked about his life, and Haqq told him about leaving Bengal, about the promises of lucre made by a recruiter, about weeding cane for twelve hours a day, how most of his friends lost feet to parasites in the always wet soil, and then he would regale Indra with stories of the sea, of the roughness of the merchant marine, of the brotherhood and isolation of life upon a ship. And when all this ran out, he explained how electroplating worked, and also of the gruesome injuries in a factory, of limbs lost, of fingers burnt, of men poisoned, and Indra listened, rapt, moved by how poverty was a curse that followed one across oceans, through nations.

"I know this about myself. Every time some big shot promises me fifty dollars, I'll always say yes. Who could say no to fifty dollars? Every time, I get all balled up. What can I do? I need the fifty."

Indra had never experienced Haqq's malady, how being poor was a vise grip that could never be escaped, how there was always a capitalist or a landlord ready to strangle the life out of the next man who rounded the corner, and it was through Haqq that Indra felt true sympathy for what had been an intellectual exercise in the library.

He had been listening for so long, and now, as he waited, half-stricken with grief, cursing himself for his inaction, he had found a way to speak.

CHAPTER THIRTY-ONE

Cora was not prepared for the clamor aboveground. The general population of women in the Tombs was a cacophony of coming and going of those in pretrial detention, every person awaiting a judge who would declare them guilty and send them to their cursed fate in another prison somewhere in the remote reaches of New York State.

The Tombs jail was only a few blocks from Wall Street, and it was a fitting location, for all around her were women crushed in some way by the great heaving wheel of poverty. *Ourselves*, one of Crothers's plays that actually dealt with real matters, told the story of women arrested for prostitution. When women fell, they were accused as individuals of some sort of grave moral failure. Men—society itself—had to shoulder an equal if not greater share of the blame. This prison was proof of that notion.

The women's portion of the jail was barely three stories high, a small block of a larger complex set off by a small courtyard surrounded by a slate-gray stone wall equal in height to the jail itself. The sun shone in the Tombs only at high noon and hid away for the remainder of the day, and without sunlight, the whole place smelled faintly of mildew. Women would wash their clothing in the sinks. They would dry only to dampness, imprinting everyone's skin with the very smell of the building around them.

Some of the women were held in the prison for hours, others days, and still others weeks or months. In the interim, a few of them spent their time crying, others were completely silent, and fewer still had the slick-grin pride of having been here more than once, knowing all the ins and outs of the daily system of detention. Most of the women, however, alternated between the three: crying when convinced no one would hear, in silent contemplation for most of the day, and ready to lord knowledge over the continual stream of fresh inmates brought into cells that never sat empty for long.

When Cora first arrived, she kept to herself—she was not ready for this efflorescence of noise, of the constant chatter coming from each and every woman, the din of humanity interspersed with the metal-on-metal crash of doors and gates, all mixed with the occasional cries from infants brought to the jail alongside their mothers. Cora was surprised at how vulgar these other women could be, but it seemed to her that their vulgarity came naturally to them because they didn't know any other language—it was a kind of coarseness that Cora hadn't heard since she was a child, a physicality that grew into a voice by way of rough hands.

Like the others, Cora wept. The worst was the first night, when she lay on her cot and arose to rest her forehead against the cold steel bars of her door. No one could tell her what had happened on the outside. No one knew if Indra had been arrested. No one knew when she would see a judge to receive her own indictment. No one knew of anything except the routinized hours of the day when each woman was simply a number, a part of a count, a dismissed object. And because of her own stupidity, her own ambition-blinded naïveté, she was left sealed off from those who had invited her through an open door. Arrested for being a woman. For the rest she needed from the pregnancy she did not want. She did not regret the abortion, only the fact that it had been needed in the first place.

To think, this all began with him.

His face half in shadow. The quietness of his voice. The softness of his lips.

His utter foolishness. His pride. The vanity of his beliefs.

They had married, and the nuptial gift given to them was fear. Sudden departure. Friends arrested. A trial begun. Hiding in a city across the nation.

New York City. At first a ghastly place, but then, suddenly and without warning, the city was anew with people and opportunities all for her, even while the maelstrom of war and hatred grew darker upon the horizon. They were being hunted, and they had moved slowly toward safety. Because of her.

She shook the bars of her door, and the cellblock matron came down the corridor with the heavy and slow thud of her footfall, and even in the darkness, Cora could see her yellowed and skewed teeth. "Now, now, don't make that kind of racket in the middle of the night," she warned.

Rules upon rules in here: Cora was made to weep silently. In the morning, around came someone who wished to speak with her, and Cora had nothing to do but entertain the conversation with a weary hello.

"When'd you check in to this hotel?" the young woman asked. Her name was Agnes, and she seemed to be scarcely older than Cora, with sunken-in dark eyes and a short, fashionable haircut. She wore a loose-fitting dress belted at the hip, and around her collar was a men's bolo tie with a turquoise amulet set in the middle, the likes of which Cora hadn't seen since she was out west.

"Just a few days ago," Cora replied. "I'm in, I suppose, for having the wrong ideas about things."

Agnes's face lit up. "Me too, me too. Just got sixty days in here, though. They're not even transferring me to the women's farm upstate. I was giving a little booklet from Emma Higgins on birth control to this poor sap who comes into the office saying, 'Wah, wah, my family is so big, I don't get paid nothin', I don't want any more kids.' And I give him the booklet, and it turns out he's from SSV, you know, Comstock's gang, and I get arrested for breaking the law on distributing prohibited literature."

Cora was thrilled to meet a fellow birth control advocate in prison and explained how she herself had just written an essay for Higgins on birth control in Japan.

"Haven't read it yet, though I've been in here a month now. I must have missed the issue, I woulda probably been in the office when you met with Emma—I'm sorry to have missed you then. I'm glad to hear you're fighting the good fight." Agnes turned to yell into the corridor: "Three cheers for birth control!"

"Hip, hip, hooray!" came a chorus of replies from some of the women throughout the cellblock.

"We've got a good crowd in here. I don't need to convince them about birth control. So is that what you're in for? Birth control? SSV?"

"Unfortunately, mine is a little worse. Military Intelligence, I think. Socialism, freedom, all the things America doesn't want to hear when she's at war."

"I'm surprised you haven't left for Mexico yet," Agnes said in a low voice.

"I had hoped to," Cora replied. "Other things got in the way."

Agnes nodded as if she knew some inkling of what Cora was getting at. "Ah, freedom. Good thing, that freedom. If only America could take some of it and give it back to the people within her borders, maybe we'd live in a better country."

IN AN INSTITUTION, A PLACE BOUNDED TIGHTLY BY BOTH WALLS AND ROUTINE, FRIENDships formed quickly and deepened. What outside could take weeks or months took only hours or days inside a jail, and Agnes and Cora were seemingly shackled to each other. Through her, Cora could feel for Hazel—she missed her old friend—for all love, especially that found in friendship, was cursed to echo throughout one's life: all new faces had a touch of the old.

Hazel had been a guide at some of Cora's first meetings across

Palo Alto, and similarly, Agnes took Cora to meet and talk with those imprisoned around them, and together, they listened to the stories of the women who passed through the Tombs, from the small-time thieves to the prostitutes to the beggars to the poor mothers to the socialists to the immigrants and every which one in between. From their stories, Cora learned that no matter her countenance or fairness or height or any of the outward and crude measurements of beauty, each and every one of those women had been made ugly in some way, women made to steal, to sell their bodies to men, to forge, to maim, to kill, all for want of some little morsel, some payday never to come.

Between the countless stories, Cora learned a bit more about Agnes, how she was born into dirt poverty in western Missouri and how she made her way west, stopping for a time in New Mexico (where she picked up the bolo tie), where she learned how to type and met (and divorced) her first husband, a man who had been a socialist and her first teacher in the cause, whose lessons she kept with her when she headed to New York and fell in with Emma Higgins. It wasn't her first time in a prison. It surely wouldn't be her last.

The two had an easy way of sharing, and so it was Agnes whom Cora went to after she woke up confused from what she had seen in a dream. The two were spending idle time in the raucous open hall, the din of others' conversations forcing the two into quiet intimacy.

"Want to talk about it?" Agnes asked.

"My father used to say that the most boring words in the English language were 'Let me tell you about my dream.'"

"Well, what does he know? He's not here. We've got time. Go on, tell me about it."

"My father appeared to me, right here in this cell, and he was thin and hollow. He looked like he did when I was a child, like when we were back out west in the mines. It was strange, because I was as I am now. We were close in age, like he was one of my friends.

"He wore a dusty brown suit, cuffs frayed at the wrists and

ankles. And he looked hungry. Not for food. Maybe for something to finally go right in his life. He folded his arms and had this twisted grimace on his face, like he was angry about something. He wasn't going to say what.

"And then, in the way dreams are, things changed without warning, and we were back west, and it was snowing, thin, light, airy stuff. There was enough on the ground for him to pull me in a sled. The cold was knocking my teeth together. And then we were at a little Christmas fair for the miners. There was a great big bonfire in the middle of it all, and there was dancing in one tent, drinking in another, and none of these men had a penny for a gift for anyone, but they had their beer, and their music, and some women brought in from God knows where.

"And my father turned to me and said, 'Why are they so ugly, Cora?'"

"Then what? Damn, what a thing to say. Real rude, if you ask me." Agnes looked offended, as if Cora's father had telephoned her in her sleep to send a message of insult to the workingmen of the past. Agnes made eye contact with another woman sitting by herself on a rough bench across the way to look for approval. The woman must have been a newcomer. She quickly looked away from Cora.

"And then I woke up," Cora said.

"Goddamn, now, that's a dream. Was it real? Did that really happen? Did he really ask you that question?"

"No, he didn't. I did. I remember that Christmas fair, and I remember taking notice of those rough and happy men, and I remember running back to my father and hanging on to him like some broken-winged sparrow lost in the rain. And I asked him, 'Why are they so ugly, Papa?' It was like I'd just noticed how unknown the adult world was to me."

"I remember being thirteen and learning, for the first time, that I was no longer a child to men. Overnight I became something that they could take for themselves. Three cheers for birth control," Agnes said quietly, a little broken. "Anyway, what did he say to you?"

"He said, 'Tell me, Cora, what makes them so ugly?'"

"Wow, wasn't expecting that. It's a great question, turning it back to you to try to understand everything for yourself."

"It was one of those questions a parent later realizes that their child will never let go of. It reappeared over and over, and I think my father ended up regretting ever posing it in the first place. It opened my eyes to a great many things. He was like that back then, able to ask good questions. Things changed later. As they do. Back then he pointed out the men as they descended into the earth and talked about the danger, all the ways the wretchedness of this grand money machine keeps the mass of men unthinking, how it keeps them happy for the small scraps handed down to them by men of such unimaginable wealth."

"Why do you think you dreamed all this last night? What do you think it means?"

As a child, Cora did not have the words to understand what metastasized within her, only the pain of endless neuromas of feeling—what was desired was always what she could not have. A day spent memorizing the multiplication tables could only heighten a need to catch a glimpse of her father, so that by nightfall, even a glance of his shadow would excite her with the possibility of feeling his love.

Her heart was built like a watch whose (sometimes sweeping, sometimes staccato) movement kept time in the hollow of her chest. And when this watch was opened, laid bare—as it was now—she was frightened by the infinite layers of gears turning upon ever smaller gears, the teeth of which were cut into place when she was a little girl.

"Don't know how I can know," Cora continued. "Freud's making a career out of dreams, but that's not for me. I just remember feeling so lonely as a child. Wanting him—wanting anyone, really. It was just me and myself, for the most part. Even when I grew older, where there were people to be found, I kept to myself even while in conversation with another, and that loneliness became part of me. But over the past few months, I finally found a way to bridge the loneliness of that little girl to the things that move me today, and yet here I am."

Cora took a moment to look around the room and caught the eye of a woman among the rough and discarded. She was a girl, really, her hair greasy and her flour-sack dress stained with spit-up, sitting in a corner nursing a plump baby of no more than three months. When the girl saw Cora looking, she smiled. She was missing two front teeth. Cora looked back toward her friend.

"I'm not sure, Agnes," she continued. "I woke up from that dream feeling like everything was for naught. That I'm here again, by myself, with nothing to say for what I've seen."

"You seem like a smart person, but damn, I don't think dreams and the like are your strength. You think this jail is a punishment. Naw, this place is a reward. It's a signal that you're doing something right. When you're like us, you don't end up here because you're a lonely coward. You end up here because you've worked with others, and what you've done is just and right. It's not our fault this country can't countenance true justice."

At first Agnes had been seated next to Cora, straddling the bench like she would a horse out west. She was breaking into a speech now and stood up, and Cora looked up as she loomed over her.

"Here's one true thing to hold on to beyond that silly little dream," Agnes went on. "Our pasts are hard places, all of them. And we'll never be able to escape them, really, so we're with them for better or worse. We keep on. We're lassoed to whatever happened back then. But more keeps coming, and you know that you can't stop what's coming. And in time, that'll change you too.

"Places like this change people, Cora. Let me tell you that. People get surprised when the worst of it all comes to test them. I've always reckoned that suffering is its own joy." With that, she smiled with a look of reaching the point she wanted to make. In truth,

Cora took in all of what her friend had to say as if she were some prophet come down from the mountain.

"I've watched you since you got here, that first night when you were quiet and weepy. And now you're talking among every last woman. That's a quick change. You're a quick study. You came into our little hotel as a matchstick flame. Trust me, when you step out of here and breathe the free air once again, you'll go back into that world blazing as bright as the sun."

CHAPTER THIRTY-TWO

Finally, two and a half weeks after arriving in Williamsburg, Indra got a real piece of news. A grand jury was going to meet to indict Cora on two violations of the Espionage Act—the same stunt they'd pulled on the Indians back in California. Indra was named as a co-conspirator on this indictment too. The good news was that they could get Cora out on bail after the grand jury met, and from there, jumping bail would be pretty easy as long as they moved fast.

He had toyed with the idea of contacting Cora's father to help her make bail. It wouldn't have been the first time Indra tried to speak with him. Even though he had chosen not to attend his daughter's wedding, there had been a check in the envelope of his reply, a gift—for all his disapproval, the man loved his daughter as well as he could, and in the face of decisions he could not fathom or respect, money was the only way to prove the tenuousness of a love that still existed: he would not consign his daughter to the poverty he once suffered.

Indra, without telling Cora, had written to her father to thank him for the gift, to try to prove that he was not some wandering fakir sent from India who had beguiled his daughter into marriage.

The reply had been terse and simple.

I did not send my daughter to attend the Leland Stanford University to fall in love with some greasy turbaned

Hindoo washed ashore in our state. If it were up to me, I'd
send the lot of you back to where you came. Thankfully,
the men of importance in this country are sympathetic to
my point of view.

Even though he had been generous with his money, in sending
that letter and not attending, he had put up a wall between them and
him. Indra would not go back and beg this man for another cent,
even if it were the easiest route to Cora's freedom. No, he would
take a slightly more circuitous route. Through Jude, he was able to
get in touch with Higgins, who started a collection with Rose Talley, who was generous with her funds. Soon they had enough money
to post bail.

Joy, of course, at the idea that she could return, that they could
be together once again. It was tacitly understood among all that this
was not a loan, was instead the price of freedom, an escape made
possible by the generosity of others who expected the two of them
to pay back not in dollars but to carry on what they had started in
America. Living in Mexico would not be an excuse. They would
have to find ways to fight for freedom elsewhere.

Indra and Cora had a debate once. He, haughty, had said that
one had to experience the pain of injustice to be able to fight it. She
had disagreed. Now she knew what pain truly was. He had no idea
what kind of woman Cora would be when got out. Fighting for
freedom in the abstract was one thing. A cold jail cell was entirely
another. And she now had lived both. Joy and fear commingled in a
great dialectic of feeling. All he wanted was to see her again.

A plan was made, passed along the grapevine to Indra—Cora
had been in New York such a short time, yet she already had a great
wellspring of support among its intellectuals and activists. This was
her gift, this was why he fell in love with her. She had a way of becoming part of something larger and then becoming integral to it.
He knew that if their spots had been reversed, that if he had been

arrested, she would have marshaled heaven and earth to ensure his release. And she would have been successful.

The plan was this: Indra would take a morning train out of the city, a few stops into New Jersey, all the way out to Newark. He would wait there until the evening train to San Antonio. Their friends were going to help her jump bail. There was a fifteen-minute stop in Newark. Cora would leave her train, and they would depart together. There would be no waiting in the city, they would do their best to make sure she wasn't followed. "Goodbye, good luck, maybe see you down in Mexico," Talley said through the messenger.

It was time to say goodbye to Haqq. "See you around," Haqq said. "You get to leave, and I'll be stuck here forever. That's the difference between you and me," a statement of fact made without bitterness. Indra perhaps felt a bit of jealousy at this idea of stability, the reality that he did not need to run halfway across the globe at a moment's notice. "You know where to find me," Haqq finally said.

"So long, I'll see you," Indra replied, and he shook Haqq's hand, and before he could think twice of it, gave him five dollars. "A gift for all the card games."

The voyage out was easy, quick. In a city like New York, a man could slip in and out among the great masses, another face to be ignored. There was no great capture, no feeling of being watched, just another body crammed among the others on the train.

Indra had hours to kill when he got to Newark, hours made slower by the anxiety, the anticipation. It was a culmination of all he had done since he had arrived in America, a way station that amounted to little more than a great arrivals-and-departures hall, and while here, he had chatted with his neighbors, listening, taking seriously what they had to say, and now he was ready, ready to leave it all, for nothing of importance to him could ever happen in America—Indra wasn't sure why, but he knew it. Maybe it was too large, a leviathan unto itself, incapable of any movement except the heaving of its own gargantuan limbs, which it used to crush others when necessary. The world outside, that was where it all happened, and he and Cora could only begin their happening outside of it.

He went from the great hall of the Newark station to the outside, walking up and down the block, a humid and sticky and disgusting day, one that smelled like piss and rotting meat. He walked back again and out and had lunch at a bar of a cold beer and a sandwich of bread, cheese, and pickles. He had learned to eat like an American in a few months.

Cora had taught him that time had no real speed, that seconds across a day tended to move at a pace determined by circumstance, and today the seconds were apathetic. The sun made its transit across the sky, men came and went on their own errands, and Indra watched it all, until the sun began to set and the train was due to arrive on platform four and he went out and peered down the track, trying to will the train into the station by looking, looking again, his body facing the direction it would come, leaning down, was it there yet, no not yet, here it came, barreling down, the great heaving machine.

The bustle of people leaving, people entering the train, and then a brief quiet.

There she was. She saw him when he saw her, and he walked to her, and she looked terrible, thin, a little greasy, her curly hair a mess, knots here and there, but there she was. It had been three weeks.

And the joy he felt upon seeing her was unspeakable, unmistakable.

In their embrace, a whisper.

"Let's leave here," he said.

"Forever," she replied.

"I love you," he said.

CODA

MOVEMENTS

LATER AGAIN, THE FIRST DAY

There were already stories Cora wanted to tell, first of Agnes, and then of each and every woman she talked to, answers to the question that had been with her since she was a child: *What makes them so ugly?*

She craved a proper bath. In the time between her release on bail and when she'd met Indra at the station, Jude had gotten her to a safe house where she could shower, but it was a quick one, just enough to wash off that sweet, loamy, oniony smell that still occasionally reached her own nose in unwelcome twists. Indra had brought her a change of clothes. She loved him even for that small gesture, so ready to be rid of the same dirty clothes. Perhaps she could freshen up in the washroom, but that was on the other side of the carriage, and nothing felt better than sitting in a seat built of cushion and comfort, a luxury she hadn't been afforded in weeks.

There had been a chorus answer to the childhood question, a unity from each woman ensconced in a vermin-infested cell: their ugliness grew from the horrible system into which they were all born. Crothers once wrote plays about women like that. Cora would take up the mantle with her essays. Each woman she met deserved to have their story printed, and she was already forming the contours of the first of them, it would be a series, perhaps she could somehow write to Rose or Emma under a pseudonym. Her friendship with Agnes had grown into a way to connect with all the women who came and went through the prison. One of the stories she would tell would be about the factory worker who once moonlighted as a prostitute and, having unceremoniously aged out of that profession at forty-two, turned to forging checks. She would clip a copy of the story and send it to Hazel in an envelope with no return address—Hazel wouldn't have to look for Cora's byline, it would go to her as a beacon, a reminder that all continued without issue. The story's opening was coming to her now, she believed she should really write it down, there had to be a pen and paper somewhere on this train. Too tired, she continued to stare out her window, little lights in farmhouse windows, structures moving about as if they were on casters in a stage play.

The sun had just set, the day had been stifling, all the windows slid open at the top, and the air that moved about the carriage felt like steam from a cooling stew. Her window faced east into the dark.

Little homes, little lives. Boys sent to die in the war. Mothers and wives and sisters pining after their memory. Arrests for all the rest. Maybe in this milk-fed part of the nation, they all played well, and no one stepped out of line, and Military Intelligence could breathe easy knowing that sedition lurked only among the swarthy and the agitated up in the cities.

It was brighter inside the carriage compartment than outside, and by pretending to look at the scenery that passed in the window, Indra was actually looking at Cora, and her eyes had this glazed-over look, and Indra couldn't decide if this meant fear or something else. He felt a great wellspring of pity for her, wished he could bridge the gap made of so many pauses and ellipses and absences, that had appeared over the past months, and the culmination, the horror and the pity, of being imprisoned. He had experienced life in a cell for a year, and when he had been granted his freedom, all he'd felt was a slight vertigo from the cadences of his life that were thrown off balance. He remembered waking up at the same time every morning for the count, and he could swear he could hear the voice of the jailer number off, but it was a rooster, or it was some voice from the street, or it was some other empty vase that had captured a memory and echoed it back to him.

That wasn't the first feeling, no, the first feeling was a question—how do I get back to the position I left behind—but when he found it again, he learned that his crown had hollowed. Nothing outside the prison had held its breath, nothing had waited for him, life had continued on, and he had to find his place in it again.

"Nothing's changed," Indra offered. "Nothing's changed at all. I love you. Your intelligence is still an inspiration. We continue to fight for what we believe to be true." He nodded, somewhat satisfied with his conclusion.

Cora seemed startled by the interjection and stared at him, offering nothing in reply.

The curse of two people who had spent too much time together, the assumption that his thoughts could trail straight from him into her. He tried again. "When I first left my cell, I went back to my comrades. We were planning to steal more weapons—it's what we did best. The plan had been long since abandoned. They were arguing over something else. New men too. Took me a long time to understand what was happening. So much had changed in my absence."

"I forgot you spent a year in prison," Cora replied. "Tell me, did you listen much to your cellmates? Did you learn their stories?"

"We couldn't talk much about our lives on the outside. You never knew who was the mole, paid off with some promise of early release by the jailers. Open talk could get you killed. When we spoke of our lives, it was at night—someone was able to get a bribe through the walls. We could pay off a guard, meet in a cell overnight, speak freely in whispers."

"All we did was talk when given the chance," Cora said. "At first I thought that none of these women would shut up. Still, it was the only conversation I could have, so I listened. I met so many, Indra. So many who speak with actual words and not tracts or speeches, the actual color we seek, the truth to our struggle, stories that have to be heard."

Indra nodded. "Your friends the Goldings sent me to Williamsburg to hide, and I met a man there called Haqq—he worked at a foundry. Before that he was a lascar, and before that he was in St. Vincent working the fields. He did every job known to man, I think. He told me he was cursed to always believe the man who could give him fifty dollars."

Cora let out a laugh. "They hid you in Brooklyn?" Indra smiled. Cora reached over to squeeze his hand. "No one would look beyond the river."

She looked down at his fingernails—he was usually so fastidious, trimming his nails down to nothing before they could grow. He had let them grow ever so slightly, and she thought it added a small elegance to his hands.

She couldn't imagine him among the rats and in the teeming life of a tenement, but she was glad to hear he had been hidden away, safe the entire time. They had been sitting across from each other, and the porters wouldn't come through to change over the seats to beds and draw the curtains for a few hours yet, though she finally felt the exhaustion, the gut punch of deleterious effect, and she got up to sidle next to Indra, and he stiffened at her proximity.

"What's wrong?"

"Can we continue this," he said in a low voice, "as the train moves through the south? Suresh told me stories."

"We're off to Mexico, Indra," she said into his ear. "We're the

children of the Mexican revolution. You're the caballero I met by
chance in Sonora, and we just introduced you to my family, and
now we're going back. Or maybe we're poets returning to our home
in Zacatecas. Or maybe we're journalists set off to Yucatán to interview General Alvarado. We're not who we used to be. There's
always a story we can tell them."

She felt him relax—briefly—at her comment. They had thousands of miles and a river before they could truly relax. There was
nothing but time ahead of them.

A train could control time itself, its comings and goings marked
cleanly on a timetable adhered to by the minute. Inside the train,
time seemed to saunter on its own, the only clock being an arrival
into a new city, a new station, where the countryside gave way to
close-packed dwellings and homes. They moved together and on
this train, there was little to separate one from the other.

"This is it," she said to him finally. "The honeymoon we never
had. From here to Mexico. And maybe Mexico too. It won't all be
work."

"It's not Halcyon, is it? It's all the same, a free moment with
you."

Next to each other, they moved through the American darkness—a nation like this was made palatable in the dark, where one
couldn't see all the knots of contradiction tied into the landscape,
couldn't hear the lip service to freedom. Outside the window was
the outline of a brilliant landscape reduced to a silhouette: rolling
hills, grand vistas, the romantic sweep of an unruly continent.

Eyes open, then closed again, and finally, she leaned upon the
soft spot on his shoulder that made for a nap. In the dream that
followed, she was back in some strange disconnected series: last to
arrive to eat and the food had all been eaten, back in isolation and
her toilet had been removed, and no one could hear her loud moans
of complaint, so then came the decision to relieve herself upon the
floor, and finally, her British inquisitor, the way the light caught

upon the thin gold frames of his glasses. He asked no questions, but in her ear came Indra's whisper: *the weight of freedom is too much for one person to bear.*

She felt the heaviness of uneasy sleep bear down on her waking mind, a grogginess that she couldn't shake.

"You were whimpering in your sleep," Indra said with a look of concern usually reserved for an invalid.

"Do you still dream of your time in prison?"

"Less now, more in those weeks after I was let out. I would dream of missing the morning count, the feeling of an officer's heavy wooden club hitting my spine on my lower back, and sometimes I would dream of the mute faces of all the friends I had made, still there, or maybe released, or maybe released and arrested again. The body may be free. The mind, unfortunately, takes its time."

"You once told me that the weight of freedom is too much for one person to bear, do you still believe that?"

"Nitin taught me that. It was a strange thing for him to say. He always insisted upon the value of being alone, of being leader among many. He never took to heart his own lesson. The weight of freedom, the weight of ambition, it's all too much for one person to bear." He paused and took a breath through his nostrils, gathering thoughts in the expansion of his chest, honoring his friend while recognizing the contradictions that would never resolve. "A reason to be glad that we love each other. It looks like the porters are here. Let us try to get you some decent sleep tonight."

THE SECOND DAY

A train was a journey, but it was always the arrangement of its passengers, alighting and departing, settling into the proper seats, finally turning to each other to speak. The question of the proper seat only became more important as the train crossed through Virginia, through the Carolinas, and into Georgia, where the air seemed to hum and shimmer with the heavy, wet heat of the summer. It reminded Indra of that moment right before the monsoon came through, an atmosphere growing heavy in anticipation of what was to come next.

The ticket collector, a short and thick man made officious and haughty by his small blue hat and uniform, walked through, and before he even checked Cora and Indra's tickets, he pointed to Indra.

"You," he said. Indra had difficulty understanding him—the southern accent seemed like a slowed-down and amplified Scottish lilt. "Move your ass. You should know them's the rules." He didn't seethe with anger, just was explaining the order of things to an inferior.

Indra nervously looked to Cora and nodded. They couldn't fight, not now, not so close to what they craved. It would be a temporary separation. They would see each other again in San Antonio. He hesitated, unsure what to do.

The collector saw that Indra wasn't going to move. "Suit yourself, asshole. You know what happens when boys like you don't obey." He waved to the conductor, who walked over.

"We gotta move him," the collector said, turning away from Indra.

"Look at him, he's foreign," the conductor said. "There's a goddamn difference and you know it, you idiot."

"He's foreign?" The collector turned to Indra. "Where you born from? You even understand English?" he asked, slowing down and increasing the volume of his voice.

"Yes," Indra replied, handing the collector his ticket. This satisfied the conductor, who continued to the next car. "I understand English. I'm here visiting from India."

"India?" said the collector. "And you're headed to San Antonio? I reckon there's a story you should know. An American story. One that a foreigner like you might notta heard in your education.

There's a hero. Named Davy Crockett. Fought them Mexicans in the war. They teach you about Davy Crockett where you're from? You know what Davy Crockett said? 'Y'all may go to hell, and I will go to Texas.'" The collector laughed and handed Indra back his ticket and moved on to the next passenger, laughing to himself. "Foreigner," he intoned over the now-quiet carriage. "Foreigner!"

What Indra had feared had not come to pass. A lesson before his departure from America—in the west and the north, he was always Asian first, some charlatan here to steal jobs, poison the well of good society. Here, in the south, he was Not Colored, and that was what mattered most. Hatred for him as an Asian would come later, perhaps. He wouldn't stay in this part of the country long enough to find out.

He needed to move, to stretch his legs, to shake off what he had just experienced. He told Cora he was going to walk to the rear of the train, to the observation car, pass the time for a bit, but really to regain his bearings.

Cora was facing the direction of travel and had to turn to watch Indra walk back. This, she thought, would make a great story, something he could tell their friends and comrades in Mexico, that one of his last experiences in America had been the dance of who was colored and who was not, who belonged on the train and who had to be punished.

And her story would be of solitary detainment, of arrest and cellmates, and of her own escape. She would recount her arrest over and over, how Indra had stepped out for only a moment, and not more than five minutes after his departure came the knock—two burly officers, as if she would pose a threat in a fight. She smiled: she could already see how they would be drawn into every last detail, how this would be proof of her mettle.

All suffering can be made useful.

To be imprisoned was a mark of accomplishment, a sign that she was on the true path and the forces of power saw her as a threat to be stamped out, but look, she was still here, she had evaded their grasp, and there was probably a new warrant out for her arrest.

Indra had brought her into the world that would lead to such gainful despair. She owed him for that.

Ambition was an act of storytelling. It was to fantasize about the future success that one could achieve, everything that was for the taking if she could just round the next corner. Ambition too was belief in the ability to weave gossamer threads of fantasy into something real, something that could be touched. She could never do this by herself. Without Indra, it would all fall apart quickly, together, the magic of the loom could spin and spin and spin.

Where was he, she wanted him back. She stood up and walked to the observation car, finding him reading the papers in a plush chair in front of a window. Outside, the bleaching sun shone down upon acres of green. "Fancy seeing you here," he said as he folded down his paper. She leaned up against the arm of his chair.

A train was a journey, but it too was its passengers.

"I saw you both get on the train at New York. Where are you headed?" It was the man in the seat next to Indra, a thin alder of a man, tall as one too, with legs that scrunched between the chair and the wall.

Cora glanced at Indra, and the look said it all: tread carefully. They were being watched.

"San Antonio," Cora replied politely, hardened with cold steel, that tone of voice she learned in New York, reserved for those who tried to talk to her on the train.

"I'm headed to Mexico," he said. "Going to take a quick vacation, if you catch my drift. Name's Charles, nice to meet you both." He stretched over to shake their hands.

"A pleasure," Cora said, still with that hard voice. "My name is Antonia, and this is my husband, Ignacio Martinez. We're headed to San Antonio, perhaps onward from there."

"Oh, sounds great. What for?"

Cora felt sure that the man wasn't being pushy, seemed only desperate for conversation, trying to strike up some sort of friendship with someone on the train.

"We're going to meet my family," Indra said. "We recently were married in New York—that's where we met. And now my family must meet my beautiful bride."

"I wish I had a glass of the old bubbly with me. Cheers to you both, congratulations!" He smiled. "I live up in New York."

"Really? What do you do?" Indra asked.

Cora was surprised to hear this question, surprised that he was so willing to speak with a stranger who was close to understanding the meaning and possibility of their travel.

"I'm an artist. Sometimes a printmaker, sometimes a painter. Sometimes I make my living teaching at the Art Students League. A little of this, a little of that."

"Lovely. My wife and I are writers," Indra said with ease. She had supplied him the basis for their story, and he was running with it, sending it across the horizon.

"Never could write a damn. Wish I could, though. Some of those magazines, phew, they pay well. Nothing like the pennies I get from teaching sketching classes. What do you write about?"

"Sometimes, if we're lucky, we write about what can be done regarding that great mass of human suffering," Indra said.

"Plenty of human suffering to be found these days," Charles muttered. "Plenty of it to be avoided too."

Indra was about to ask another question, but Cora felt that the conversation had run its course. "Ignacio, dear, let's head over to the restaurant car. It was lovely talking to you, Charles."

As the two of them left, Cora had to stifle a giggle, the levity of making something new in the moment.

"Antonia and Ignacio. I'm impressed," Indra said. "Only now does another invention come to me. We could make do with the romance of the Orient. I'm the Indian prince escaped under the threat of persecution, and you're the woman I fell in love with in America. Partially true. It's up to them to figure out where's the truth and where's the lie."

Cora laughed. "Why, I never knew you were an Indian prince."

They could be anyone, as long as they were together.

THE THIRD DAY

They were getting closer, and they both felt the restlessness of departure. There was a chance to begin anew, to leave behind all the sediment that had accumulated upon them both, but this was a silly thing to think—they had begun anew three times in six months. A new start meant nothing, the only thing that mattered was the break, the chance to leave, everything after that was chance. Indra thought of playing cards with Haqq: get dealt a bad hand and leave, find some job elsewhere.

The heat was unbearable the closer they got to San Antonio.

Indra listened to the other passengers, learning that it would get worse the closer they got to Laredo, becoming so oppressive that to go out in the day would be to risk exhaustion. That old saying, only mad dogs and Englishmen go out in the noonday sun. Indra purchased a newspaper to give to Cora as a fan. Even in this heat, he felt a lightness. Freedom soon.

"I keep hearing it called the canicula," Indra said.

Cora folded the paper into thirds and began to fan herself. She hadn't heard that word since she was a child. She recounted to Indra that she had first heard it from the cowboys who came up from New Mexico. They called this time of year the dog days of summer—her father had told her that the phrase had its origins in the Dog Star, Sirius, a star that rose above the sun during the worst of the heat. "Always starts in the beginning of July, right around now," she said.

They arrived in San Antonio, and she saw the columns of doughboys making their way through the station. The sight of so many men in uniform made both of them nervous. They couldn't wait to leave. Another train, this one three hours, down to the border.

Outside their next train, it was as if they had scoured the topography from her childhood. The same endless and dry plain, not a tree in sight, just emaciated scrubs peeking out of the ground, each trying to poach what little water it could from an unforgiving, ever clear sky. Gone were the mesas, gone were the striations of stony earth, and in their place was pure nothingness, nothing to catch and break the wind that swept through, and Cora felt a curious fear that if the wind were to blow hard enough, she would fall over and be carried forever into that which stretched on, nothing to catch her.

Six months ago she had been Cora Trent. Now she was Cora Mukherjee, or Mrs. Pierre Thomas, or Antonia Martinez, or maybe she was nothing but the sum total of a need to leave.

The train station was a small building, whitewashed walls and terra-cotta roof tiles, a faded memory of Stanford's campus. The border was a mile away. The heat was unbearable. They decided to check in to a small hotel to spend the hottest hours of the day. They were in America still, yet the only language they heard as they moved through the town was the romance lilt of Spanish. Get used to this language, she told herself. It's all that you'll hear from today onward.

Cora took a hot shower, her first in weeks, it felt like what the early evangelists must have felt when they were dunked in the waters of the River Jordan.

She washed their clothes in the bathtub, and they lay naked on the bed while waiting for them to dry. They hadn't been able to stretch out together in ages, and they made love in a desultory way as the heat drove beads of sweat down every crevice of skin made slick by every passing minute. Every kiss against skin salty but mouths never dry, oh, to love again, until the heat finally made it so the only way they could was through the smallest possible movements, both on their sides, his tall body cupping and enveloping hers.

They went to the border in the early evening, past the worst of the warmth. Their clothes were stiff from the washing, and it seemed like their gait too lacked the proper creases.

The Americans were trying something new out. They wanted to stop Mexicans from crossing the border wherever and whenever they wanted, so they'd made a few new bridges, small official channels for crossing over. Most ignored these paths and chose to cross wherever at will, for whoever dared to enter the newly built American building was to be stripped naked and sprayed down, deloused of the imagined layer of filth brought in from the south. Or so they said.

No one cared about going the other way. Leave the country, don't come back. So long, see you another time. Cora had never left the country before. Indra seemed so at ease. He had crossed borders, hidden himself away, changed identities when needed. This was his life.

What was his was hers. She had earned this.

She held his hand.

They took a step onto the planks of the wooden bridge of the Laredo crossing. Farmhands and traders and small-time merchants who made their money in American dollars were heading home. Even in the early evening, the canicula bore down upon them like a smothering blanket, sapping them of life, but this was their chance. Indra had Dawson's letter in his pocket.

Beyond the river was Nuevo Laredo, another human settlement dropped into the arid desert. A desert was an emptiness built of stories, a could-be place where no one knew what the difference was between a mirage and an oasis until it was too late.

A story was a lie with more structure. It didn't matter if that lie consecrated some greater want or ambition. The risk was always the same. Their marriage, and perhaps all marriages, plodded ever forward with the help of (sometimes everyday, sometimes extraordinary) lies, for the truth was by its very nature shaped as an ogive, quick and capable of piercing deep into the matter of things. But if these lies were meant to protect or distract from without, they didn't make for safekeeping within, for they were nothing more than a bomb placed close to the heart, necessitating some sober watchfulness for the ever present danger that could envelop one or the other. Or both. A story was a lie with gears and fuses and petty jealousies and timers and love and switches and charges and shrapnel and tender care and heat and fire and concussive power. And the rising smoke.

Beneath them, the lazy flow of the Rio Grande carried water between two countries. A river made a perfect border. One embankment per nation, and in the middle, two people, brought together by some invisible thread and, once bound, remained, one step for the other, in sickness and health, in freedom and imprisonment. They were together. They were nowhere. In between for only a little while longer, and in front of them, the endless desert filled the horizon, their lives ceaselessly emerging anew from the deadening heat of the summer star.

ACKNOWLEDGMENTS

I owe a great debt of gratitude to those who made this book possible. Jamie Carr shepherded this book from idea to draft and onward. Sara Birmingham treated it with care as its first editor and Rachel Sargent did truly magnificent work stepping up and stepping in to see it to publication. Amelia Possanza helped me in understanding how this book could find an audience, as did Cordelia Calvert and Meghan Deans.

I am grateful to Professor Lauren Thompson at Kennesaw State University for taking the time to speak with me about the history of contraception and abortion in the United States. Steve Staiger, historian at the Palo Alto Historical Society, was incredibly patient with my queries about life around the Stanford campus in 1917. Hanna Ahn, assistant university archivist at Stanford University, kindly pointed me to digital material about campus history.

Thank you to Ryaan Ahmed, Samuel Fury Childs Daly, Lauren Aliza Green, Tracey Rose Peyton, Mayukh Sen, and Sam Sussman for forming a network of solidarity when I needed it most. I am grateful to Akil Kumarasamy, Sarah Thankam Mathews, and Morgan Talty for believing in this book at an early juncture.

To Sylvie, Sanjh, and Emily: my days find their cadence in your warmth and love.